Make

Feel Again



PS. BLACK
Romance Author

Edits: Dee's Notes: Editing and Proofreading Services

Cover Design: Coffin Prints Designs

Formatting : PS. Black

Proofreaders: Toni McPherson & Claire Buckley

"One good thing about music,
when it hits you, you feel no pain."

– Bob Marley

# Playlist

"Unsteady" By X Ambassadors
"Empty Space" By James Arthur
"Dancing On My Own" By Calum Scott
"Falling Like The Stars" By James Arthur
"How Could You" By Jesse Murph
"Bleeding Love" By Leona Lewis
"If You're Not The One" By Daniel Bedingfield
"Stone" By Jaymes Young
"Act Like You Love Me" By Shawn Mendes
"Here With Me" By Dido
"Time After Time" By Eva Cassidy
"You Proof" By Morgan Wallen
"Rock and A Hard Place" By Bailey Zimmerman
"Wings" By Birdy
"Fast Car" By Luke Combs
"Helium" By Sia
"Rescue" By Lauren Daigle
"Yours" By Ella Henderson
"Last Night" By Morgan Wallen
"You Are The Reason" By Calum Scott
"Love Again" By Alex Isley, Jack Dine
"Feel Again" By Kina, Au/Ra

Make Me Feel Again has subjects that some readers may find difficult to read. Please also note, there is mature content.

If you would like the trigger list, please email me - authorps.black@outlook.com.

"You don't know what you're made of until you're forced to let go of someone you love." — R.M Drake

Dedication

To myself.
I embraced the pain and chose to make
something heartbreakingly beautiful with it.

# Prologue

## Cash

"Jace is brain dead."

Everything stops. My whole world crashes to the floor in a thousand pieces. My blood runs cold. Never in my life did I think I would hear those four words while on this earth. How can it be, how can I be living in a world where Jace doesn't. I stare at the doctor in front of me, his mouth is moving, but no sound reaches my ears. My stomach curdles, so I place my hand over my mouth. It can't be my boy.

"My boy. Not my boy," I choke out on a sob, trying to hold in the sickness threatening to come out. Pressure lands on my arm, and through blurry vision, Bohdi falls to the floor before me, gripping my shirt and tugging me into him. The pain seers through my chest, causing me to grasp Boh harder. Boh's shoulders shake with mine as we cry into each other's arms.

"My baby." I zone back into the world, pulling away from Boh enough to look over, and one of the most amazing women to ever walk this earth falls to her knees beside Jace—the most amazing sister and auntie anyone could ever ask for.

"Bridge," I croak out. Boh leans back as we open our arms to her. She crawls along the floor; I doubt any of our legs could carry this pain at this moment. She pushes up to her knees and falls into us, and our pain combines as we all cry together.

"How are we going to do this." She sniffles into our chests. "How are we meant to go on without him, Cash." The pain intensifies, the words cutting like razor blades over my heart. I can't say anything because this is all I could think about the entire week. How do I go on in life without him. My son, my best friend. The light in all our lives, the bigger-than-life smile that lit up every room he walked in, the sense of humor that brought smiles to people's faces on their worst days. How can this world exist without my son. All I know is my life, all our lives, won't ever be the same without him. My mind flashes to Rylee, and with blurred vision, I scan the room for her, but she's gone.

# Chapter One
# Rylee

"James?"

I stay rooted to the spot and stare into his soulless eyes. My vision becomes hazy from tears, and I open my mouth, then close it again, unable to say a word. I just want to ask him why he has done this.

"You're probably thinking, why, am I right?" He smiles at me. My heart rate picks up, as the smile on his face does not make me feel safe in any way. I want to answer, but I can't get any words out, so I nod.

"When I first saw you in that club, Ry, I was mesmerized." He walks toward me, and my body freezes, as though I am being held down. The closer he gets, the louder my brain screams for me to move, to do anything, but I can't.

"You were and are so effortlessly beautiful. It was like seeing an angel. I knew, from that moment, you were mine." He says it like he believes I have been waiting my whole life to hear him say it. What is happening right now? This can't be real. He crouches in front of me, so I drop my head to my chest. I can't look at him. The smell of his aftershave makes me sick to my stomach.

"Look at me," he whispers.

I keep my head down, shaking it side to side, tears trailing down my cheeks.

"Rylee," he snaps, so I flinch away from him. "Look. At. Me." He grips my arm, making me wince. I lift my head slowly, the endless pools of black stare at me as he leans down, and I stop breathing. *What the fuck is he going to do?*

His lips skim my cheek. "Fucking beautiful."

A sob escapes my mouth before I can stop it, and then I find my voice. "James, please. Stop." I don't know what else to say, but I want him to get away from me. I don't want him anywhere near me.

He huffs in my ear, as if my reaction is an inconvenience to him.

He pulls his head back a few inches so he is nose to nose with me, and his eyes, which represent the pits of hell, flicker between mine. A tinge of sadness flashes in his eyes.

"Get some rest, this has been a lot for you. I'm sure it will all make sense once you have slept and eaten something, my beautiful girl." He slowly stands. I shake my head back and forth. *All make sense? None of this will ever make sense, what planet is he living on?*

"No," I choke out. "James, what is happening right now? What have you done, and why am I here?" My whole body shakes as the fear flows through me at not knowing what he will do.

"I told you, Rylee. You belong to me. I was hoping you'd come to the realization on your own, but that fucking prick Cash made me recognize I needed to push this along." His face turns an alarming red, his chest heaving, then he takes a few deep breaths as if he is trying to calm himself down.

"That prick always tried to get involved. I don't know how Jace put up with him," he grits out.

Jace's name leaving his lips sends a jolt of sadness through me. I need to keep him talking.

"What do you mean he always tried to get involved, get involved with what?" I keep my voice quiet and as uninterested as possible. If he picks up on me trying to gather information, then he may not give me anything, and I need to know as much as possible.

He sighs like he doesn't have the energy to get into it. "It doesn't matter now." The smile he flashes makes me sick; it's like a mask has been lifted off James's face and I'm finally seeing him for who he is. I have never seen so much coldness, so much evil in his eyes before. "I have you now, so I won. He didn't." His thumb grazes my cheek. I stay frozen to the spot, waiting for him to continue or give me more.

"James, please tell me what is happening." I hold eye contact with him, even though I'm trying to hold the sickness at bay.

He stares at me with a blank expression for what feels like an eternity and then speaks. "You want to know everything?" he asks, raising his eyebrow.

I nod because I don't think I can speak without breaking down. He crouches again.

"I don't think you can handle the truth, Rylee. I can promise you, it's so much deeper than you could possibly imagine." He smiles, then stands, spins on his heel, and walks back toward the door.

"Wait. James. Don't leave me on my own. What are you going to do?" The words leave my mouth before I can even think. Panic is taking over my body. I can't sit here without knowing what or why. He doesn't even bother turning around to look at me.

"Make sure you eat the food I left you; you have lost a lot of weight recently. I miss those curves," he deadpans, before walking out the wooden door and closing it behind him.

The locks click in place, then I lean to the side and liquid burns my throat and nose as I finally retch. *I miss those curves.* I cover my mouth, trying to hold back the sobs wanting to escape. There's no way I'm getting out of here, and I have no idea what James will do. By the things he was saying, and the way he was looking at me, whatever he does, it will happen whether I want it to or not.

# Chapter Two
# Cash

I pace the length of my house, tugging my hair till pain sears my scalp. When I got a call from James's ex-girlfriend, Casey, an hour ago, my heart sank. I always knew something wasn't right with James, and after what Jace and I saw on his phone a year ago, my thoughts were confirmed.

Rylee is a stunning girl, and Jace knew everyone knew that, but he had the attitude of they can look all they want, but she's mine. He was a lot calmer than I ever could have been. Yes, I was a hypocrite, and I still am, but back then, I only ever admired Rylee's looks and personality. I bet that slimy prick James admired a lot more. When James was flicking through pictures on his phone to show Jace and me his holiday pictures, he accidentally scrolled too far and a picture of Rylee came up. Anger simmered through my veins. I have never struggled so much to hold back anger like I did that day.

If Jace hadn't done something about it, I would have. Jace's eyes narrowed, and his face got red before he snatched the phone out of James's hand. I grasped James so he couldn't grab it back. With the fury flowing through me in that moment, I could have crushed his worthless bones with my bare hands. Anger filled Jace as he flicked through the pictures. I only saw the one, but Jace said there were at least twenty of Rylee, all pictures he had saved from her Facebook. I wanted to rip his fucking head off. Jace was a calm man, but he could hold his own. I knew that from the little scraps he got into at school, and he always came out on top, but he was a lover, not a fighter. Rylee brought the loving side out in him more, but when he saw pictures of her on one of his closest friend's phone, he lost it.

One minute, Jace was staring down at the phone, trembling in anger; the next, I was pushed out of the way and Jace was on top of James, raining blow after blow down on him. I was happy to sit back and let it play out. The slimy prick needed a beating, but Rowan pulled Jace off while some staff from the bar helped James up off the floor. Jace had a few firm words to say before we left and was raging on the way home.

The thing is, James didn't even try to plead his innocence or make any excuses. He just looked angry that Jace had reacted the way he did, and never showed any mercy, as if he had the right to have those pictures of Rylee. I told Jace then he needed to kick that prick to the curb and keep him far away from her. I had no doubt in my mind that he would try and take Rylee from him. The thought sends me spiraling even more.

The heartbreaking truth of the matter is, Jace isn't here anymore to stop him, but is what I'm doing any better? No, it isn't. As much as I said I wasn't sorry the other night, it's plagued my mind since being at home alone more than I ever thought it would. I can't stop thinking how sick and wrong it is of me to do what I'm doing. I've told myself it's the grief. We gravitated toward each other because of Jace—the one person we loved more than life itself—but I know for me that's not the reason. I just have to say that to stop hating myself more than I already do. All I want is for Rylee to be safe, and I know Jace would want me to do everything I can to make that happen.

I send Rylee a text to know she is safe, and I also need to explain to her why Jace stopped talking to James and why I told her to stay away from him.

**Me:** It's urgent, I really need to speak to you. Pick up your phone.

I know deep down why she isn't answering, it's the guilt of what happened the other night. The guilt is eating away at me. I have barely slept since, not that I sleep much these days. My dreams have turned into play-by-play memories of Jace growing up. When I open my eyes and I am back to reality, the pain hits harder each time. So I try and keep busy with work, or just drink myself into oblivion to the point my brain is too fucked up to dream. It usually works.

My phone shows she has read the message. After this, I will go back to the way things were and keep my distance. Well, try, but I need to explain everything first. I try ringing her again, but this time, it goes straight to voicemail. I get she doesn't want to talk, but there's no way I can leave this after what I've found out today. I grab my coat and keys and head out to the car. As much as I don't want to step foot back in that apartment, I need to see her.

"Rylee," I shout through the door. I've been banging on the door and she hasn't answered. Maybe she is out with Toni or Rachel. I rub the outline of the key in my pocket, not wanting to cross that line but the bad feeling in my gut hasn't left me since that call. I pull the key out of my pocket, flip it between my fingers and glance back up at the door. I pound on the door one more time before opening it, then shout Rylee's name again, but it's deadly silent.

The horrible feeling in my stomach intensifies from being back in this apartment. "Stop thinking, Cash, just look for Rylee." I step into the apartment some more. "Rylee!" Her keys aren't hanging on the hook. She's clearly out, but this isn't something that can wait. I pull my phone out of my pocket and dial Toni's number.

"What do you want?"

"It's Cash."

"Yeah, I'm aware. Like I said, what do you want?" Toni is a character, but she's not rude, so I'm not sure why—

"You have some nerve ringing me, Cash. You best believe if you were standing in front of me, your cheek would be stinging from the hardest slap you have ever received in your life." Then it dawns on me, either she heard what happened at the bar or Rylee told her what happened in the apartment and they're both disgusted with me right now.

"Look—"

"No, you look, Mr. My Rylee is a good girl. She certainly does not need you calling her out in front of people and talking down to her like she is a piece of shit on the bottom of your shoe. She isn't one of these flavors of the week you parade around. She respects herself and would certainly not go with the likes of creepy as fuck James. Especially after everything that has happened." Her voice dims down on the last bit.

I sit in silence because I know what I did at the bar was disgusting, and she is right. I acted like Rylee is one of these girls who jumps from person to person when she is not even in the same galaxy as those women.

"Cash." Her voice is low and calm. "I know you're hurting; I can't even imagine what you and your family are going through right now. We all lost a huge part of our lives, and things will never be the same, but please, I beg you, give Rylee a break. You have always acted a certain way with her, but this is not the right way. Go back to being your moody-broody self toward her, but please, don't be nasty to her. She's fighting this uphill battle alongside you, and I don't know how much more she can take." She sighs.

She's right, everything she said is right, and I have nothing to say back to her. "We all miss him." Her voice cracks as sniffles come through the phone. My jaw clenches as I try and hold back my emotions. Now is not the time to break down. I can't.

"Toni, everything you have said is true. Rylee knows I'm sorry for what happened the other night. There is no excuse for it, I was a complete prick and I own that." She sniffles and chuckles.

"Never did I expect to hear Cash Stiles admit he was wrong."

"Don't get used it. Listen, Toni. I called for a reason. I'm worried about Rylee."

"What, why?" Her voice peaks.

I explain the call I received earlier, and she screams down the phone, "I fucking knew it. Ahh, when I get my hands on that fucking creep, it's game over for him."

"Yeah, same, but right now, I can't find Rylee. She read my text earlier, and then her phone went off. Do you have any idea where she could be?"

"Yes! She put a picture up on her Instagram of the sea. She is at the beach, Cash!"

"Okay, I will head down there now."

"Cash, please keep me updated and let me know once you are with her."

"Will do, Toni. Thanks." I put the phone down and sigh at knowing where she is. She loves the beach, so I don't know why I didn't think of it.

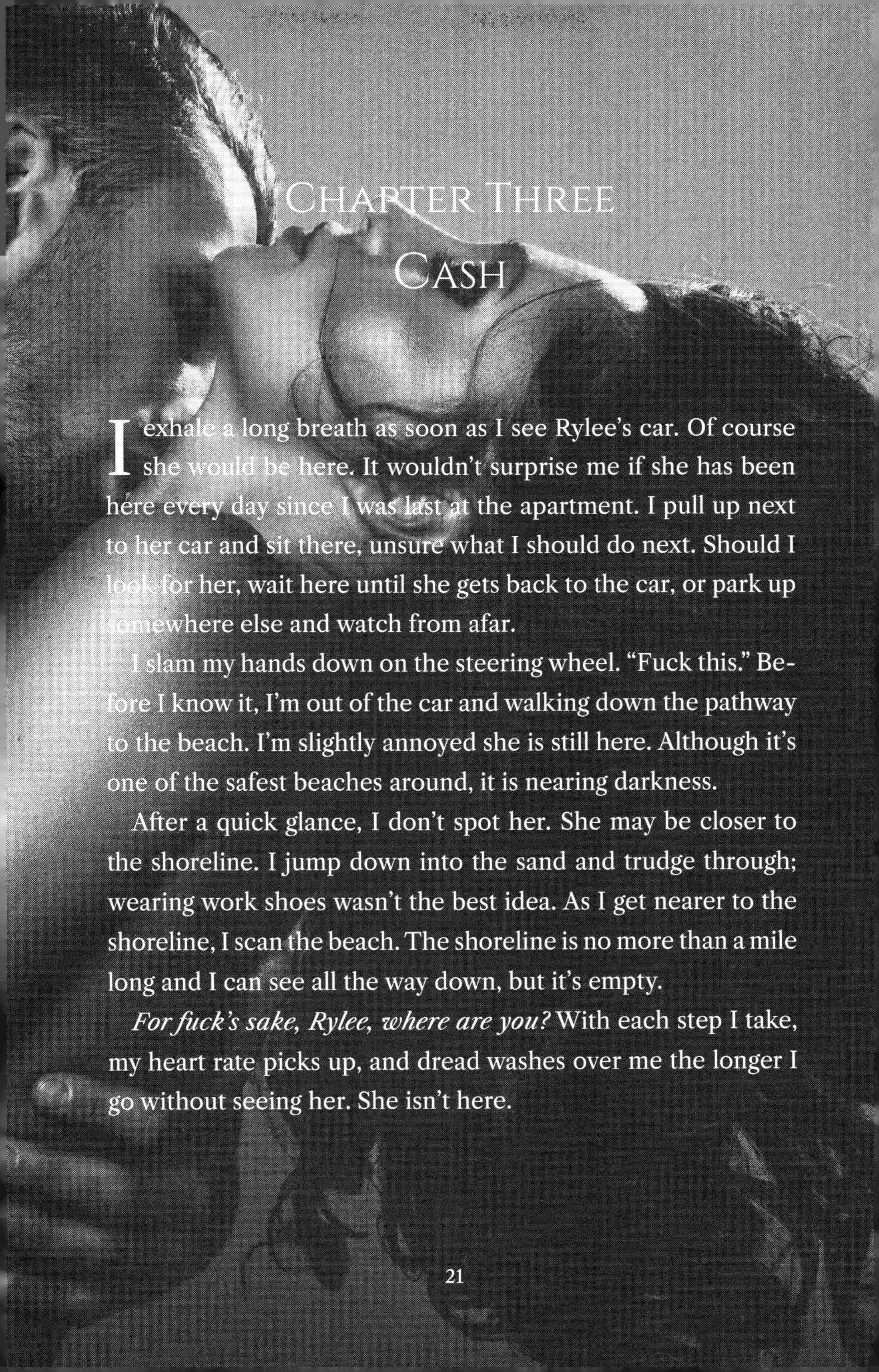

# Chapter Three
## Cash

I exhale a long breath as soon as I see Rylee's car. Of course she would be here. It wouldn't surprise me if she has been here every day since I was last at the apartment. I pull up next to her car and sit there, unsure what I should do next. Should I look for her, wait here until she gets back to the car, or park up somewhere else and watch from afar.

I slam my hands down on the steering wheel. "Fuck this." Before I know it, I'm out of the car and walking down the pathway to the beach. I'm slightly annoyed she is still here. Although it's one of the safest beaches around, it is nearing darkness.

After a quick glance, I don't spot her. She may be closer to the shoreline. I jump down into the sand and trudge through; wearing work shoes wasn't the best idea. As I get nearer to the shoreline, I scan the beach. The shoreline is no more than a mile long and I can see all the way down, but it's empty.

*For fuck's sake, Rylee, where are you?* With each step I take, my heart rate picks up, and dread washes over me the longer I go without seeing her. She isn't here.

"Fuck!" I scream, looking up at the sky as if it will give me the map to her. I reach into my pocket, knowing I need to ring Toni, as I walk back through the sand toward the car.

"Cash? Are you with her," Toni rushes out.

"She's not fucking here," I grit out.

"What do you mean, not there?" she screeches.

"As in, no where to be fucking seen, Toni. Her car is here, she is not." I don't have time for her questions. I jump up into the parking lot and pace toward Rylee's car. Toni is still screeching and panicking, but I don't take in anything she says. As I get closer, something glistens near her car. My pace picks up, then I crouch down, and there lies Rylee's keys. Sweat beads on my forehead as my gut tells me something isn't right.

"Toni, I need you to shut the fuck up and listen to me." She goes deadly silent, as if shocked by my tone. Normally, Toni would tear me a new one, but I assume she knows I'm not fucking around.

"Her car and apartment keys are lying on the ground near her car door. I need you to call around to everyone and ask if they have seen her. Do you understand me?"

"Ye-Yes. Cash?"

"Yes?" I sigh out.

"She will be okay, won't she?" Toni's sniffles fill my ears. I stay silent, and her cries get stronger.

"If he has hurt one hair on her head, I will make sure he pays, Toni. I promise." I put the phone down before Toni can ask too many questions. My need to protect Rylee is how any father-in-law would react, isn't it? But why do I feel like I will tear every single person's head off until I find her. Why do I feel like I will tear a whole fucking city apart until I find her? Something tells me that isn't very father-in-law of me. Even though I was never technically her father-in-law.

"Breathe, Cash. Think. Think." I bring up Rylee's number and call her again, but it goes straight to voicemail.

I need to ring Bridge and Boh to let them know what's going on.

I couldn't bring myself to call Bridget. I don't want to worry Bridge, she is a huge worrier and with being away, this will send her over the edge. I called Boh and asked him to call Bridge and explain everything. I know she will freak out, and I can't deal with that headspace. I need to think straight. Think where she could be. Has she even been taken?

I pace the length of Rylee's car, back and forth, and my gaze keeps flicking out to sea. She wouldn't. No. I can't think like that. She wouldn't leave us like that. I exhale a long breath, and I lean on the hood of Rylee's car. I need to ring Casey.

"He-hello." Her anxious voice gives away she's worried. I don't blame her. The things she told me make my skin crawl knowing he could have Rylee right now.

"Casey, it's Cash."

"Look, I told you everything I know. I don't want to be involved anymore, please don't call me again."

"No, wait. It's Rylee. She's missing."

"Wha-what?"

"After what you told me earlier, I came to her apartment to speak with her about it. She wasn't there, I called her friends. They haven't seen her. So I came to the beach where she likes to go sometimes. Her car is here, but she isn't." I sigh. "Also, her keys were on the ground near her car." Saying it out loud sets the panic in me. He must have her. *What the fuck is he going to do to her?* Thoughts race through my mind, causing my stomach to turn. I need to find her.

"I . . . I don't know what you want me to do," she whispers. I know she is scared, but she said how lovely Rylee seemed, so she spoke up because she didn't want Rylee in danger.

"Have you seen or spoken to him?" I spit. I can't even say his name, it makes me sick.

"No, I haven't seen or heard from him in about a week."

"Okay. I'm going to his house to see if he's there." If he is, I will make him wish he wasn't born. The sick freak.

"Cash, please be careful. I'm not joking when I say he is sick in the head. Please just keep your wits about you."

"Yeah, yeah, in the meantime, I need you to think on anything else he may have told or shown you. If he isn't home, then I guarantee he has her, and if he does, we have no idea where, so please think, Casey."

"I will, of course I will."

"Thank you." I put the phone down and jump in my car, ready to head to James's. I put the hands-free on and dial Rowan to see if he has seen James.

"Rowan!" I shout as he picks up.

"Cash, are you okay?" He sounds skeptical, probably because I've never called him before.

"Yeah, I just need to know if you have seen or heard from James?"

"Ahh, nah, man. Probably about a week ago was the last time I heard from him. Why?" I don't want to go into everything, but I need him to know this is serious.

"Look, some shit has come to light about James. It's not good, and now Rylee is missing. If you see or speak to him, can you let me know?" The laugh that comes down the line shocks me, as if he thinks I'm joking.

"What would James have to do with Rylee missing?" He laughs again. If only he knew how deep James's obsession for her is. If only everyone saw something wasn't right about him. All the signs were fucking there. Thinking about him makes me tighten my grip on the steering wheel.

"Trust me, Rowan. A lot. I don't have time to get into it right now, but I had a call from Casey and—"

"The stripper James was seeing?" I didn't know she was a stripper, not that, that matters. I don't care. All I care about is the information she provided me with.

"Yes, whatever her job is, I don't care. She had a lot to tell me about James, and I'm worried he has taken Rylee."

"Look, I don't know wha—"

"Rowan, I don't give a shit what you think right now. Can you just see if anyone has heard from James, and if so, call me straight back. Got it?"

"Yeah bu—" I hang up to stop from hearing any of his bullshit about how James wouldn't do anything to hurt Rylee. I like Rowan, I always have, but he never saw the bad in James and always remained friends with him. I never understood that.

Ten minutes later, I'm pulling up outside James's. His car isn't here. I knew it wouldn't be, but I was hoping otherwise. I jog toward the door and bang on it. Adrenaline rushes through me at the thought of seeing him. The thought of raining punches on his face has my hands twitching. I keep banging and shouting his name, but no one comes. I know he has her.

I put my face to his front room window, but it's empty: no sofa, no TV. Nothing.

"Fuck!" I shout. I rush back to my car and dial Casey's number. She has to know something.

# Chapter Four
# Rylee

I sit there waiting. For what? I don't know. James hasn't come back yet. I have no sense of time, but I assume it's been a few hours. I can't stop thinking about what it is he will do to me. He said it goes deeper? Deeper than what exactly? My mind is all over the place. How can my life go from being so perfect, to everything crashing down within a few months?

Scanning the room again, I hope something will pop out that will help me get out of here. But there is nothing. I want to know what's going on, but I don't want to see him. He terrifies me, and I don't know how far he may go. I have never seen this side of James. Why did I not see it? Toni knew something wasn't right with him. Cash always had a problem and then . . . Just the thought of his name makes my heart crack all over again. Jace. Something happened between them, and he never told me.

As if he was listening to my thoughts, he unlocks the door. My head snaps up, and I focus on the door as it opens. My breath hitches as I wait for him to walk through. When he appears, a cold flush takes over my body. There is nothing warm about him. He's like a whole different person.

"Where has the kind James gone?"

His eyebrows raise to his hairline, and then he throws his head back and laughs. He closes the door behind him, then turns and stalks toward me.

"Oh sweet, sweet Rylee. You don't get it, do you?" He tilts his head to the side and then juts his bottom lip out.

"The James at the bar the other night. He doesn't exist. He's fake."

He stops a few feet away from me and brings his arms out to the side.

"This right here is the real deal, and fuck me, I've missed him." The smile that forms on his face fills my entire body with dread. He was lying all along. The James I knew doesn't exist. Tears leak from my eyes, one after the other, as I drop my head and bring my hands to my face. He's not going to let me go no matter what I say.

I hear a scurry before his cold hands land on mine, then I jump back on the bed as much as I can.

"Don't touch me," I spit, pushing my hands out in front of me, as if they will shield me from him.

"Oh, princess." He sighs. "You're mine, I'll touch you whenever the hell I feel like it." My anger quickly forms as he leans forward and grabs my face with one hand, his fingers gripping my cheeks so hard, I know he will leave fingerprints behind. My eyes squint from the pressure.

He gets nose to nose with me, and the pain evaporates. What is he doing? I stay as still as a statue. I don't even want to breathe. His breaths hit my lips, making me feel sick.

"You're mine," he whispers against my lips before pushing himself forward and presses his lips to mine. I don't move. It takes me a few seconds to catch on, but when his tongue enters my mouth, I punch him, and he lets go. I jump off the bed and run for the door. I know he didn't lock it, and as I approach the door, a feeling of hope floods me.

A harsh grip pulls at my shoulder, and I fly backward. My back and head hit the floor, and I cry out from the pain.

I hiss, rubbing at the spot, trying to get rid of the sting.

"That's what you get for acting silly, Rylee," he scolds. "You can never just behave, can you. Jace always said you had fire in you. I see what he means now." His eyes roam me as if he enjoys me not being compliant. *Who the fuck is this person?*

"Don't say his fucking name. His name does not come out of your mouth again, you don't deserve to speak his name."

He points to his chest. "I don't deserve, no? Of course I don't. Jace was too perfect, wasn't he, Rylee. Tell me"—he holds his chin and looks up to the ceiling—"if he was so perfect, then why did he overdose, clearly something wasn't right." He smiles down at me.

Tears prick my eyes at the reminder. "He didn't overdose," I say through clenched teeth, trying to delay the breakdown my body is approaching.

"No, no he didn't, did he." James crouches down in front of me and glares at me dead in the eyes.

"Then ask yourself, Rylee. How did those drugs get in his body." His eyes flicker between mine as a small smile creeps on his face.

My whole body starts to tremble.

"No. No. No." I shake my head as I crawl backward.

"You." I point at him. I can't even say it. Please, please tell me this isn't happening.

"Ding. Ding. Ding." He smiles as if it's an achievement and something he's proud of.

"It finally sets in. It took you a while, Rylee. But yes, it was me. I spiked Jace's drink that night. I'm the reason he crashed. I'm the reason he's dead." His sinister smile is back, and I get lightheaded as the room spins. My heart beats so fast, and a panic attack encroaches on me. Black spots fill my vision as my body becomes a dead weight and I fall to the ground. The monster who ruined my life and took everything from me looms overhead as darkness takes me under.

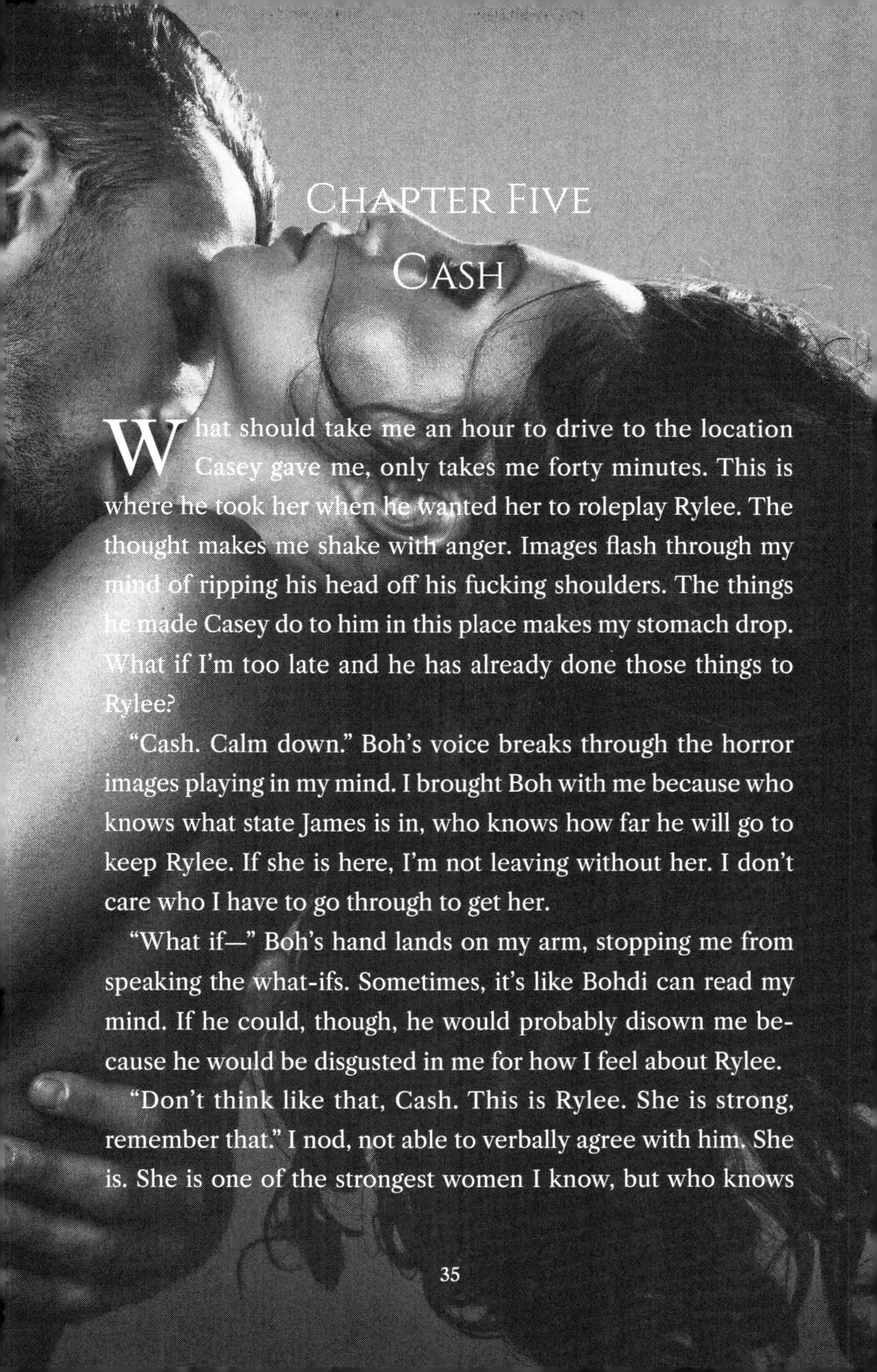

# Chapter Five
## Cash

What should take me an hour to drive to the location Casey gave me, only takes me forty minutes. This is where he took her when he wanted her to roleplay Rylee. The thought makes me shake with anger. Images flash through my mind of ripping his head off his fucking shoulders. The things he made Casey do to him in this place makes my stomach drop. What if I'm too late and he has already done those things to Rylee?

"Cash. Calm down." Boh's voice breaks through the horror images playing in my mind. I brought Boh with me because who knows what state James is in, who knows how far he will go to keep Rylee. If she is here, I'm not leaving without her. I don't care who I have to go through to get her.

"What if—" Boh's hand lands on my arm, stopping me from speaking the what-ifs. Sometimes, it's like Bohdi can read my mind. If he could, though, he would probably disown me because he would be disgusted in me for how I feel about Rylee.

"Don't think like that, Cash. This is Rylee. She is strong, remember that." I nod, not able to verbally agree with him. She is. She is one of the strongest women I know, but who knows what James has done to her. He could have drugged her. Hurt her.

We creep toward what looks like a barn converted into a modern-looking house; except all the windows have been blacked out. I park the car down the pathway, out of sight. If my head wasn't so all over the place, it would have probably been a good idea to park well away from here, but it's too late now.

Boh pulls on my arm as we creep up the drive. "We should have called the police, Cash." He keeps his eyes on the only door we see to the house.

"We will, but I can't have them startling him if he has her in here. We need to catch him by surprise." We edge more and more toward the door, it's dead silent, and I feel in my gut that something isn't right. Something tells me she is here. I gently try the handle, but it's locked. I look over my shoulder at Boh and shake my head.

"Help!" A scream comes from inside the house—Rylee's scream. The adrenaline sears through me quicker than it ever has before. I scan my surroundings for anything that will help me knock this door down. There's fucking nothing. Boh kicks the door, and I join him, hoping doing it together will break it down.

After what feels like hours, of kicking but it's not even a minute, the door splinters. My adrenaline skyrockets, and Boh's leg goes straight through, taking half the door down with it. We push through, then scan the hallway before we kick out each door.we come across. The next door opens to an extremely large room, and the high ceilings and wooden beams that go across prove this used to be a barn.

"Cash . . ." My eyes land on Rylee, devastation mars her face as her eyes fill with tears and her mouth drops before she is tugged by her arm through another door at the rear, a door you wouldn't know was there unless you were really looking. Bohdi and I run across the large open space. The door closes, and I pray with everything he didn't lock it. She is here, in front of me. I can't lose her now. Boh reaches the door before me, and as soon as we get through it, there is another wide open door at the end of the empty room. It leads out of the house. We take off through it, and a hooded figure runs toward a parked car.

"James!" I bellow at the top of my lungs. I know it's him. I don't have to see his face to know. He falters a bit before he continues to pull Rylee. Her gaze locks with mine. She cries my name, and her eyes beg for me to help her as we chase him down the path. Rylee flails her arms and drops to the ground, making it harder for James to drag her. She screams out more as she's dragged along the rubble before leaning forward and biting his hand.

"Ahhh," he shouts as he lets her go. He glances back enough for me to see it's for sure him.

"You piece of shit," I scream as I get closer. Rylee scurries away on her ass, staring up at him, but he doesn't do what I think he will do. He doesn't try and get her, he leaves. He takes off running toward the car. I approach Rylee, dropping to the ground.

"Rylee." I cup her cheeks with my hands. "Please talk to me. Are you okay?" I examine her face, checking for any visible injuries.

"Cash." Her arms fly around my neck, and she grips me with every bit of strength she has.

"Ry," Boh whispers crouching down. She jumps when the car starts and rubble kicks up behind it as he speeds off. I didn't want to let him go, but this is going to the police now. All I care about is having Rylee in my arms. James will get caught; I'll make sure of it. She wails into my chest, gripping my top. I frown at Boh. What the fuck has he done to her?

"Ry, I need to call the cops. Boh is going to take you to the car." I run my hands through her hair and hold her as tight as she is holding me. I don't want to let her go, but I need to call them and get them here. They need to see this place and find out what James has been doing. She nods into my chest, peeking up at me before moving her gaze to Boh.

"Boh," she weeps as he pulls her away from me and buries his face into her hair.

"We got you, Ry, he's gone, we are going to get you home. Can you stand for me?" She continues sobbing into his chest. He doesn't ask her again, he just hooks his hands under her legs and picks her up. She clings to him, not moving her face from his chest. I want to rip her out of his arms, hold her, and make her better and safe.

I call the cops, explaining everything that went down, and they send out a unit. They wanted us to wait here, but I told them no. Rylee needs to be back with familiarity, not here. I said

I would bring Rylee to the station first thing tomorrow morning. She's staying with me so I know she's safe. The cop protested, but I hung up on him. He can turn up at my house, but I won't be letting him in. I know him through Bridge anyway, so I'm hoping he takes my word and leaves it at that.

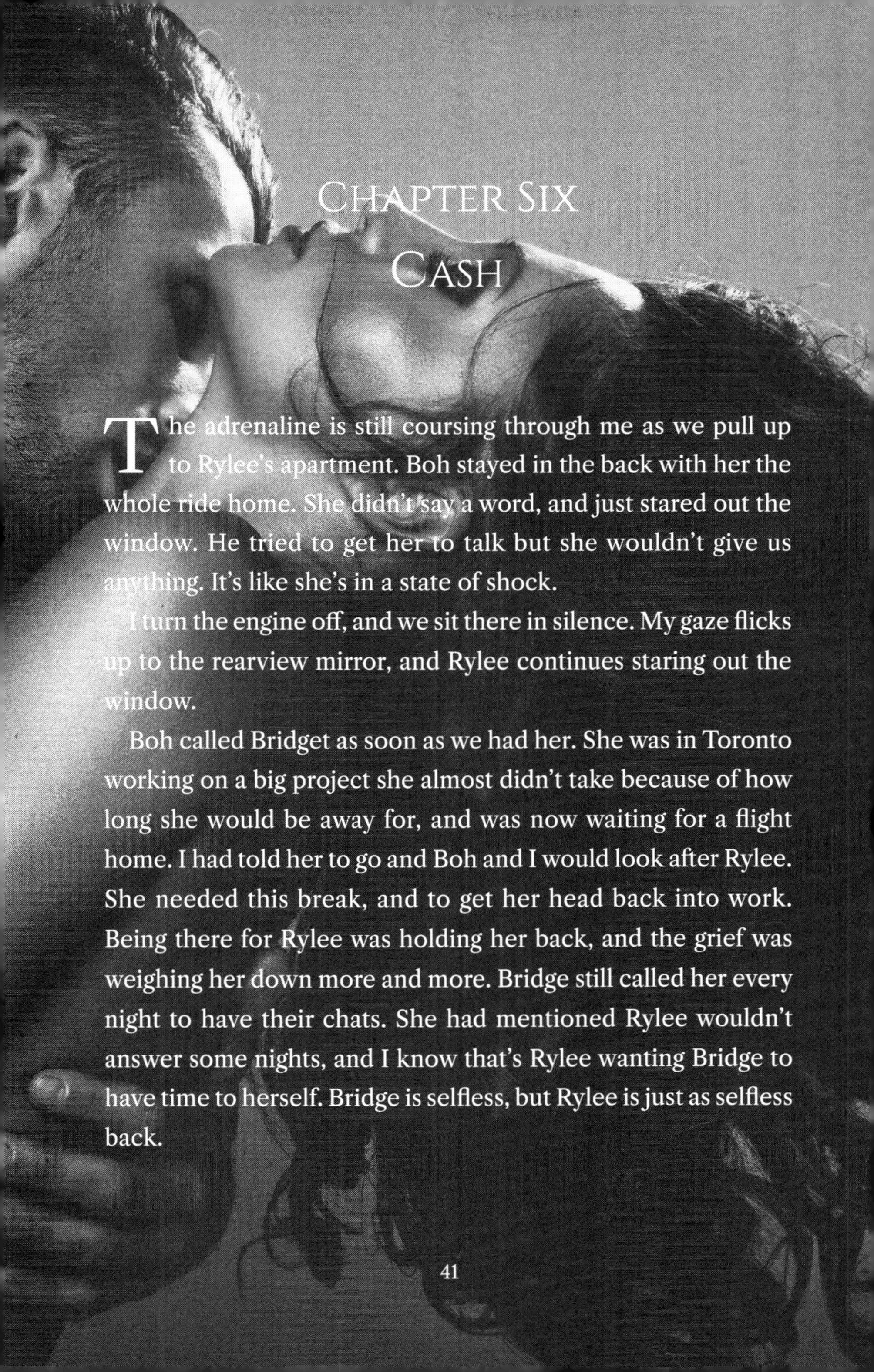

# Chapter Six

## Cash

The adrenaline is still coursing through me as we pull up to Rylee's apartment. Boh stayed in the back with her the whole ride home. She didn't say a word, and just stared out the window. He tried to get her to talk but she wouldn't give us anything. It's like she's in a state of shock.

I turn the engine off, and we sit there in silence. My gaze flicks up to the rearview mirror, and Rylee continues staring out the window.

Boh called Bridget as soon as we had her. She was in Toronto working on a big project she almost didn't take because of how long she would be away for, and was now waiting for a flight home. I had told her to go and Boh and I would look after Rylee. She needed this break, and to get her head back into work. Being there for Rylee was holding her back, and the grief was weighing her down more and more. Bridge still called her every night to have their chats. She had mentioned Rylee wouldn't answer some nights, and I know that's Rylee wanting Bridge to have time to herself. Bridge is selfless, but Rylee is just as selfless back.

"Rylee. We are home, come on." Her head turns to Boh, and her eyes are glazed over. What the fuck has he done to her? My teeth grind. All I want to do is scream at her to tell me what happened, but I know I can't. My mind is in overdrive, trying not to imagine all the things he did. Why didn't we catch the fucking creep? I get out of the car and walk toward the entrance, not even glancing back at the car. My mind and body are too pumped to be calm enough to talk to her and get her out of the car. If I have to go over there, I will drag her up the stairs, and she most definitely doesn't need that.

I pull the door and hold it open, waiting for her or Boh to take it. When I realize no one is there, I turn and Boh is crouched at Rylee's door talking to her. She stares down at him, but I don't even think she is hearing what he is saying. My heart sinks in my chest. I stay there for a few more seconds, then walk over and stand next to him. Boh peers up at me, frowning, not knowing what to do with her. I nod my head to the side and bend down so I'm eye level with her.

"We are going upstairs, okay, you can either walk or I'll carry you." Her head falls forward, so I guess that is my answer. I place my hands under her legs.

"Cash," Boh interjects, but I don't listen to him. I place my hand around her back and lift her into my arms, and the minute I do, I know I made the right decision. She grips my arms and lays her head on my chest. The adrenaline leaves my body in an instant. Having her in my arms and knowing she is safe douses the fire raging inside me. Boh regards Rylee like he wants to take every bad thing that's happened to her away. I wish someone could take it all away.

I walk up the stairs, hugging Rylee tighter to my chest to make sure she doesn't smack into anything. She grips me even tighter and cocoons herself into me more. As much as I shouldn't, my chest beams knowing I am the one she wants. I place her down on the sofa, but she doesn't let go of my arms as I go to stand.

"Rylee, you need to let go, I won't leave, I promise you," I whisper into her ear so only she can hear me. She nods, and relief floods me.

I look up at Boh. "Can you call Toni for me please, let her know we are back and ask her to come over. Rylee can't be on her own tonight." Tingles race through me at her delicate touch on my arm.

"Please, no," she whispers. Her teary gaze penetrates me. I want to see the fight back in her eyes again, it's like the day Jace took his last breath; she looks so defeated. I know how she feels, maybe this is a mirror, this is how everyone sees me. Boh stands there flicking his gaze between Rylee and me.

"You need to tell us what you want, Rylee." She eyes me and then Boh before a tear falls down her cheek and drips from her face.

"Ca-can you just stay with me, please." She looks down, as if she's ashamed, but my heart soars knowing she trusts me to keep her safe.

I nod. "Yeah, okay." I glance back up at Boh. "Just let Toni know we are back and to come over tomorrow, and I'll stay here to keep an eye on her." Boh nods before pulling out his phone and heading out of the room.

"Boh." I stand and Rylee's eyes follow me. Like she is scared I will walk out and not come back. "You can go, I'll call you if I need anything." His brows draw together as he looks at Rylee again.

"Cash, can I have a quick word out in the hall?" Boh's eyes gravitate toward Rylee again as I look down. Her eyes are blown wide.

"I will just be outside that door, Rylee. I promise I'm not going anywhere." Her eyes flick between Boh and me again and then she nods before bringing her knees to her chest and resting her chin on them. I pace over to Boh and stand just on the inside of the door, and Rylee doesn't take her eyes off me. Where the fuck has our Rylee gone?

"Ca-Cash." He picks at his fingers. I swing my gaze to him, searching his, trying to work out what's wrong with him.

"Boh. What is it?" He glances up at me, and defeat stares straight back at me.

"What's going on with the cops?"

"I told them I would bring Rylee to the station, but I can't in this state. They can wait until tomorrow." I glance over at Rylee, who has her face lulled to the side resting on her knees, eyes fixed on me.

"Look at her, Boh." I don't take my eyes off her. "She isn't in a fit state to talk to the cops."

He huffs.

"What is it?"

"They may have to see her tonight, Cash. They may need to run some tests." His eyes narrow and his shoulders slouch as if he has the weight of the world on them. Then I realize what he means.

"I swear to fucking God, if he has touched her, I will fucking kill him," I whisper as close to him as I can.

"I will be right behind you, brother. But we need to ask her." He grips my shoulder as we walk back into the room.

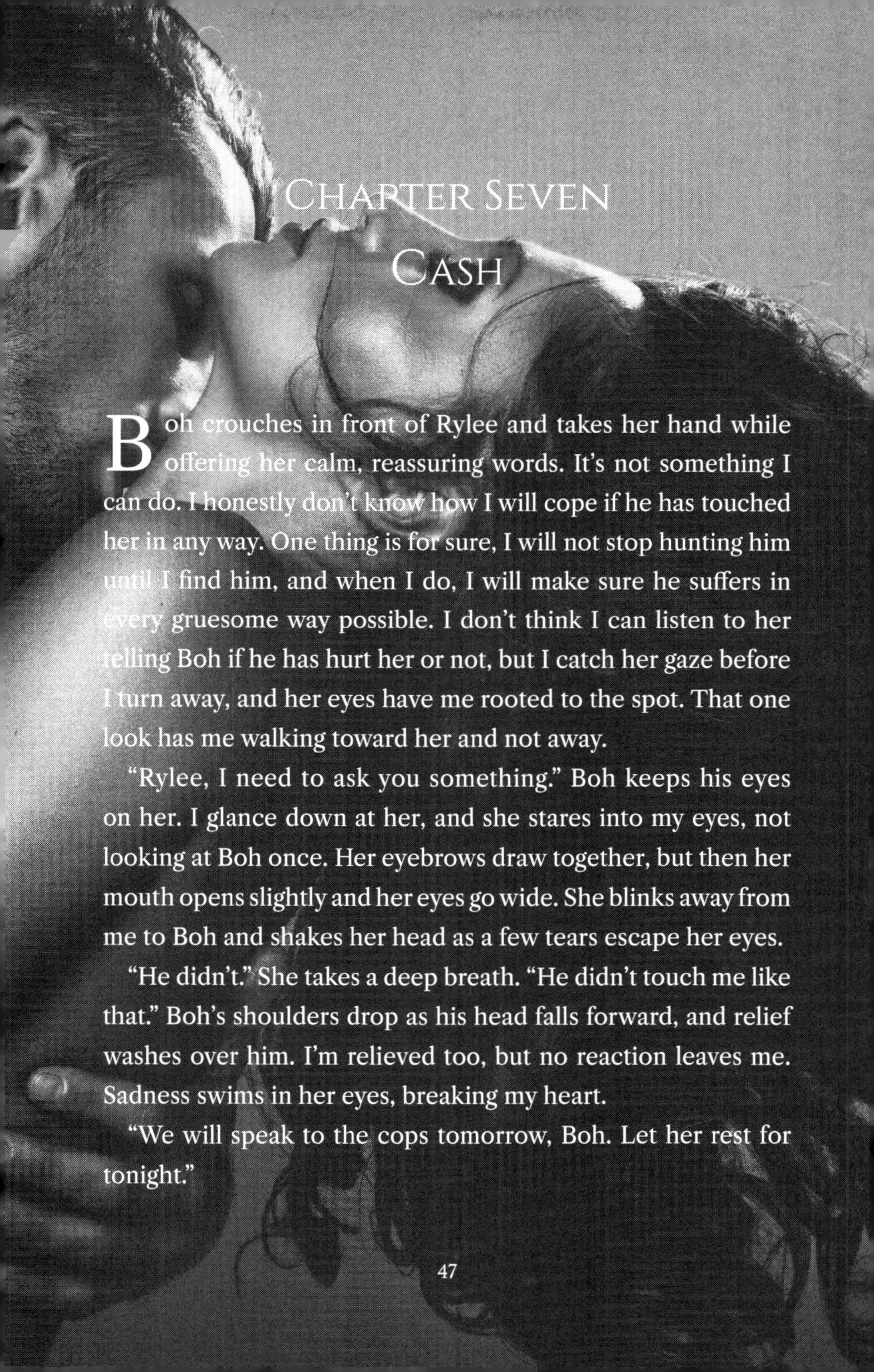

# Chapter Seven

## Cash

Boh crouches in front of Rylee and takes her hand while offering her calm, reassuring words. It's not something I can do. I honestly don't know how I will cope if he has touched her in any way. One thing is for sure, I will not stop hunting him until I find him, and when I do, I will make sure he suffers in every gruesome way possible. I don't think I can listen to her telling Boh if he has hurt her or not, but I catch her gaze before I turn away, and her eyes have me rooted to the spot. That one look has me walking toward her and not away.

"Rylee, I need to ask you something." Boh keeps his eyes on her. I glance down at her, and she stares into my eyes, not looking at Boh once. Her eyebrows draw together, but then her mouth opens slightly and her eyes go wide. She blinks away from me to Boh and shakes her head as a few tears escape her eyes.

"He didn't." She takes a deep breath. "He didn't touch me like that." Boh's shoulders drop as his head falls forward, and relief washes over him. I'm relieved too, but no reaction leaves me. Sadness swims in her eyes, breaking my heart.

"We will speak to the cops tomorrow, Boh. Let her rest for tonight."

"Is that okay with you?" She gives me a sharp nod. Boh leans forward and places a gentle kiss on her head, and a small smile graces her lips as he steps away.

"I'll be back tomorrow, Ry."

"Bye, Boh." He goes to walk away, but she grabs his arm, halting him. "And thank you." More tears escape her eyes. She lets go and curls into herself on the sofa, as if she is protecting herself.

"Let me know if you need anything." Boh slaps me on the back and heads for the door. The door shuts, and then silence fills the room. It's rare I feel awkward, or I'm at a loss for words, but I have no idea what to say or do. I want her to tell me everything, but I need to wait for her to tell me in her own time, although I've never been a patient man. I want to tell her everything I found out from Casey.

"Can I get you a drink or something to eat?" I don't even know if she's eaten or drunk anything in the last twenty-four hours.

"Some water, please," she whispers.

I walk into the kitchen and grab the filtered water from the fridge before seeing an open bottle of her favorite wine. I fill up a glass of water but also a glass of wine for her. This may calm her a bit and help her sleep. She wears a small smile as I bring both glasses into her. White wine has always been her favorite. She takes a couple of sips of the water and then reaches out for the wine.

"Thank you." She takes a few pulls, and her shoulders drop as a little bit of stress leaves her body.

Rylee wavers as she gets to her feet.

"I think I need to go lie down." She walks toward her bedroom. Anxiety courses through me when she turns the corner and is out of sight. I pour myself a glass of wine and drop onto the sofa. My body relaxes and I let my head drop back, and stare up at the ceiling. With every sip of this wine, the stress leaves my body more and more.

I'm happy we found Rylee, and I have her back here safe, but knowing he's still out there has me on edge. We won't be able to relax until he's found. I jolt upright at a noise breaking me from my thoughts and place my glass on the table. I stare at the front door until I hear the sound again. Crying. I storm toward the bedroom and knock on the door.

"Rylee. Rylee. Are you okay?" The crying continues. "Rylee, if you don't answer me, I'm coming in." She doesn't answer, so I open the door and scan the bedroom, not knowing what I'll find, James maybe?

But what I find is Rylee curled up on her bed, her knees pulled to her chest with her hands wrapped around them, and she cries into her lap. Her shoulders tremble with the hysterics of her sobs. I stand still, not knowing what to do. I want to console her, but my body freezes.

"I'm so sorry, Cash. I'm so fucking sorry." The pain in her voice pulls me toward her, and then I crouch down next to her and place my hand on her back.

"Talk to me, what's going on? You don't need to be sorry for anything," I whisper. Her head rises, and her bloodshot eyes pierce my heart. She's so broken, and I don't know how to fix her.

"I do, Cash. It's all my fault, the whole thing is my fault." More tears leave her eyes.

"Rylee. I don't understand what you're saying. What's your fault?"

"Jace." Her voice cracks, along with my heart as she says his name. "He's dead because of me." The sobs echo against the walls. She stares me straight in the eyes as tears run down her cheeks. "If it wasn't for me, Jace wouldn't be dead."

I rear my head back. What is she talking about? It has nothing to do with her.

"Rylee. Are you okay? I think you're tired. What happened to Jace was a freak accident, it has nothing to do with you." I try and coax her back from crying. I'm sure she hasn't slept and is confused right now.

"He . . . he—" A sob breaks from her throat as she looks at me again. "James killed him."

I drop back onto the floor, landing with a thud.

"Wha-what." I shake my head. "Rylee." Tears continue to track down her face.

"James had it in his head that I was his all along, from the night I met Jace. He believed I was his, so to get me, he killed Jace. He drugged his drink the night at the bar, that's what caused the crash." She takes a deep breath as her nose wrinkles and her lip curls in disgust.

"Jace is dead because of me. If he had never met me that night, you would still have your son here now."

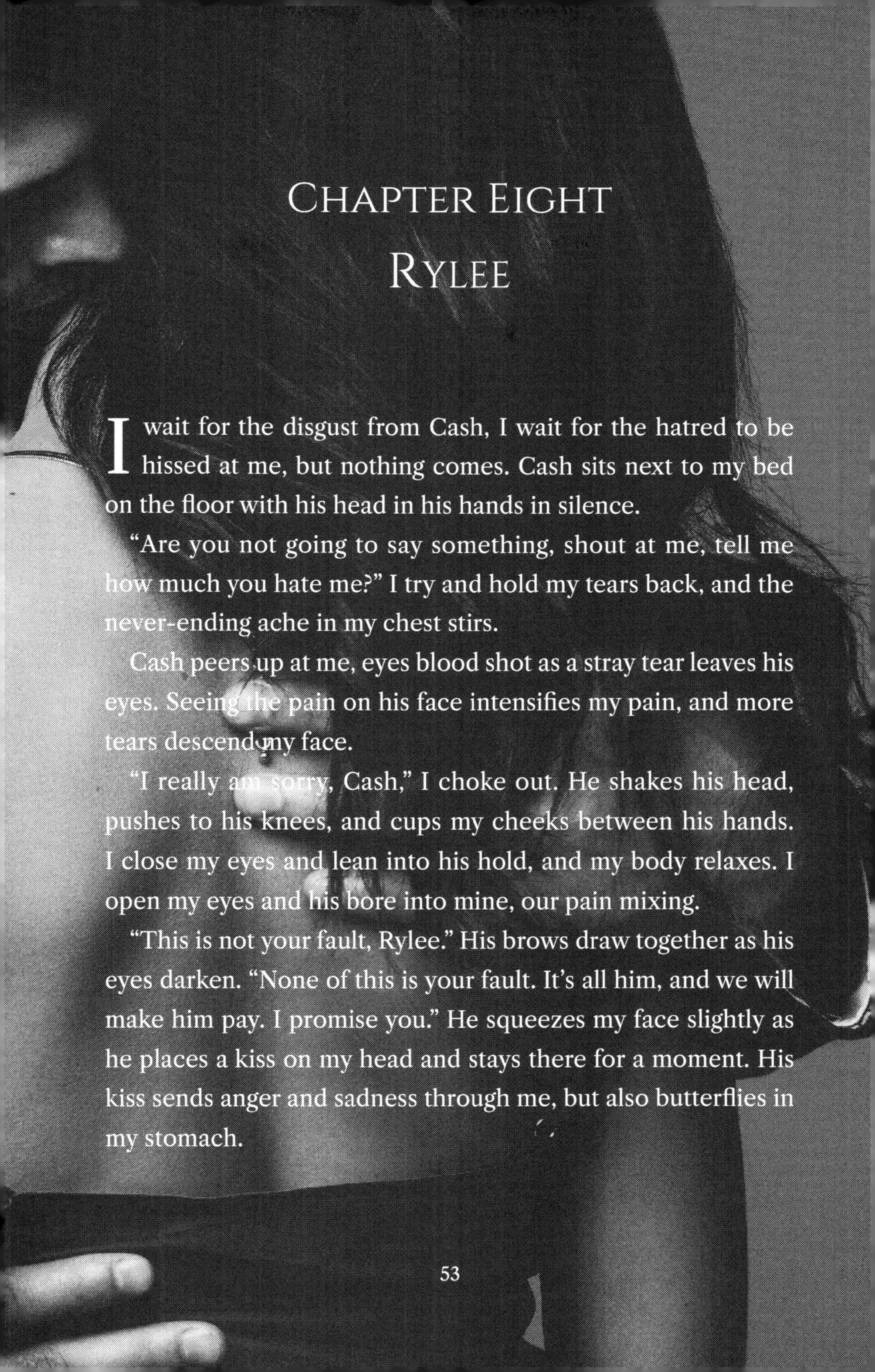

# Chapter Eight
## Rylee

I wait for the disgust from Cash, I wait for the hatred to be hissed at me, but nothing comes. Cash sits next to my bed on the floor with his head in his hands in silence.

"Are you not going to say something, shout at me, tell me how much you hate me?" I try and hold my tears back, and the never-ending ache in my chest stirs.

Cash peers up at me, eyes blood shot as a stray tear leaves his eyes. Seeing the pain on his face intensifies my pain, and more tears descend my face.

"I really am sorry, Cash," I choke out. He shakes his head, pushes to his knees, and cups my cheeks between his hands. I close my eyes and lean into his hold, and my body relaxes. I open my eyes and his bore into mine, our pain mixing.

"This is not your fault, Rylee." His brows draw together as his eyes darken. "None of this is your fault. It's all him, and we will make him pay. I promise you." He squeezes my face slightly as he places a kiss on my head and stays there for a moment. His kiss sends anger and sadness through me, but also butterflies in my stomach.

"You saved Jace. Don't ever believe anything else," he whispers as he slowly pulls away. "You promise me you will not blame yourself, Rylee?"

I nod. "I promise, Cash." I say it to make him feel better because I know how much this must be killing him, but how can I not blame myself when James told me it was my fault? He told me he wanted me, so he had to get rid of Jace. No matter how fucked up the situation is and how fucked up James is, his decision boiled down to me.

"Go sleep, Rylee. We are going to the police station tomorrow. It's going to be a long, emotional day telling them everything, so you're going to need some strength." He stands and walks toward the door.

"You can sleep in the spare room, don't sleep on the sofa."

He stops and takes a deep breath before looking over his shoulder at me. "I'm staying in here tonight. There is no way I'm letting you out of my sight after what happened today and after what you just told me." His voice cracks. "Go sleep. I'll be back here soon. Don't worry, I'll sleep on the floor." He walks out, closing the door behind him.

In a way, I'm glad he's staying in here. I don't think I could stay here on my own, and not just because of what happened with James but because of what I just told him. I feel like the closer he is, the more I realize he doesn't hate me for what happened. Maybe he does still care for me if he wants me safe.

I sigh, lying back on the bed, my mind rushing and processing everything that has happened in the last twenty-four hours. I can't believe this is my life. My life wasn't getting better, but I had started to accept what life had dealt me and that I was only ever going to have Jace in my life as a memory and nothing more. Now I'm back to square one. My boyfriend was killed because of me. How am I meant to get over this? Tears fall down my cheeks as I think back to what James said, but then I remember what else he said. *"It's so much deeper than you could possibly even think."* The more I think about that, the more I think he isn't referring to what he told me, and something tells me there is more to this, but what?

Cash walks in wearing only his pants, interrupting my overthinking, and I feel like the world falls beneath me. He glances up at me, then looks away.

"I thought you may have been asleep," he says, placing down a quilt he must have grabbed from the spare room. I can't help my gaze lingering on his body. His broad shoulders and muscular arms, there's no way you can't look. I feel his eyes on me, and my cheeks redden as I lie back on the pillow while hoping the world will swallow me.

"I couldn't sleep," I whisper.

"Do you need anything?" I want to ask him to come lie next to me. Just lie with me and hold me. Make me believe this isn't my fault. I feel so weak right now, and I hate it. I hate that this is my life.

"No, I'm fine. Night, Cash." I roll to my side and turn off the lamp, dreading tomorrow and the days to come.

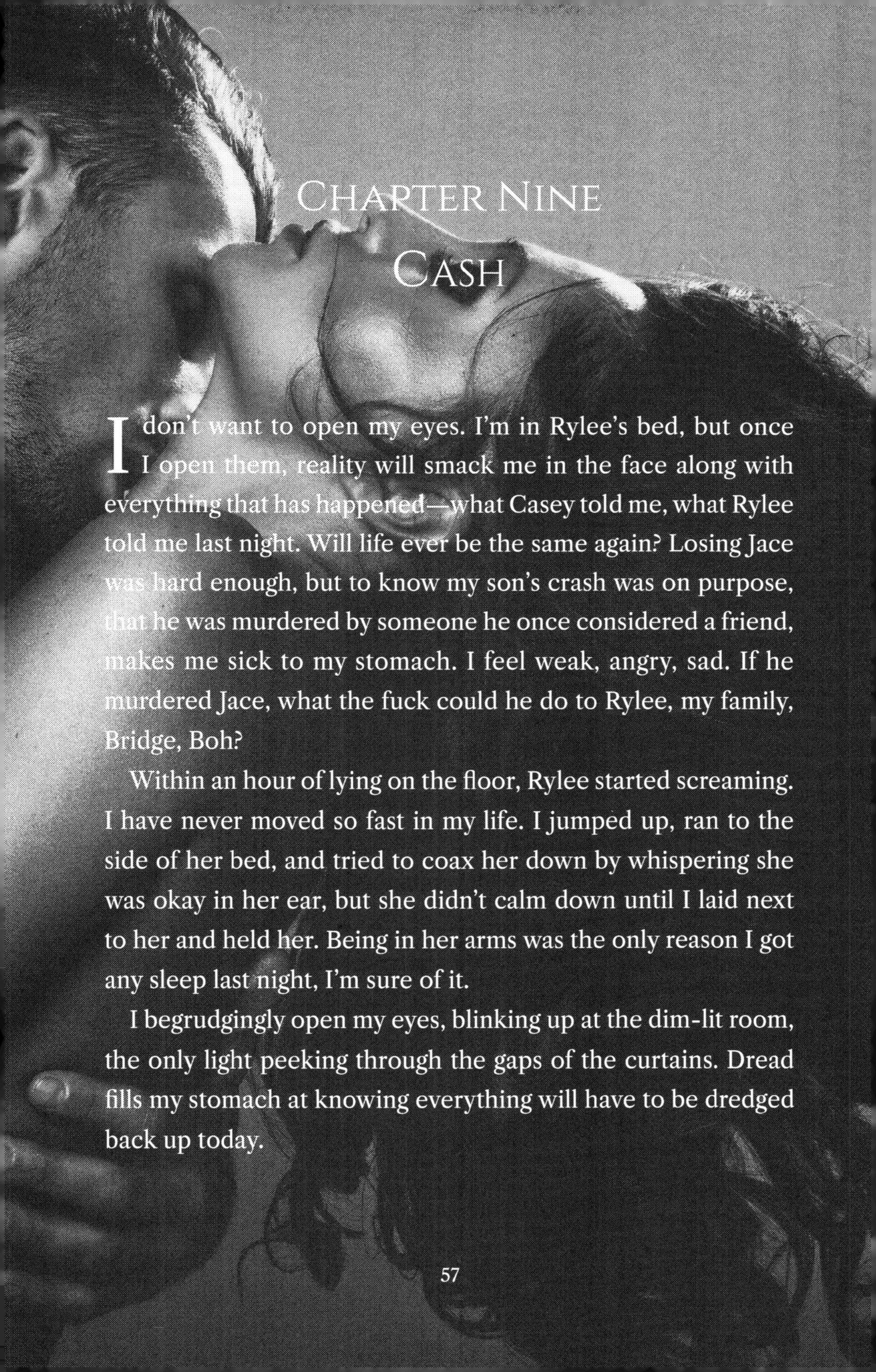

# Chapter Nine
## Cash

I don't want to open my eyes. I'm in Rylee's bed, but once I open them, reality will smack me in the face along with everything that has happened—what Casey told me, what Rylee told me last night. Will life ever be the same again? Losing Jace was hard enough, but to know my son's crash was on purpose, that he was murdered by someone he once considered a friend, makes me sick to my stomach. I feel weak, angry, sad. If he murdered Jace, what the fuck could he do to Rylee, my family, Bridge, Boh?

Within an hour of lying on the floor, Rylee started screaming. I have never moved so fast in my life. I jumped up, ran to the side of her bed, and tried to coax her down by whispering she was okay in her ear, but she didn't calm down until I laid next to her and held her. Being in her arms was the only reason I got any sleep last night, I'm sure of it.

I begrudgingly open my eyes, blinking up at the dim-lit room, the only light peeking through the gaps of the curtains. Dread fills my stomach at knowing everything will have to be dredged back up today.

I glance down at Rylee clinging to me around my waist, and her leg hangs over mine. It brings me back to that night Toni called me from Freedom when Rylee went mad and hit her thinking she was seeing Jace. She clung to me like I was her lifeline that night too. I remember the feeling then and it's the same now. Weightless, like everything will be okay. Whenever she's near, everything seems easier, life feels easier. Having her in my arms reminds me I can get through anything.

Her head lays on my chest with her face pointing up at me, her mouth open slightly. She's painfully beautiful. Without makeup, Rylee is a vision. Her natural long brown, glossy hair, her high cheekbones, the freckles which dust her nose and cheeks. I can picture those emerald-green eyes that would have me falling to my knees, offering her anything she wanted.

I stay here for a little while longer, soaking in her touch. The control freak in me wants to spin her around, pin her down, and demand she is mine and has to accept it. I don't care how fucking wrong it is or what people think of me when I'm with her. No one else matters. The alarm bells in my head know what this means. It goes so much deeper than a crush, and I have never felt so fucking fucked in all my life. The thought has me grinding my teeth because I don't know how much longer I can stay away from her. I don't even know if she wants me, but I don't care, I'll make her want me.

When I realized she had been taken, it felt like losing myself all over again. I didn't think I could bring myself back after losing Jace. Bridge and Boh helped, and I'll always be thankful to them for what they have done for me. They kept me standing, but

Rylee brought light back into my life and doesn't even realize it. I know if anyone could read inside my head, they would think I was the biggest piece of shit to walk this earth, and the funny thing is, I know it, but I can't turn off this obsession I have for her. It's not happening, and with what happened between us, I know deep down she feels the same fucked-up way. That's why I'm staying.

I let my eyes get their fill of her one last time before I place a gentle kiss to her head, breathing in the vanilla scent of her hair. Then I lean back and take a deep breath before peeling myself from her grip.

Even if I would prefer James to be six feet under instead, something tells me that would be too easy for him. I want him to suffer. I want him to fucking rot in prison for what he has done to my family, and I won't stop until he gets the hell he is owed.

---

I take a quick shower, and when I return to the room, Rylee is still fast asleep, no doubt exhausted from everything that has happened. I still haven't explained to her everything Casey told me and don't know when the right time will be. Boh or Bridge being here will help because I don't think I can tell her without losing my head. And then on top of that, I still need to break it to Bridge and Boh about what Rylee told me. When did life become such a mess.

Boh text me last night to tell me he had work covered. He wants to come with us today.

I'm about to wake Rylee when her name is screamed through the apartment. *Toni.*

"Ryleeeeee!" Rylee shoots up, eyes wide but looking like she doesn't know what month it is. The bedroom door flies open, and I'm surprised it doesn't come off its hinges. Toni barges in, runs toward Rylee, and throws herself at her. She bursts into tears while peppering kisses all over Rylee's face.

"I don't know what I would do if I lost you, Ry."

I walk away and let them have their moment. Rylee will want a coffee, so I head to the kitchen. I glance over my shoulder, and Rylee is staring at me over Toni's shoulder while they hold each other, tears tracking down her face. Her eyebrows are drawn downward, like she's waiting for something bad to happen. I give her a reassuring smile; whatever she goes through today, I will be right beside her. She gives me a small, relieved smile back. I know Rylee better than she thinks, and even though I asked her not to blame herself for James, she will.

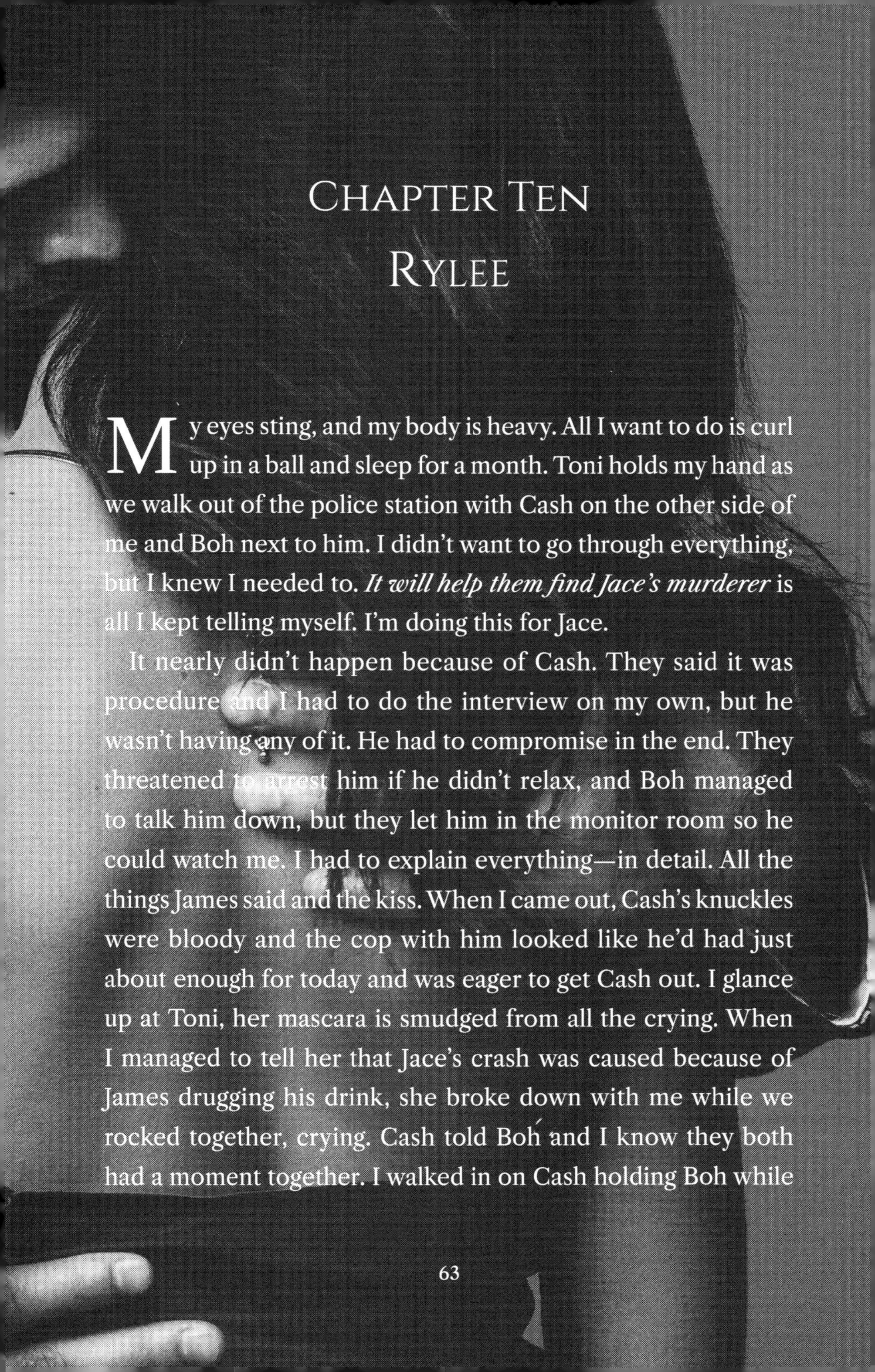

# Chapter Ten
## Rylee

My eyes sting, and my body is heavy. All I want to do is curl up in a ball and sleep for a month. Toni holds my hand as we walk out of the police station with Cash on the other side of me and Boh next to him. I didn't want to go through everything, but I knew I needed to. *It will help them find Jace's murderer* is all I kept telling myself. I'm doing this for Jace.

It nearly didn't happen because of Cash. They said it was procedure and I had to do the interview on my own, but he wasn't having any of it. He had to compromise in the end. They threatened to arrest him if he didn't relax, and Boh managed to talk him down, but they let him in the monitor room so he could watch me. I had to explain everything—in detail. All the things James said and the kiss. When I came out, Cash's knuckles were bloody and the cop with him looked like he'd had just about enough for today and was eager to get Cash out. I glance up at Toni, her mascara is smudged from all the crying. When I managed to tell her that Jace's crash was caused because of James drugging his drink, she broke down with me while we rocked together, crying. Cash told Boh and I know they both had a moment together. I walked in on Cash holding Boh while

Boh silently cried into Cash's shoulders. Boh then turned to me, and walked over pulling me into his arms whispering none of it is my fault.

"You're staying at my place tonight." Cash's words break me from my thoughts and bring me to a halt, along with Toni.

Before I can even respond, Toni interjects, "She's going to stay with me tonight. I will take good care of her, don't worry."

Cash looks between Toni and me. "I'm sorry Toni, but until we know what's going on, I don't want Rylee out of my sight."

Toni's glare burns into the side of my head as I stare at the ground. I don't know what to say right now. I want to be with Toni, but of course I feel safe with Cash. But he doesn't go about situations in the right way. Four months ago, he treated me as if I didn't exist most of the time, and now he's nearly getting himself arrested for me and demanding I stay at his place. To prove my thinking right, I glance up to Boh, and his eyebrows are drawn together, his gaze roaming Cash's face for some sign as to why he's acting like this. Toni is frowning at me, waiting for me to reply.

"Rylee." Toni speaks up. "Are you okay with this?" She has a slight bite to her voice, probably annoyed Cash hasn't given me a choice and told me what I was doing.

I grab Toni's hand and give it a slight squeeze. "He's right, Ton, I don't want to put you in any danger, who knows where he is." Toni has always been able to see when I'm lying or hiding something, and with her staring at me like this, I feel it's written all over my face what Cash and I did. Is it written over my face that every time he's around me, my heart beats a little faster and my stomach swarms with butterflies. Is it written all over my face that I've had thoughts of him I most definitely shouldn't be having?

Cash is also staring me down. I shake my head at Cash and frown for him to stop looking at me. The whole moment is awkward.

"Okayyy, but can we meet up tomorrow, please? Rachel is going out of her mind." I smile at her, thankful she let this go.

"I would love to go for some coffee." I squeeze her hand before dropping it.

She pulls me in for a hug, but before letting me go she whispers, "We're talking tomorrow." Like I said, Toni always knows when I'm hiding something, and I know she won't let this go until I tell her everything. She won't judge me; she never does. I could do the worst thing known to man and she would somehow justify what I did and argue with anyone as to why I'm right for what I did. Toni likes to dig deep and will want to know how I'm feeling about Cash, how I'm feeling about everything, and right now, I don't know. If someone pushes me, I may say what I don't think I'm ready to admit out loud yet.

"Bridge's flight lands in a few hours, I'm going to pick her up from the airport." Boh interrupts my spiraling mind.

"Can I come with you?" Cash stiffens next to me. I don't know what he thinks this is, but he will not have me locked up in his house like I'm some damsel in distress. I'm safe with Boh.

"Of course, you can, Ry. She is going out of her mind and will be relieved to see you." He smiles at me. Then his eyes flick to Cash again which causes his smile to falter slightly.

"I'll pick you up from Cash's at three, okay?" His gaze stays on Cash. He knows something is up.

"Perfect." I smile, shifting from foot to foot. The tension is building rapidly.

"I need to go back to my place to get some clothes," I say, aiming it at Cash and hoping he will defuse the situation and get us out of here quickly.

"Yeah, okay. Let's go." He walks toward his car without a goodbye to anyone.

"I love you Toni. I will speak to you later, okay?" I give her a reassuring smile.

"I love you too, baby. I'll see you tomorrow." She points at me.

"Tomorrow, I promise." I blow her a kiss, and she catches it, placing it in her pocket. I get a little lighter, and Toni's shoulders drop, and we laugh at the same time. The girl is my anchor. She gives me one last smile before turning away and walking toward her car. I swing my gaze to Boh watching Cash walk off.

"See you later, Boh."

His gaze softens. "Yeah, see you soon, Ry." Cash is stopped near his car and watching me walk toward him. He scans the area like he thinks there is a threat ready to jump out and take me any minute. My heart speeds up as he watches me. Is he just being a protective person of someone who has been in his family for six years, or is it more? We haven't spoken about what happened before I was taken. I don't know how to approach the subject. Will I be happy if he says now that he's had time to think it over, he realizes it was a mistake, or will I be sad? What if he says it wasn't a mistake and he doesn't regret it? There is so much going on in my mind, I feel like I could close my eyes and shut down. Shut myself away from it. It's physically and mentally exhausting.

"You look deep in thought," Cash says as I stand next to him.

"Yeah, I'm just tired." I do not have the energy to get into this with him now.

"We will go grab your clothes and then head back to my place. You should be able to get a nap in before Boh picks you up."

I nod, mustering up a smile before opening the passenger door and slipping in. I'm already done with the day. If it wasn't for Bridge, I would go back to Cash's, lock myself away in the guest room, and not come out until next year.

# Chapter Eleven
# Rylee

I didn't sleep a wink. Once I grabbed my stuff from my apartment and got back to Cash's and took a shower, I was too keyed up to sleep. Cash didn't say a word the whole way, and since walking into his house, he showed me where I would sleep and then walked away, and I haven't seen him since.

Boh text me to tell me he will be ten minutes, so at least I can get out of here for a while. I hate when Cash does this hot-and-cold shit. He knows how guilty I feel and how much this is killing me, with everything going on, so why is he now giving me the cold shoulder, making me wonder what I did wrong, and I can only think of one thing. What I told him about James. I don't know how long I'll be able to keep up with this silent treatment before I escape and go stay with Toni.

I grab my jacket and bag and slip out of the room, trying to be as quiet as possible, but within a few seconds of heading down the stairs, Cash appears at the bottom.

"Is Boh here?" he deadpans.

"No," I say as I walk past him and toward the door.

"Then where are you going?" His footsteps thump behind me.

"To wait outside, he will be here in a few minutes." I grab the door handle, and Cash's hand lands above it, slamming it shut.

"You can wait in here until he arrives."

I'm done with his moody shit. I spin on the spot, giving him a death glare. This exact moment reminds me of when he turned up at my apartment drunk and told me he couldn't stay away from me. He stares down at me, and the blue in his eyes has darkened and his eyebrows drop into a sharp point.

"I would rather wait outside, thanks."

He steps in behind me so I can't get to the door.

"Like I said," he grits out before bending down to look me directly in the eyes. "You can wait in here for him."

"What is your fucking problem, Cash?" The doorbell rings. "Saved by the bell, I guess." I shoulder check him out of the way, and he moves away from the door as I yank it open. Boh eyes us both, and the tension could cut glass right now.

"Perfect timing, Boh. Let's go." I slam the door behind me, and Boh winces. I don't even try to justify or make out it was an accident. I'm too pissed off.

On the way to the airport, Boh makes small talk with me, but I hate the tension in the air. I have never had this with him before. He was always the person to break the tension, to turn everything into a joke. Since Jace left this world, his light has been missing. Life is dull without him.

"Rylee, can I ask you something." *Don't panic, Rylee, it could be anything.*

"Cash seems . . ." *Oh hell.* "I don't know, different." I keep looking out the window. I have always been a terrible liar.

"I think we all are, Boh. Including you." It's not a lie, he is, we all are. Who would be the same after everything that has happened.

"Yeah." He sighs. "I guess you're right."

"He just seems different with you." *Fuck my life.*

"How do you mean?" As much as I want to defuse the situation, I want to hear what others see.

"He's gotten extra protective of you all of a sudden. Don't get me wrong, Cash has always been protective, he was hell to grow up with." He laughs.

I smile to myself because I bet it was actual hell growing up with an older brother like Cash. I bet he was nightmare for poor Bridge.

"And please don't get me wrong, we are all here for you, Ry. We will always protect you." He grasps my hand, and I look over at him as his gaze flicks to me and then back to the road. "Maybe it's just me, but he's just different, I can't explain it really."

I can't either, Boh. I wish I knew what was going on in that man's mind.

We wait at the gate for Bridge, and the minute she walks through and her gaze lands on me, she bursts into tears, abandons her luggage, and runs toward me. I sprint toward her, and we jump into each other's arms. Bridge's hold is all it takes for me to break down. Everything in my life is a mess, and with Bridge here, I feel like she can make it all better, even if at the back of my mind I know she can't. Cash called her and told her what happened and what James had done. He didn't want to wait until she was here, he felt she had to know when everyone else did. Bridge called me, while we both cried and she reiterated it wasn't my fault and that I shouldn't blame myself. It's easier said than done.

"My darling girl, I'm here, I'm here," she whispers through sobs. I grip her tight, taking in her smell that grounds me like nothing else.

"God, I'm never leaving you again, Rylee." I stay in her arms, letting her hold me. I never want her to leave me again, but a niggling feeling stirs in my body. Would she leave me and never talk to me again if she found out I kissed Cash? The thought has me holding her a little tighter. She would hate me if she found out, I know she would. Some days I hate myself.

"You can stay with me tonight, we can have a girls' night and eat lots of snacks, what do you think?" She continues to hold me. I know Cash will cause a scene if I do this, and I don't want to cause any more suspicion. Boh is already questioning stuff, and Bridge will clock within an instant. It always scared me how well she knew me and Jace, so I have no doubt if she saw the way Cash acted today, she would know something has happened. I pull myself away from her.

"Maybe tomorrow, Bridge. I'm so tired. I think I'm just going to go back to Cash's and crash." My eyes snag on to the floor and then the wall, everywhere but at her.

"Cash?" *Oh no.*

"Yeah, he, uh wants me to stay there for the time being. Just until James is found." I brave it and look at her, and her eyes soften, and she gives me a gentle smile.

"Always the protector, that man." Boh walks up to us with Bridge's bags in tow. He bends down and kisses her on her head.

"Let's get you both back," Boh says as Bridge and I turn around and walk out of the airport while holding each other. I have no idea what I'm going to do with Cash. I can't lose this family. Apart from a handful of friends, they're all I have.

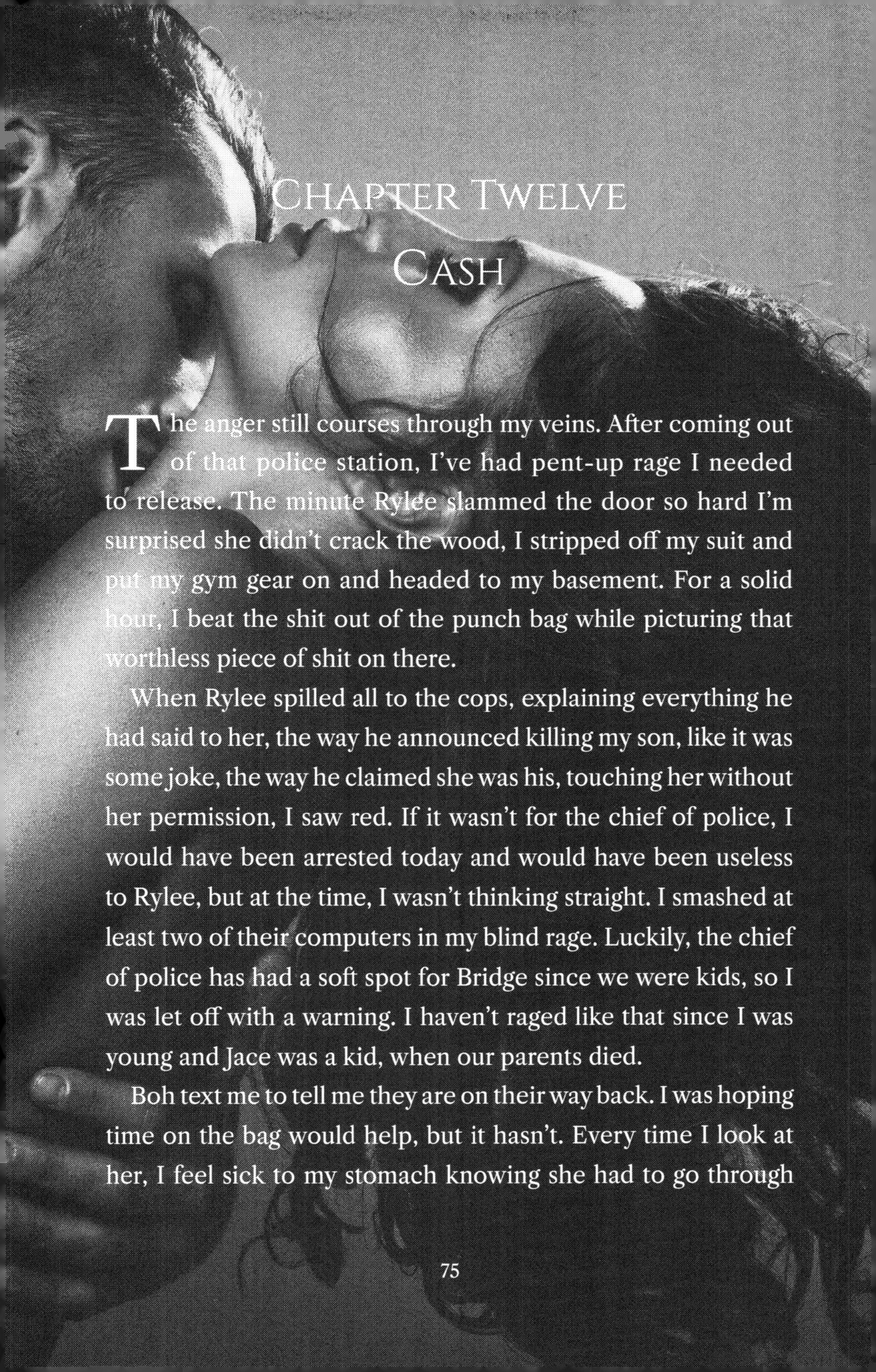

# Chapter Twelve

## Cash

The anger still courses through my veins. After coming out of that police station, I've had pent-up rage I needed to release. The minute Rylee slammed the door so hard I'm surprised she didn't crack the wood, I stripped off my suit and put my gym gear on and headed to my basement. For a solid hour, I beat the shit out of the punch bag while picturing that worthless piece of shit on there.

When Rylee spilled all to the cops, explaining everything he had said to her, the way he announced killing my son, like it was some joke, the way he claimed she was his, touching her without her permission, I saw red. If it wasn't for the chief of police, I would have been arrested today and would have been useless to Rylee, but at the time, I wasn't thinking straight. I smashed at least two of their computers in my blind rage. Luckily, the chief of police has had a soft spot for Bridge since we were kids, so I was let off with a warning. I haven't raged like that since I was young and Jace was a kid, when our parents died.

Boh text me to tell me they are on their way back. I was hoping time on the bag would help, but it hasn't. Every time I look at her, I feel sick to my stomach knowing she had to go through that and I couldn't help her and be there for her. I couldn't be there for my son.

Rylee is strong, and I know she will get through this, but I don't know how I'm meant to let her get on with her life knowing he could take her at any moment. It's not going to happen. Until he is found, she is staying here, and I don't give a shit what she has to say. Over my dead body is he getting his hands on her again.

Boh and Bridge stayed for takeout, but I could barely stomach anything. Bridge asked a couple of questions regarding my mood, so I told her I was tired. Boh kept looking at me funny. I could tell earlier he was questioning things in his head with the way he was watching me outside the police station. I don't care though. I'll always protect the ones I love, and I failed this time. Miserably. I head into the kitchen to pour myself a whiskey, hoping it might take the edge off, and I'm taken back when I see Rylee standing in front of the fridge filling up her glass.

She looks at me over her shoulder. "I'm just getting some water, then I'll be out of your hair," she mutters.

I don't reply, because what do I say to her. She sighs and then spins on her feet.

"No, actually I won't get out of your hair, what is the fucking problem, Cash?" she spits, slamming the glass down on the counter, and I'm surprised it doesn't shatter. "If you keep this up, you can bet your ass I'll be out of here quicker than you can blink. I didn't ask for this." She points to the floor. "This is all you. You wanted me here, yet you treat me like I've done something wrong."

Her voice cracks and makes me feel like the biggest piece of shit. "I'm sorry, okay, Cash. I'm sorry for what happened with James. I'm sorry you had to hear all that at the police station, and I'm sorry your son is dead because of me, but if you hate me for it, then you need to let me go because I can't stay here knowing you're angry with me." What started off as anger, has now turned into pure torment. Her tears track down her cheeks, one after the other. I storm toward her and grab her by the back of neck.

"Listen here and listen good," I say, inches from her face.

"It. is. Not. Your. Fault. Jace. Is. Dead." My heart cracks open whenever I have to say my son's name in the same sentence as the word dead. I will not have her beating herself up over this. "Do you hear me." Her eyes flick between mine, tears welling. She looks so sad and defeated.

"Then please stop treating me like it is," she whispers, with her gaze to the floor. Her words crack my heart. I was struggling to look at her after the station, but I never thought how me being cold toward her would make her feel like I blame her for Jace's death.

I grab her chin. "Look at me, Rylee." She is desperately trying to hold back her tears. "I'm sorry. It's no excuse, but hearing what happened and then what Casey told me it sen—"

"What do you mean what Casey told you? Casey who?" The slight bite to her voice has me taken back.

"Did you not wonder how we found you?" It hasn't been spoken about, but I wondered if she had questioned it. I told the police what Casey told me, and they said they would bring her in for questioning as well.

"I haven't really had time to think, but who the fuck is Casey?"

"Wow, what's wrong?"

"What's wrong? You have been acting funny with me since the station, making me feel like complete shit, and now you have been talking to someone named Casey about me. What the fuck?" I'm completely thrown by her reaction, and the way she blinks and opens and closes her mouth, I think she is as well.

"I-I'm sorry. I don't know where that came from."

I nod. "Casey was James's girlfriend, well, not girlfriend but—"

"Casey," she whispers. She nods. "I remember her, I met her once when I was out with Toni. They were at the same place we were."

I grimace. Casey told me James has logs of Rylee's favorite places, and somehow always knew where she was going. I explained all this to the police. They checked Rylee's phone while she was at the station, but nothing came back. When we went to collect her stuff, I grabbed her laptop, and Boh took it back to the station so they could check for tracking.

Her brows are drawn together. I know this will be hard for Rylee her to hear, but I have to tell her. "Let me pour you a glass of wine and we will talk, yes?" She nods and walks into the living room. I pour us both a glass of wine because I know this will be hard for me to tell her without losing my shit.

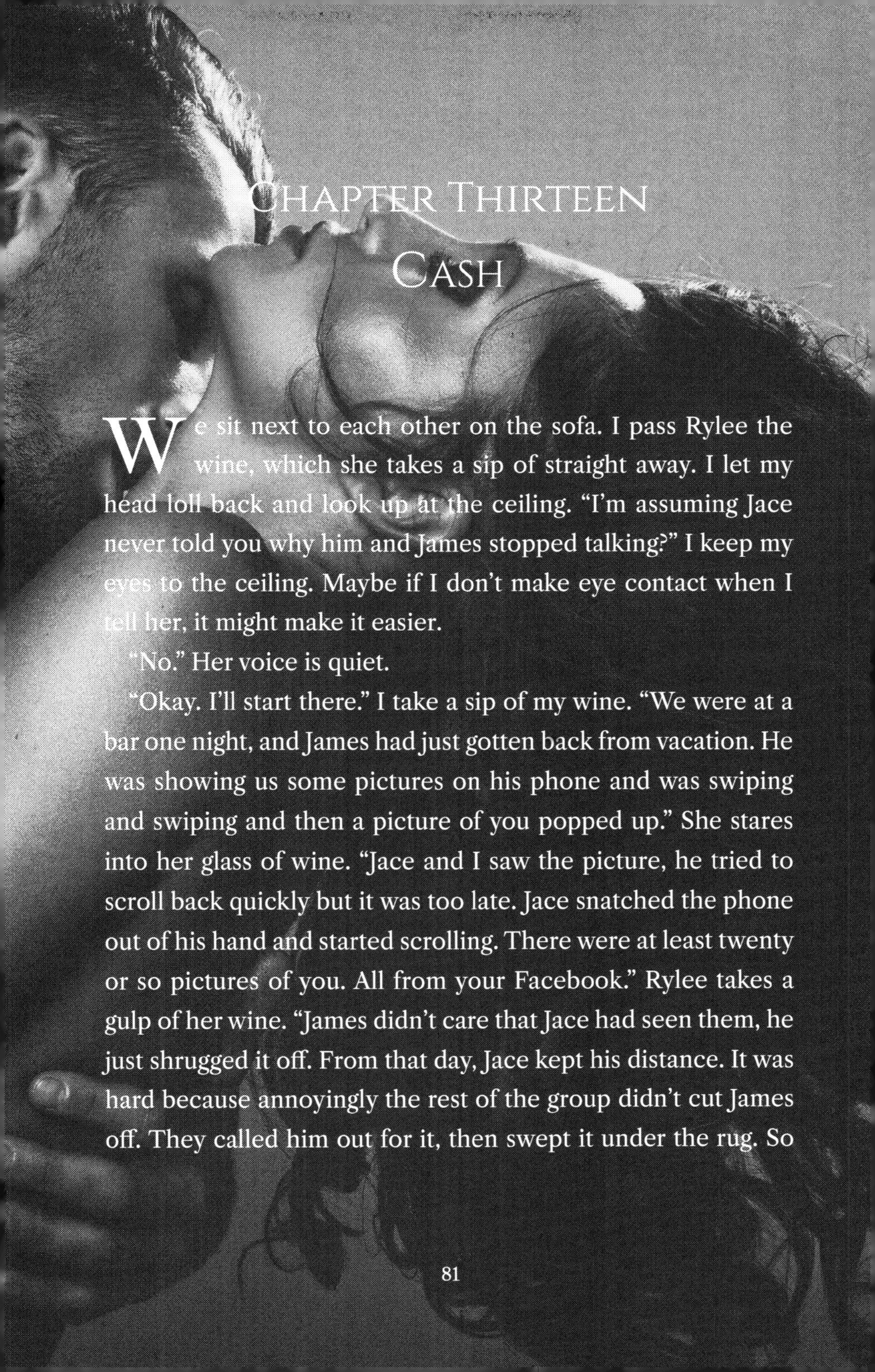

# Chapter Thirteen

# Cash

We sit next to each other on the sofa. I pass Rylee the wine, which she takes a sip of straight away. I let my head loll back and look up at the ceiling. "I'm assuming Jace never told you why him and James stopped talking?" I keep my eyes to the ceiling. Maybe if I don't make eye contact when I tell her, it might make it easier.

"No." Her voice is quiet.

"Okay. I'll start there." I take a sip of my wine. "We were at a bar one night, and James had just gotten back from vacation. He was showing us some pictures on his phone and was swiping and swiping and then a picture of you popped up." She stares into her glass of wine. "Jace and I saw the picture, he tried to scroll back quickly but it was too late. Jace snatched the phone out of his hand and started scrolling. There were at least twenty or so pictures of you. All from your Facebook." Rylee takes a gulp of her wine. "James didn't care that Jace had seen them, he just shrugged it off. From that day, Jace kept his distance. It was hard because annoyingly the rest of the group didn't cut James off. They called him out for it, then swept it under the rug. So

Jace still had to see him, but he did everything he could to keep James away from you."

"That's why he acted the way he did when James dropped me home."

"Yep."

She takes a couple more gulps of her wine. I point to the glass. "Do you want me to top that up for you?"

She shakes her head. "No, thanks. Please carry on."

"I got a call yesterday afternoon from Casey. I don't know how she got my number, but I'm glad she did." I focus on the stem of my glass, running my finger up and down, then close my eyes, recalling everything Casey told me on the phone. I've never wanted to hurt a man as much as I do James.

"She had split from James. He told her she did what he needed. She said she was hooked by James, he got his claws so deep into her she was like his puppet, and it wasn't until he chucked her that she snapped out of the trance she was in."

I sigh, knowing I need to get the rest out.

"James made Casey do things. Act things out for him. He would make Casey pretend to be you." She gasps and stares at me with wide eyes and her hand over her mouth. I want to console her, but she needs to know everything. If I stop now, I'll never tell her the rest.

"She had to dress like you. He would show her pictures of you to recreate hairstyles. She said this was all before she had met you. He would call her Rylee. He—" I take a deep breath before saying the next words. "When they had sex, or did anything sexual, he would call her Rylee."

She chokes on a sob, so I grab her hand and hold it, squeezing it tight.

"The day at Blossoms wasn't a coincidence. He knew you were going there. He knew you had a booking. He made Casey take the morning and afternoon off work so he could take her there. When Casey was with James that night, he hit her because she wasn't acting enough like you. He then began to talk down to her, telling her she would never be you, so he didn't know why she tried."

"Cash, please stop. I can't. I think I'm going to be sick." Rylee jumps up from the couch and runs out of the living room and up the stairs.

She slams the bathroom door, and as I approach, I hear her gagging, so I open the door.

"Cash, please leave me."

I sigh while crouching next to her and gathering her hair up. "I'm not going anywhere, Rylee." I rub her back as she cries and heaves into the toilet.

I tear off some tissue and place it in her hand. She mumbles a "Thank you."

She flushes the toilet and slumps next to the toilet and cries in her hands. Her uncontrollable sobs cut through me like shattered glass.

"Why has he done this, Cash. Whyyy?" she wails. I gather her in my arms, and she crawls into my lap and holds me while crying into my chest.

"First, Jace, now this. He needs to be stopped." She sniffles.

"He will. I won't stop until he's found and locked away. I'll make sure he never sees the light of day again."

"Let me run you a bath, Ry." She nods into my chest but doesn't move.

"Can we just stay here a little longer?" What she doesn't know is I could stay like this all night.

"Of course," I reply. Five minutes later, when her tears dry up, her head slowly rises. Her gaze penetrates me like she can read every thought in my mind. She is so close I would only have to lean forward slightly for our lips to touch. The lips I dream about, the lips I crave every day.

"Thank you, Cash. Thank you for everything you have done for me." She gives me a sad smile before standing up.

"I can run my own bath, yo—"

I shake my head while jumping up onto my feet. "No, go get yourself sorted. I will start it for you now."

She nods, and before she walks out, she turns around. "Cash."

I nod for her to continue.

"Jace was lucky to have you as a dad. Never forget that." The words make me sad and happy all at once. I give her a tight-lipped smile to keep my emotions in check. I was a good dad, but if he ever found out why I was the way I was toward her, I would have been the worst dad to walk this earth.

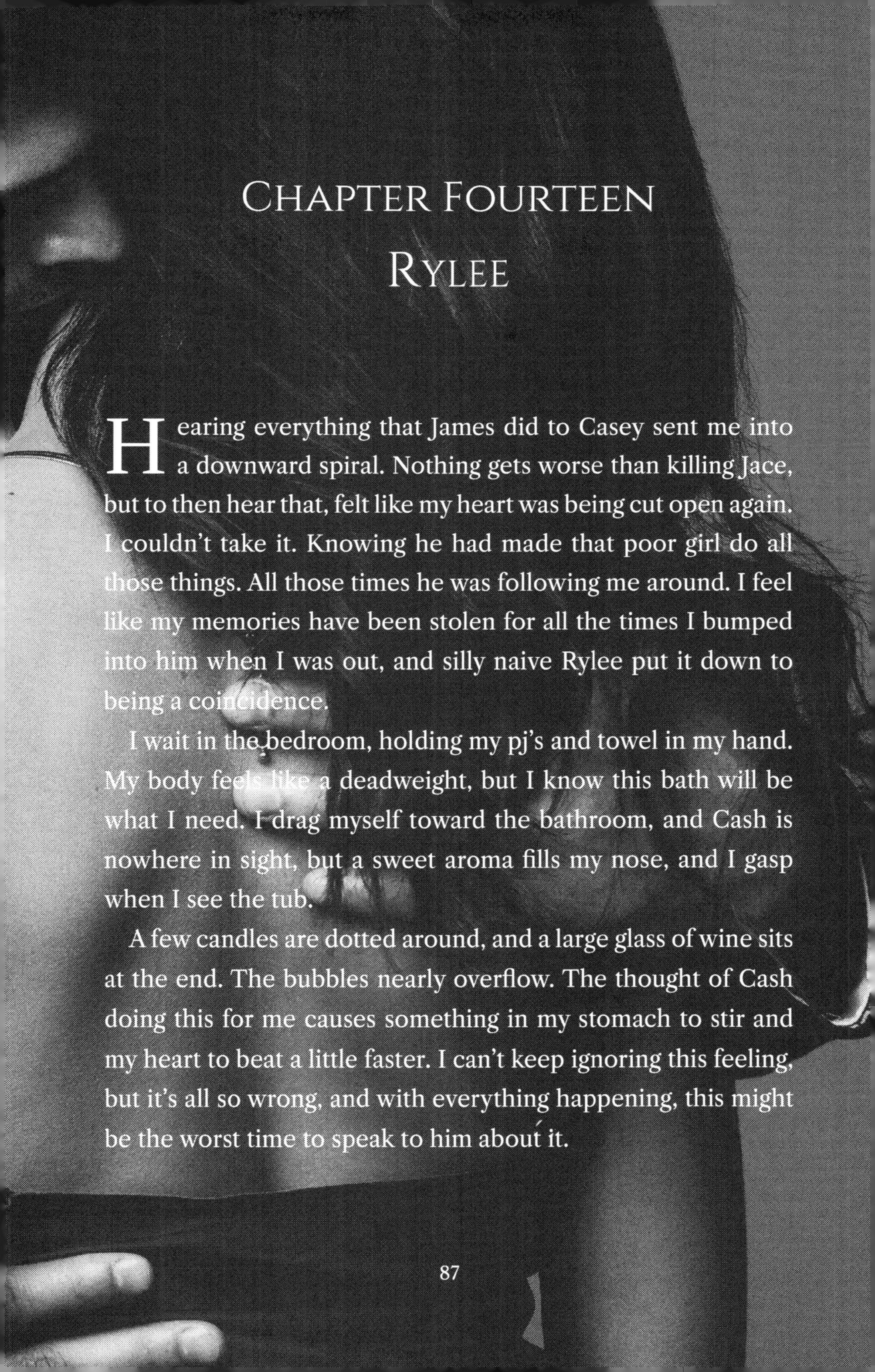

# Chapter Fourteen
## Rylee

Hearing everything that James did to Casey sent me into a downward spiral. Nothing gets worse than killing Jace, but to then hear that, felt like my heart was being cut open again. I couldn't take it. Knowing he had made that poor girl do all those things. All those times he was following me around. I feel like my memories have been stolen for all the times I bumped into him when I was out, and silly naive Rylee put it down to being a coincidence.

I wait in the bedroom, holding my pj's and towel in my hand. My body feels like a deadweight, but I know this bath will be what I need. I drag myself toward the bathroom, and Cash is nowhere in sight, but a sweet aroma fills my nose, and I gasp when I see the tub.

A few candles are dotted around, and a large glass of wine sits at the end. The bubbles nearly overflow. The thought of Cash doing this for me causes something in my stomach to stir and my heart to beat a little faster. I can't keep ignoring this feeling, but it's all so wrong, and with everything happening, this might be the worst time to speak to him about it.

I step into the bath, the water is the perfect temperature. I ease myself down and let out a long sigh as I lie back. That's the thing with baths, they can either take it all away or bring it all to the surface. Right now, I feel content but sad. Like I could lie here blissfully but still cry. What is wrong with me? I close my eyes, and let the bubbles consume me, pretending the water removes every weight holding me down in life. If only it was that simple.

Out of nowhere, a wave of sadness crashes into me. I didn't think I could cry any more, but it floods out of me. I cry for everything in my life: for Jace, for the life he can't have back, I cry for us, for our future we will never have. I cry for his family that will never get to see his lightness again, for Casey who had to endure all of James's torturous games, and then I cry for myself. I lost the love of my life and now I sit here in his dad's house, in this messed-up situation, knowing these feelings are not going to go away. Then I have to admit I have feelings for Cash Stiles and my life is so fucked up, I don't know if it's ever going to get better.

My breath lodges in my throat as the sobs come too fast for me to let them out. I don't hear Cash approach, but when the arms that I have been craving wrap around me, it's like all the pain seeps out.

"Shh, Rylee. I'm here. Let it out."

I grip Cash's arms. My head rests on his chest as he leans over the bath rocking me until the cries get softer.

"How do you do it, Cash." I don't know what I'm asking: deal with his son's death, deal with the fact his son has been murdered, deal with the fact he's kissed me.

"Deal with what?" he whispers.

"Life. This shit card life has dealt you."

"Lie back, Rylee." I don't even think, I just do what he says. He eases me down into the water, and my trust in him takes over, and my mind doesn't even need to work. I allow him to lead my body and mind. I keep my eyes closed as he runs his finger through my hair in the water, and then he pulls me back up, bringing my knees to my chest. Wrapping my arms around my legs, I lean my head on them. A bottle cap pops open and then his fingers are massaging my scalp. The simple act has me choking on another sob. He's taking care of me when I need it most.

"Life can be real shit, Ry." he says, still massaging my scalp. "I learned that when I lost my parents within the same week." Jace told me about his gran dying of cancer and his grandad having a heart attack five days later. He was only seven, so he didn't remember them well enough, but he had pictures of them. Bridge always spoke about them and what incredible parents they were and how they worshipped the ground Jace walked on.

"I didn't know what life was without them, Ry. They had always been there. Always helped me, guided me. Losing them was the hardest thing I've ever had to deal with, especially having a little sister who was more heartbroken than I'd seen anyone. She lost both of her best friends within five days of each other. It was tough."

He presses on my shoulder, pushing me backward. He uses both hands to rinse the shampoo out of my hair. I open my eyes and gaze over Cash's face as he concentrates on what he's doing. He lifts me back up to sitting, then runs the conditioner through my hair.

"The one thing I remember was crying for weeks, feeling as if my whole life had stopped. Everything goes dark, but when you look around, the world is still spinning and doesn't stop to grieve with you. People get on with their lives while you're stuck in your head not knowing how to get on with yours. You're expected to just build up your walls and fall back into routine. Your clients don't wait around for you to build yourself back up, you still have to pay bills. You still have to go shopping and live life. Nothing stops for you.

"Then there was Jace. Being a single dad didn't just stop at that moment. I still had to bathe him, feed him, put him to bed. I had to build up my walls, even if they were jagged and broken, and get on with life, just like everyone else. It's not that easy for some people. This is the shit side of life, and this isn't going to be the last time my walls fall and crumble. This won't be the last time I crash and burn, but I'd done it once so I knew I could do it again. I think having Jace helped. It was a distraction. I couldn't just give up, because I had him, and what a distraction he was." He chuckles.

I smile through more tears as Cash slides me back down to rinse the conditioner out of my hair. This should be awkward, but it's actually the most at ease I've felt in a long time. I close my eyes, relaxing at the feel of his fingers running through my hair, and hoping all my troubles wash away with his actions.

Cash pulls me gently back up, and I feel the moment slipping through my fingers. I don't ever want to lose this moment, but Cash doesn't stop. He soaps up a loofah and scrubs my back. I smile to myself while resting my face on my knees again.

"I would wake up every morning with Jace lying next to me, cuddling me, it was like he knew I needed him. I woke up every day with a smile because of him. He took the pain away and brought back the light in my darkness. I knew then I had to pick myself up, not just for me, but for him and my family. I had to accept the harsh reality that is life and had to accept my parents were no longer here and were just a memory. I had to say goodbye to that part of my life because it was no more. That doesn't mean I don't still think of them, every day I think of them, but I couldn't wallow in self-pity anymore, I couldn't drag through life. I had to remember the good times, hold onto the amazing memories they gave me, and say goodbye.

"Is that what you have done with Jace?" I'm not judging him in the slightest, what he says makes sense because that is what I've been doing for the past few months—dragging myself through life. I just want to know if it feels different with Jace.

"It's different. The love you have for your children is a love you will only ever have once. It's a different kind of love, a unique love, but it's also the strongest of them all." He goes silent for a minute.

"It cut deeper than anything I've felt before. The shock lasted a while before the grieving kicked in, but this time, I didn't have

Jace there to distract me, so I turned to drinking. Alcohol was my best friend. I grieved into every bottle I opened and with every sip I took, but every morning, that anxious and panicked feeling was there when I opened my eyes. The pain I had nursed the day before would be back again, and drinking was the only thing that took the pain away, even if it was temporary. It would until I saw a picture of him or had a memory of him." He pauses, long finished rubbing my back and arms. He doesn't touch me anywhere else, just stays resting on his knees, arms leaned over the rim of the bath. We sit there in comfortable silence.

"The night before I ended up at your apartment, I had a dream." I think back to the dreams I used to have of Jace every night through my grieving. They were painful, but I felt so close to him in those moments.

"It was just us at a bar after a long day at work, like we always used to do. Talking about work, laughing, joking. Then he just stared at me and stopped talking. Then he started disappearing. First it was his hand and then one arm. I was frantic, not knowing what to do, and the more I touched him, the faster he faded. His last words—" Cash clears his throat as he looks down to the floor. "He said please look after her." My breath hitches. He means me. "Then he was gone." Cash take a deep breath before continuing.

"I don't believe in the afterlife, and I know it was just a dream and concoction of my own thoughts, but when I woke up that morning, I felt a pull to you, Ry. I tried drinking it away, hence why I ended up at your place that night. I wanted to sit in Jace's office, and in my drunken state, I thought he might show me a message to confirm my dream, but he didn't. I then realized it was just my own selfishness wanting to be near you." He whispers the last part. My heart beats out of my chest with that small confession. He stands, drying his hands on the towel. I keep my head rested on my lap, watching him as he walks toward the door.

"You want to know how I do it, Ry? How I get through losing my son." He stops at the door and turns toward me, keeping his eyes on my face.

"You. You're the light in my darkness." He walks out the door, closing it behind him and leaving me stunned and feeling more confused than I ever have. But what I do know is, all the pain I felt half an hour ago is no longer there. He made it stop.

# Chapter Fifteen
# Rylee

I think I saw every hour on the clock last night. My head was swarming with thoughts of Cash. Everything that should bother me, isn't anymore, it's just thoughts of him and everything he said. How it all made sense and then "*You. You're the light in my darkness*." That has changed everything.

It wasn't until I was in bed that it hit me: I was in the bath naked, and Cash washed me. No one has ever done that for me. I cried in bed, but not because I was sad, but because of how overwhelming the whole situation was: his words, his touch, his gentleness. I have missed that feeling.

My nightstand clock reads 5:52 a.m. I sigh heavily, rubbing my eyes. I'm not meeting Toni until eleven, and there's no way I will be able to sleep now, so I may as well start the caffeine intake. I drag myself to the end of bed and sit there, pushing the bags under my eyes while staring at myself in the mirror. They're probably worse because of all the crying yesterday. I run my fingers through my silky hair, and the memories of Cash massaging my scalp flash through my mind. My whole body erupts in goose bumps. I let out another sigh before pushing myself up off the bed. Coffee will be my only friend today.

As I turn the corner into the kitchen, I gasp at Cash sitting at the island, with the lights on dim. My breath hitches when I realize he's in plain navy lounge pants and no top. The dim light above him makes him stand out more than he normally does. The light bounces of his muscular arms leaning on the countertop, his back muscles are bulging. His hair slightly curled at the ends, stick up like he has run his fingers through it multiple times.

Then his head moves, and he stares at me. He always reminded me of someone, and I could never pinpoint who until now—a sexier version of Henry Cavill, if that's even possible. He eyes me up and down, taking me in. It's like his gaze is burning into my skin as it runs up my body. I don't even move, I just stand there. When our gazes meet, then he looks away. It feels like he just rejected me. *Ouch.*

"You're up early," he mumbles.

I tiptoe into the kitchen, wanting to get this coffee and head back to my room.

"Yeah, I couldn't sleep," I say as I pull a cup from the cupboard. He doesn't say anything, so I follow up with "You?" I glance up at him as I pour the coffee.

He nods, finishing the coffee in his cup. "Same." He places the cup down and pushes his chair back. Why does he have to leave just because I'm here? He's so hot and cold all the time; I never know what he's thinking. The Cash from last night is long gone, and back is the moody, unpredictable Cash.

He starts to walk out of the kitchen and then turns back. "I have some work to do in the office. I'm going to work from home."

I nod while taking a sip of my coffee. "Okay, well, I'm going out at ten thirty."

His jaw is clenched as he asks, "Where?"

"I'm meeting Toni for coffee." If he wants to be hot and cold, then so can I.

"Where?" he grits out again, sounding like he's losing his patience with me. My eyes meet his in a sharp swing.

"Pearls," I grit out. He stares at me but then spins on his heels and walks out of the kitchen.

*Ahhh, he's such a fucking asshole sometimes.*

Cash is nowhere to be found once I'm ready. I thought I would do the decent thing and say bye before I left. I'm surprised he didn't lock me in the room. My phone goes off to let me know my ride is here. Once I'm in the Uber, I drop Toni a message to let her know I'm on my way. I have this niggly feeling in my stomach, and it gets more intense the farther we drive away from the house. I was hoping getting out of the house would make me feel better, but so far, I feel sick.

I stare out the window, watching the world go by. Baltimore is a stunning city. The sun beams down on the tall buildings, bouncing off the glass, creating starbursts. The Uber pulls up at

Pearls, only a short five-minute drive from Cash's house. Cash wanted to be close to the office, so he chose smack dab in the middle of all this beauty.

I smile at the driver and say, "Thank you" as I step out of the car and shut the door, but all I want to do is get back in. I stand on the edge of the sidewalk watching people rush past, my heart racing.

*Come on, Rylee get a grip.* I speed walk to the door.

"Rylee!"

I jump out of my skin, spinning on my heels. My heart beats so hard, I can hear it. "God, Toni. Don't do that."

Her brows draw together. "Are you okay, Ry?"

I sigh. Lack of sleep and being out on my own since James, is not a good mix.

"Yeah, sorry. I just, I don't know." I sigh out.

"Hey, let's get inside and get a coffee." She brings her arm around my shoulder, ushering me into Pearls, and her comfort eases me.

"So . . ." Toni eyes me over the rim of her coffee cup as she takes a sip.

I squint at her. "We have literally just sat down."

"And you have a lot to tell me. I had to go all last night not being able to find out what is up. Do you know how hard that was for me?" she says, not smiling. If something is up with me and I don't tell this girl straight away, it's normally hell to pay.

"Ton," I groan. I don't even know where to start.

"Okay, hold that thought." She puts her finger up to me and digs through her bag, scanning the room like she's about to pull a gun out of her bag and point it at someone. Why does she look so suspici—

"What are you doing," I hiss. Now it's me scanning the room. Toni pulls a small flask from her bag and drops some liquid into our coffees before placing it back and putting it under the table. She picks up the spoon and stirs our coffees while I just stare at her, mouth agape. Picking up her coffee, she takes a sip, then her eyes roll back as her shoulders move up and down a few times.

"Perfection," she says. "Okay, shoot."

I sometimes wonder where I found this girl.

"What the fuck was that you just put in my coffee?" I eye her.

"Taste it and find out." She wiggles her eyebrows.

"Sick bitch," I mumble before taking a sip of my coffee. I choke when the alcohol burns my windpipe as I swallow.

"What the fuck is that?" I wheeze.

"Rum. Now, get that tongue moving, miss." She wags her finger at me. I freeze with the cup midair, trying to work out why she is acting like drinking rum in coffee is an every morning occurrence for her. Hell, it probably is, I wouldn't put anything past this girl.

"Toni. Why are you spiking our drinks with rum?"

Holding the coffee in one hand, she waves the other in the air. "Call it a . . . sixth sense. It's needed." So much for my coffee to wake me up.

I sigh. "I have no idea where to start."

"How about you start at what the fuck is going on with you and Daddy, huh?" I stare at her wide-eyed. How did she know?

One side of her lip tilts. "I'm not stupid, Rylee, and quite frankly, Daddy isn't great at hiding how crazy obsessed he is with you."

Emotion clogs my throat, and a sob escapes at the relief I feel knowing I can finally talk to someone about this and everything else that has happened in the last twenty-four hours.

"Oh, my baby." Toni drags her and her chair next to me and pulls my head into her chest while I cry.

"It's such a mess, Ton. Everything is such a mess." She holds me for a little while longer before leaning back for me to lift my head.

"Listen, baby girl. I hate seeing you cry, you know I always want to make it better for you, but I can't do that if you don't tell me what's going on in that pretty little brain of yours." She wipes away my tears with her thumb and then passes me the coffee.

"See, sixth sense. I know these things." She smirks and winks. Toni is the only one who could make me laugh while crying. I sigh, knowing I need to get this off my chest.

"I have feelings for Cash, like deep feelings."

"Well . . . okay, I think we need to forget the coffee and head back to your place for this conversation." I nod and grab my bag. She downs her coffee as we stand.

"Wait, hold up." She jogs back to the table, downing my coffee, then she shivers as she walks back. She smiles as she approaches me.

"It's needed."

# Chapter Sixteen
# Rylee

Ton and I curl up on the sofa. I wanted to be close to Jace, so I got some photo albums out of us over the years. Many people don't collect photos in albums anymore, but I do. I love looking through them; it means more than flicking through albums on your phone.

"He was so beautiful," Toni says, stroking a finger down one of the pictures.

"I did good, didn't I?" I smile at the one of him leaning against a bar at someone's birthday.

"He did just as good." Toni nudges my side. I smile down, flicking through the pictures. One after the other guts me each time, but I need to see him.

"I can't believe he's dead, Ton," I whisper, and a tear slides down my cheek. She lays her head on top of mine as we stare at a picture of Jace and me smiling into a kiss.

"Have the police said anything?" she whispers.

I shake my head. "No. They are still looking for him."

"You haven't spoken about what happened? You know you shouldn't hold that in. I'm here to listen."

I take a deep breath. "I know, I just don't want to relive it all. I told the police everything and now I'm trying to put it to the back of my mind." I pause, wondering whether I should say something but then internally beat myself for ever thinking I should hold something back from her.

"He did say something that keeps playing in my head."

"Mm, go on," she whispers.

I continue flipping through the pages. "He said it's so much deeper than I could possibly think." I haven't stopped thinking about it. What could he mean?

"What is?" Toni questions, lifting her head to look at me.

"I don't know, that's the thing. Something doesn't feel right."

"Leave it to the police, baby. They will get him, you know that, don't you?" I nod. I'm sure they will, but what if they don't, what happens then? I have to live my life looking over my shoulder everywhere I go? Toni brushes through my hair with her fingers and grips my face.

"What am I going to do with you, my Rylee."

I smile. "Tell me about it. I ask myself this every day in the mirror." We laugh and then fall silent. What am I going to do, though?

Toni lets go of my face, sitting up a little straighter. "Are you going to tell me about what happened between you and Daddy, then."

I squint at her. I don't think she will ever stop calling him that. I roll my head back, groaning. "Where to even start."

"Ow, that hurt." I rub at the spot she just smacked me.

"Stop deflecting just spill, verbal diarrhea me." Her word choice is worrying sometimes, but I do just that, I explain everything from when Cash turned up to my place drunk, to the night at the bar, and then to last night. I explain through tears everything I have been feeling: the confusion, the guilt. By the time I have finished, I'm sobbing into her chest.

"The guilt is eating me up, Ton. It's been nearly four months since losing Jace, four fucking months," I cry out. "How can I have feelings for his dad, and the worst part about it, I don't feel any guilt when I'm with Cash. It's like he takes all the pain away, but then as soon as he's not around, it hits me like a ten-ton truck."

"Okay, baby. Let it out," Toni whispers, holding me tight and stroking the back of my head.

"I don't want you to just agree with me, but please tell me how sick and wrong this is. Don't sugarcoat shit." She pulls me away from her chest.

"First, I am your best fucking friend, okay. I will never sugarcoat shit for you, if I think you're wrong, I will call you out quicker than you can blink." Her shoulder rises as she leans in closer, keeping strong eye contact with me until I nod in understanding.

"And second." She sighs, her shoulder drops, and her face softens. "I will also tell you when you're right and . . . What you're feeling, there isn't anything wrong with it, but I do think you need some time."

"What do you mean some time?" I wipe at my tears.

"Some time to yourself, time away from Cash. This guilt won't go away until you have accepted it yourself. I also think." She grabs my hands, lacing her fingers through mine and frowning down at her hands.

"Go on." I urge, wondering what she's going to say.

"You know you will always love Jace, right?" Her eyes flicker between mine.

I nod. "Of course."

She smiles. "Then one day you will have to accept that you can love him forever but also let him go."

I nod, letting my head drop. "You're right, I think I'm just scared that I'll never be able to even though I know I need to."

Toni's phones pings for what feels like the hundredth time since I've been with her. She keeps her eyes on me, giving me a tight-lipped grin.

"Why are you looking at me like that?" I raise my eyebrow at her. "Are you not going to check that, it won't stop pinging."

"Uh-huh," she says, pulling her phone out of her bag. She huffs, typing something out, her fingers punching the screen, and then she chucks it back in her bag and her eyes swing and meet mine straight away.

I narrow my eyes at her. "Who was that?" I gesture to her bag.

She waves her hand in the air. "Just some guy. So, when are you back to work." She attempts to change the subject, but I know Toni, if it was just *some guy*, she would be shoving a picture of his dick in my face or telling me how big it is.

I tilt my head, and her eyes widen. "Who was it?"

Her eye twitches.

"God, I hate how well you can read me, it's annoying as fuck sometimes, you know. God forbid anyone wanted to throw a surprise for you, you would have it out of me within five minutes." She rolls her eyes, huffing.

"It's Cash." I rear my head back, and then it clicks into place.

"Is he checking up on me?" I frown at her. She winces but then puts her hands out in front of her.

"Hold on. He's not checking up on you, more just . . ." She twirls her hand in the air.

"Checking up on me, Toni. That's the only explanation." She slaps her hands down on my lap, causing me to wince with the sting.

"No, but it's not what you think. He's worried about you, can you blame him?" She's right, but I hate how he's rude and then checks up on me.

"It just annoys me. After the way he was with me last night, telling me I'm his light and then today can barely be in the same room as me," I mumble, feeling more irritated now that I've said it out loud.

"Ry, he is falling for his son's girlfriend. I bet his head is messed up more than any of us can imagine." Ton's eyes soften. "I think he needs time as well. If these feelings are real, then they will bring you back together, but you both need time away, to try and work through everything on your own that is going on in your heads. A lot has happened over the last three months. It's a lot to unload, and although you two helping each other is amazing, you can't work on each other's guilt together. It won't work."

I side-eye her. "Have you ever thought about being a therapist." We laugh because Toni as a therapist would be hilarious.

"Honey, I'd end up sleeping with half my clients. Let's not." We lean into each other, laughing to the point tears well in my eyes, but this time, they're not sad tears, they are happy ones.

"This is true," I say, still laughing. We fall silent, both sitting on the couch staring at the wall.

"Have you spoken to Rachel?"

"Not face-to-face, just over text. The company said I don't need to rush back, but I think I want to. I miss my lunches with Rach."

"I think it will be good for you too. Ease yourself in though, don't go storming back into that office and working stupid hours again, you need to work on your feelings, not bury them." She points at me.

"Okay, counselor."

"Piss off." She laughs. "You know what I'm in the mood for." A devilish smirk graces her lips.

"I would say sex, but there are no men around, so, erm wine?" I squint, questioning her.

"Henry Cavill." She squeals. I raise my hand in the air for her to high-five me.

"I second that."

She claps. "Oh my God, have you seen *Night Hunter* with him?"

I tilt my head, trying to think if I have. "I don't think so."

"Ahhh," she shouts. "Girl, you will *never*!" She claps while dragging each word out. "See him look so fine as you do in that film. We are watching it tonight. Wine and takeaway, you down?"

"I'm down, but I need to do something first." I wince, not wanting to bring the mood down. Her eyes meet mine as her whole demeanor softens.

"I will order an Uber, I'll wait outside while you talk to him." She smiles. I don't even have to say anything, she can read my mind.

# Chapter Seventeen
# Rylee

The minute I enter Cash's house, relief washes over me. The chat with Toni today was exactly what I needed. That girl always knows how to make everything better.

"Cash," I shout through the townhouse, my voice wavering from the sudden nerves or maybe excitement, I don't know. All I know is I need to see him. I hear shuffling and then the basement door open from the kitchen.

I walk toward the kitchen, but Cash comes barreling out, eyes wide. "What's going on?"

Every single word I had rehearsed in my head, everything Toni and I spoke about, goes out the window. Cash stands in front of me, in gray tracksuit bottoms, no top and sweat dripping from every inch of him. My stomach drops, and I have to clench my thighs to stop the ache.

"Rylee," he snaps, making me jump, and my eyes flicker to his.

"I-I." Next thing I know, I'm on him, smashing my lips to his. He opens for me like this is what he was waiting for all along. My whole body craves him. His large hands grip my waist before running over my ass and clutching my thighs, hoisting me up, and my legs wrap around him. He squeezes my ass hard, holding me there. I bring my hands around his neck, running my fingers through his hair while our tongues lace around each other's.

This, this is what I have been wanting, needing. My whole body feels like it's on fire, and the butterflies in my stomach are fluttering over my entire body. I tighten my legs as Cash brings his hands up to my face, caressing my cheeks, and he deepens the kiss. I never knew how much I longed for this. Being in Cash's arms washes away every bad emotion and kissing him makes me feel like I'm on the top of the world, like I can do anything. Cash stops kissing me but leaves his lips on mine. We breathe heavily into each other.

"Rylee, what is going on," he whispers. His hands have now moved back to my thighs, holding me. I shake my head while closing my eyes and leaning my head against his.

"I really don't know. This wasn't the plan." He grips my thighs tighter, causing a small pinch.

"What was the plan?" There's a slight edge to his voice.

"To talk," I whisper into his lips. I place one last kiss on his lips, but he doesn't let me pull away, his lips cling to me as his tongue caresses mine. He kisses me slowly, like he's reaching into my soul and claiming it as his own.

As much as I needed this kiss, this is making the reason I came here so much harder. His tongue continues to stroke over mine. I pull away slightly. "Cash," I breathe out.

"Don't," he grits. I pull my head back, looking into his eyes.

"I don't know what you're thinking right now, but please just hear me out."

"Talk, then." He doesn't make a move to put me down, and there is no way I'm doing this with him holding me. I will never leave.

"Put me down, please." He hesitates before lowering me. When my feet hit the floor, he sits back, leaning against the island. His arms cross in front of him as he watches me, waiting for me to speak.

His muscles pop and the veins bulge. I can't talk to him like this. My gaze meets his, no emotion on his face.

I raise one eyebrow at him. "Can you at least put a top on?" An ever-so-slight lift of his lip tells me he knows what he is doing, but I need him to be serious. "Cash, please." All I ever do is beg this man and say please because he can never do something when asked the first time around. *Typical man.*

He walks toward the stairs and disappears up them. Moments later, he reappears while pulling a top over his head. He comes and stands back in the position he was in before. He nods for me to continue, so I take a deep breath and let everything out.

"This has been so hard for me, and I know not just me, but for you as well." I walk beside him, and lean on the back of the island so we are next to each other. I glance down, playing with the sleeves on my top.

"I can't deny my feelings for you anymore." I sigh out, feeling relieved I got the words out even though I can't look at him when I say it. "Every time I think of you, the guilt eats away at me. It's wrong, in so many ways, and I know that, but I can't help it. The feelings won't go away. When I was taken, I was scared and closed my eyes, and it was you I saw. You." Everything feels like it's coming out faster than I expected, but I want him to know this isn't me leaving. I just need some time.

"When I left the house today, I had this anxious feeling, and I couldn't pinpoint what it was. It wasn't until I spoke to Toni that I realized it was because I wasn't with you. I wasn't around you." My voice breaks as the tears build up. "That scares the hell out of me, Cash." A tear falls, and Cash doesn't react or move in any way, and I'm so happy he doesn't. I can't have him touching me or looking at me right now.

"I have no doubt in my mind that these feelings are real, they're too strong not too be, but it's too soon." I admit. "I hated being out today and feeling like I couldn't go anywhere unless you were with me. That isn't me, and I won't be that person, but also, I'm still grieving for Jace. I need to sort my head out and get myself back because right now I'm not the Rylee I once was, and I miss her." Cash doesn't say a word. It then dawns on me that maybe I have this all wrong and he doesn't think of me in that way, or he did but no longer does. I take a breath before turning my head to look at him. He stares at a spot on the wall. His chest heaves as he takes deep breaths.

"Cash, say something."

"So, what is it you're actually saying." His stare moves to me, cold as ice.

I let my gaze flicker between his, hoping my eyes show him how much I need this.

"I'm saying that I need to be on my own for a while. Not staying here. Not having any contact with you."

His stare hardens. "You think I'm letting you go home on your own when that psycho is still out there, over my fucking dead body," he grinds out, the veins in his arms more pronounced than before. His shoulders are hunched. I stand straight and push my shoulders back before turning toward him to give him my sole attention so he can see I'm doing this and he's not stopping me.

"I'm going home. On my own. Toni knows a guy that installs good security systems who she called today, and he is going to come over this afternoon and see what he can do," I say in a clear and calm voice. His eye twitches at that, knowing that I made this decision before walking in here, has already pissed him off.

"I will be fine, I will text you now and then, I just need to get my head sorted. Please understand this." I grab his hand and the tension slips away. Small steps.

"How long?" He scrutinizes me.

"I don't know." I sigh. "I will text you to check in."

Cash rubs at the back of his neck, and then he drops his hands beside him, clenching his fists. His eyes close as he takes a deep breath. "I don't think I can let you go Ry." He opens his eyes, his forehead scrunching, and his eyes manically flicking between mine. "What if something happens, what if a security system doesn't keep that creep out? Then what?" His eyebrows draw down as his gaze softens and he lets out a sigh, his shoulders dropping. If he keeps looking at me like this, I will never leave.

"I will hardly be on my own. I will be at work most days with everyone in the office. I will be seeing Toni, Bridge, and Bohdi."

He runs his hands through his hair and paces back and forth in front of me, his hand on the back of his neck again. "It's not enough. I won't sleep at night if I don't know you're okay." I reach out, stopping him, and he brings himself in front of me, pushing between my legs. He cups my face in his large hands, and I place my hands around his neck. He pulls at my face for me to look up at him and then places a gentle kiss on my lips.

"It will have to be enough. It's all I can give you," I whisper into his lips.

"Let me make you a counteroffer," he says, placing another kiss on my lips. I freeze and then pull my head back, biting my lip, wondering what he is going to say.

"How about you text me each night before you go to bed so I know you're safe and then drop me a text each morning?"

"The whole point is to get my head straight, speaking to you every day won't do that."

"You don't have to engage in conversation with me, just a morning and night text, that's all I ask. Please." He begs with his eyes. I sigh, my gaze bouncing across his. It's sweet, how can I say no to that.

"Okay, but that's it." He nods, standing up, holding my face between his hands.

"I hate everything about this, but just promise me one thing." He places a kiss on my lips and rests his head against mine.

"You best fucking come back to me. I swear to God, I will hunt you to the ends of this earth if you don't." He clutches my cheeks, placing his lips on mine as he opens my mouth with his tongue. He caresses my tongue with each swipe, and I swear it makes it harder for me to let go.

I don't doubt for one minute he wouldn't hunt me to the end of the earth to get me back, but he won't need to. I don't know how I will do this without him, but I have to. These feelings have crept up on me. It's like I knew they were there but I didn't realize how strong they were. I pull myself away; the longer he kisses me the harder it will make this.

"I'm going to grab my stuff from upstairs, and then I'm going, Toni is downstairs in an Uber." Cash closes his eyes, his nostrils flaring as he takes a deep breath, then gives me a slow nod before bowing his head and walking toward the basement.

I take the stairs two at a time, knowing I need to get my stuff and get out of here. As I pack the few clothes and toiletries I brought with me, a dread fills my stomach. What if he won't wait for me, what if he moves on and finds someone else?

I grab my phone out of my pocket to text Toni that I'll be a few minutes and we need to stop to get more wine. She's staying with me tonight whether she likes it or not.

I pad down the stairs, and once I get to the bottom, I hear loud bangs and grunts. What the fuck is that? I walk toward the basement and realize it's Cash hitting the bag. Hard. I was going to go down and say bye to him, but I think it's best I just leave. I have always thought of myself as strong, but he makes me feel so weak for him, and if I had to face him again, there is no way I would leave this house.

Once I walk outside, my phone pings. I pull it from my pocket, and Cash's text leaves a smile on my face.

**Cash:** Don't you dare forget that you're mine, Rylee. I'll be here when you're ready.

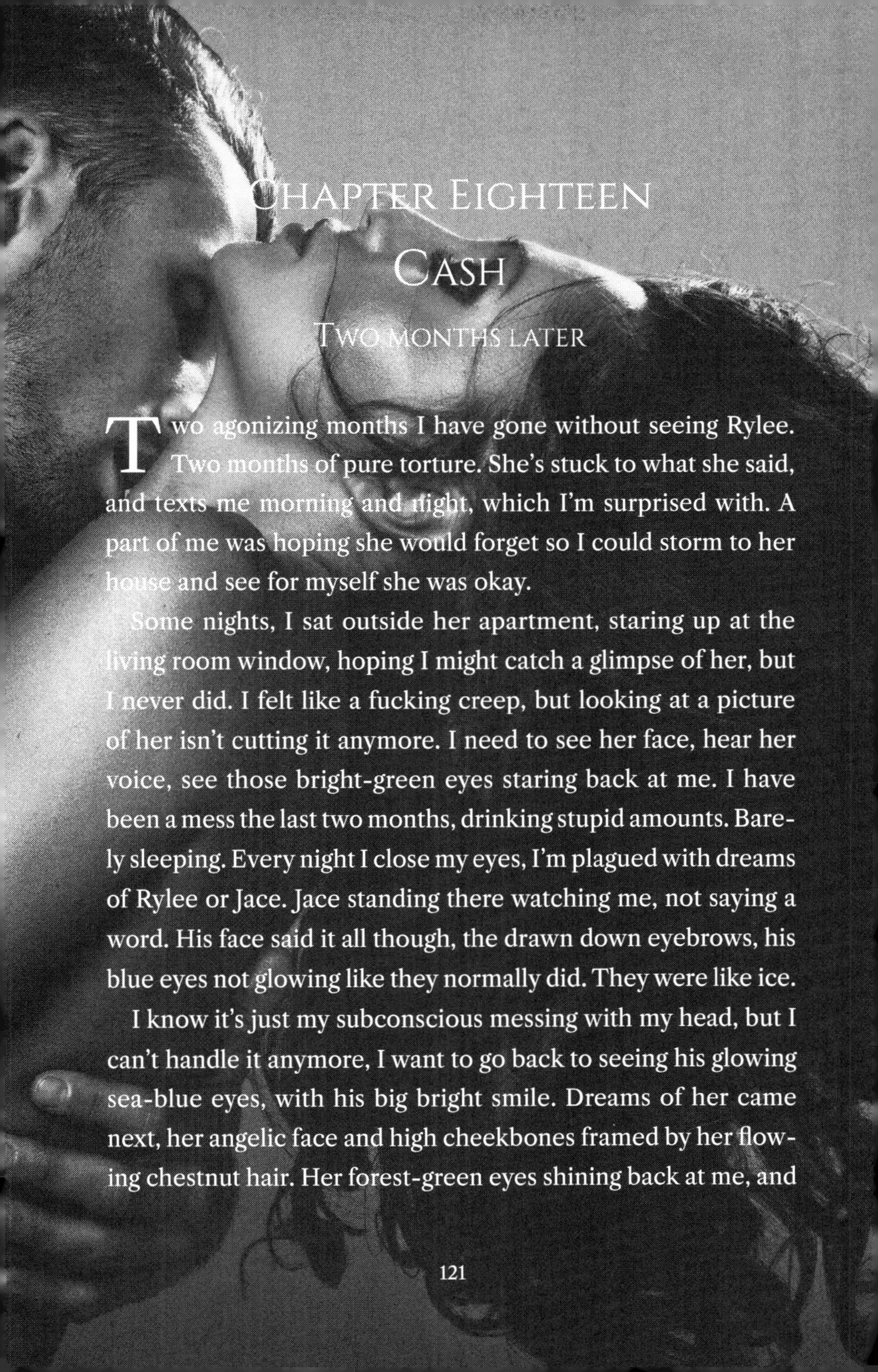

# Chapter Eighteen

## Cash

### Two months later

Two agonizing months I have gone without seeing Rylee. Two months of pure torture. She's stuck to what she said, and texts me morning and night, which I'm surprised with. A part of me was hoping she would forget so I could storm to her house and see for myself she was okay.

Some nights, I sat outside her apartment, staring up at the living room window, hoping I might catch a glimpse of her, but I never did. I felt like a fucking creep, but looking at a picture of her isn't cutting it anymore. I need to see her face, hear her voice, see those bright-green eyes staring back at me. I have been a mess the last two months, drinking stupid amounts. Barely sleeping. Every night I close my eyes, I'm plagued with dreams of Rylee or Jace. Jace standing there watching me, not saying a word. His face said it all though, the drawn down eyebrows, his blue eyes not glowing like they normally did. They were like ice.

I know it's just my subconscious messing with my head, but I can't handle it anymore, I want to go back to seeing his glowing sea-blue eyes, with his big bright smile. Dreams of her came next, her angelic face and high cheekbones framed by her flowing chestnut hair. Her forest-green eyes shining back at me, and that smile. The smile that could have any man dropping to their knees while praying to spend a lifetime with her. You can tell with one look at Rylee, her soul is pure. Light shines out of every pore on her face. I knew it from the moment I first met her, then once you get to know her, you're fucked. Because she is one of the most precious souls I have ever encountered, and I know my son felt the exact same, so I had to do the best thing and keep her at arm's length. The longer I blocked her out, the easier it got. The less I spoke to her, the more I forgot how mesmerizing and funny she is. I slowly forgot how beautiful she was. I even had to stop myself from looking at her because one smile is all it took with Rylee. One smile and you're done for.

The thing is, Rylee doesn't know how amazing she is, and that's what makes her even more special. The guilt has hit me more over the past two months than it ever has done. I wasn't lying when I said she was my light because now that she's not here, my life has been hell—one deep pitch-black hole I can't get myself out of.

Boh and Bridge have been asking why Rylee is staying away from me, what I did wrong, why am I reacting the way I am. I just grunt at them; they never get much of an answer out of me. I know I can't tell them the truth. They will hate me and will never look at me the same. No one will, but when I'm with her, none of that matters. It's just her.

It's her birthday tomorrow morning, and I don't care what she says, or about these fucking rules of her staying away, I'm seeing her whether she likes it or not. I have something for her, and I want to be there when she opens it. I keep trying to find out odd things from Bridge. I don't bother with Boh; he's been distant with me, and I don't know why.

I asked Bridge, but she said he has just generally been like that. I text Toni a couple of times, but she only gives me few-word answers. She called me once and said no matter how much information I try and get out of her, she won't give in and to just give Rylee space. Fucking space. I have given her two fucking months of space. I hired a private investigator; the police aren't doing enough, but this private investigator came highly recommended and has found absolutely fuck all. Not a thing. No trace of James. There is no trace of him from when he was younger, he magically appeared in the systems when he was eighteen. Something isn't right with him, and I plan to find out what it is.

"Rylee." My voice echoes through her apartment. There is no reply, no sound. You could hear a pin drop in here with how quiet it is. I was always coming here today, but it's the first morning in two months I haven't received my morning text from her. Even on days she slept in, I always had it by 10:00 a.m. It's now midday, and I tried calling, but the phone keeps going to voicemail.

"Rylee," I shout louder this time, but there is still nothing. I pop my head into the dining room and then walk down the hallway to check her bedroom. I would knock, but her door is wide open, the bed is untouched. Her en suite door is also wide open. Nothing seems out of sorts. Maybe she's out, but something doesn't feel right, the house feels empty like no one has been here for a while.

I take hesitant steps toward Jace's office. The last time I was in here was with Rylee when I was drunk—the night I confessed what a fuck up I am. I take a deep breath before placing my hand on the knob, knowing the flood of guilt that will wash through me when I enter this room. A sigh leaves my lips when the handle doesn't move—the door is locked.

I walk back to the living room and get my phone out before dropping down on the sofa. I glance up at the shelf that Jace's picture sits on but it's not there. I draw my eyebrows together. I focus on the spot before running my gaze along the other shelves, but it's not there. I know Rylee, and she wouldn't remove that picture. What the fuck is going on? My heart rate kicks up. I dial Toni's number. I don't want to ring Bridget about Rylee; she will only panic and be over here within seconds. We promised Rylee wouldn't go anywhere on her own while that piece of shit is still out there.

"Cash," Toni answers, panicked. Dread washes over me like a tidal wave as my stomach turns.

"Toni, where is she?" I demand, not trying to let my voice crack with how sick I feel right now.

"Sh-she text me saying she needed time to herself and that she would be safe." She sniffles. "Where the fuck could she have gone, Cash, surely nowhere is safe with that maniac on the loose." She sobs down the phone. I know how much of an effect this has had on all of us. She was hit hard when Rylee was taken.

They have this unbreakable bond, like when one is in pain, the other feels it too.

"Okay, breathe, Toni. I need you to think. You know her better than anyone. Think!" I shout out the last part, trying not to let my temper get the best of me. It's not Toni's fault, but the thought of anyone hurting Rylee makes my heart ache.

"Cash," Toni cries out, "I really don't know. Let me ring Rachel, she may know something, I'll call you back." She hangs up before I can reply.

I chuck my phone back on the sofa, tug my hair, and take a deep breath. *C'mon, Cash, think. Where would she go that is safe?* I rack my brain, but the panic is taking over and won't let me think straight.

"Fuck!" I fall to the sofa and let my head drop in my hands. I know I need to ring Boh and Bridge, but the minute I do, the reality kicks in that she's out there on her own thinking she is safe, when nowhere is safe. What part of this doesn't she understand?

I stand up, pacing again, my eyes land on a beautiful portrait of a beach in Brazil, with a quote in bold writing that says, "The beach is cheaper than therapy." Jace bought it for her a couple of years back. Rylee has always loved the beach, according to Jace. It was where she was when she was taken. She always said to Jace, "If you're ever stressed or sad, just go to the beach." I smile. He started going on his own, but also sometimes with Rylee. It was their thing; they loved the beach and the sea. My eyes bug out as it dawns on me—the vacation. I grab my phone, knowing who will know the location of the beach house.

# Chapter Nineteen
# Rylee

Waves—my favorite sound. That is all I hear when I wake from my broken sleep, but I can't quite bring myself to open my eyes yet. If I keep them closed, I can create this false sense of reality. It all feels so peaceful and weightless. I want to live in this forever, like there are no worries in the world and everything in life is perfect. I open my eyes, knowing this will come crashing down, and reality will settle in thick and fast.

Staring at the ceiling, ice fills my veins, and the sound of the waves blurs into the background. There is no warmth next to me, I am alone—just me and my thoughts. I glance around at the white walls and baby-blue furniture. It's all meant to be light, fresh, and happy, but has the opposite effect. The large patio doors are open to the sand and sea. I can't appreciate the beauty of it because everything seems dull. Like there is a black-and-white filter on my vision. I shouldn't have come here, but I thought it would make me feel something. If anything, I'm worse, and the guilt comes rushing back because all I can think about is Cash.

Letting out a long breath, I roll to my side and slip out of bed, with a weight on my shoulders, and my whole body aches. I have no idea why because I have done absolutely nothing since I got here yesterday. I pad to the kitchen on bare feet, welcoming the ice-cold tiles, and head straight for the fridge. My stomach has been growling since yesterday when I picked at the food on the plane, but I haven't had an appetite. I have this horrible taste in my mouth that no amount of water or toothpaste will get rid of, so I need to eat something.

I open the fridge and see all the fresh food along with platters of fresh fruit. A maid comes each day, according to the lady who let me in and handed me over the keys, to stock up the food. Jace went all out with this place. I put some melon, strawberries, and grapes into a bowl and add some plain Greek yogurt on top and head to the terrace to look out to sea. I take a deep breath and take my first bite, and honestly, I thought this would taste like cardboard, but the flavors are exploding in my mouth, and it's delicious. Maybe this will make me feel something, food always used to make me happy . . . among other things.

Cash's face appears in my head. I have gone to call him at least five times since being here but stopped myself each time because I know the minute I hear his voice, I will cave. I head back into the kitchen and place the bowl in the fridge; maybe I will try again later. I'm tired, even though all I have done is sleep, but being asleep is much better than being awake at the moment. At least in my dreams I'm happy—I'm the old Rylee. I head back to the bedroom and slip back into bed. My body gets heavy and I drift off, then his beautiful face appears.

I hear knocking, but it seems far away; I'm not sure what it is but my body is too exhausted to care right now. The knocking gets louder and more aggressive, then I bolt up and realize it is the villa door. I glance over at the clock and it's past noon, but the maid comes around 3:00 p.m. and has a key. Maybe she came early and forgot it.

I make my way to the door, but I dread having to speak to her. Opening the door, the first things I see are trainers. Men's trainers. I look up and gasp at the set of ocean-blue eyes staring right at me—the same color eyes I fell in love with all those years ago.

"Hi, Rylee."

I suck in a sharp breath, not believing who is standing in front of me.

"Cash." I look him up and down to make sure what I'm seeing is real. He's here in front of me, in Tulum.

"Wha-what are you doing here?"

His eyes zone in on mine, squinting. "What the fuck do you think you're doing?" he snaps through gritted teeth, raising one eyebrow at me.

I don't know who this fucker thinks he is, but there is no way he is making this vacation worse than it already feels. "Don't start." I'm not in the mood for his whiplash personality today. *Wait. How the fuck did he find me?*

"You answer me first, what are you doing here, how did you fi—" I know exactly how he found me. Bridget. She is the only person who knew the location of this beach house. Well, other than Jace.

"Bridget." I sigh, dropping my shoulders. No matter what happens on this earth, I cannot be annoyed at Bridget. Every decision that woman makes benefits other people.

Cash barges past me into the beach house, and I close my eyes trying not to get lost in his smell. I can't have him this close to me. My head is so messed up, and him being here makes it worse.

"Cash," I say as gently as possible. His gaze runs over the open-plan living room before he places one hand on his hip, then runs his other hand through his stubble and drops his head, staring at the floor like he doesn't know what to do or say. Neither of us do. I know he knows he shouldn't be here.

"You need to go," I whisper.

"I can't," he says as his gaze meets mine, his shoulders droop and his eyes scrunch together. I take a controlled, deep breath as the lump forms in my throat. I can't cry, I can't break in front of him. I need to be strong.

I glance up. His squinted eyes penetrate me as his brows furrow. Every ounce of strength leaves me as a tear escapes and slips down my cheek.

"Please, Cash. Please."

He takes a few steps toward me. "Stop." I put my hand up.

His hands raise in front of him as he stops. "Look, I know I shouldn't be here. You don't think I haven't beaten myself up on the flight here. Do you know how much it took for me to come here." He points to his chest. "You promised us, after what happened, you wouldn't be anywhere on your own." He levels me with a glare.

I huff out a laugh. He's being ridiculous. "Cash. C'mon. I'm safe here. No one know—"

"You're not safe anywhere," he bellows, his hands tightening into fists. He scoffs, throwing his hands up in the air before dropping them to his sides again. "You were kidnapped, Rylee." The reminder has me dropping my chin to my chest.

"What part of that don't you understand? He is still out there, his sick obsession with you won't stop. He's still hunting you. You will never be safe until he's found." Cash's heavy breaths are all that can be heard in the silence that follows. He has brought everything to the surface again, the kidnapping, the obsession James has with me . . . the price Jace paid because of me. The tears fall freely and land on the tiled floor at my feet.

"Rylee." Cash's voice cracks. "I don't mean to shout. You worried us. Toni has been beside herself." That little bit of information makes me feel bad. I knew if I told her where I was going, she either wouldn't let me or would've demanded to come with me. I needed this time on my own, but it looks like that isn't going to happen.

"I'm sorry I worried you." I glance up at him. His blue eyes, that stand out even more due to the sunken shadows underneath, stare back at me.

"I'm sorry I worried everyone. I just needed it. I need this time on my own. To think, to grieve. So much has happened since losing Jace, I didn't think it could get any worse, but it has, and I don't know how to process it all." Cash stands there in silence, staring at the floor near my feet.

He sighs, raking his hands through his overgrown wavy ball of hair on top of his head. It's normally styled to perfection. "I know, but I'm sorry, I can't leave you on your own." He looks down at his feet, and rocks back and forth while pushing his hands into the pockets of his gray sweat shorts.

"If you still want to stay and have your alone time, that's fine. I will stay out of your way as much as possible, but I'm staying. I'm not leaving this island without you." He walks toward the front door before disappearing outside. I hesitantly follow, thinking he has rented somewhere nearby. There are other beach houses along the shoreline, but they are at least fifty yards apart. I'm stunned when he grabs a suitcase and walks back toward the door.

"Ahh, what are you doing?" My eyes flick to his suitcase and then to him.

"I'm staying here. In the beach house with you."

# Chapter Twenty
## Rylee

"You, what!?" My eyes nearly leave their sockets. There's no way Cash is staying here with me. I block the entrance to prevent him moving past me. He raises one brow at me. I cross my arms over my chest. Then he huffs and stands in front of me with his suitcase to one side and his duffel in the other hand.

"You're not staying here on your own. I will sleep in the bedroom next door. You will barely know I'm here." His eyes flick between mine.

"Having you here won't make it easy for me to relax," I grind out, slightly annoyed because I know I won't be winning this. Cash does what he wants.

"I have lots of work to do. I have my laptop; I will be on calls and meetings most of the time. If you need to pop into town to grab some things, that's the only time you will have to spend time with me." As much as I don't want him here, it makes me sad that he feels he has to say that. Our gazes meet in a silent battle, a frown appears on his face, showing me anything but annoyance. His tired eyes that move between mine and his deflated shoulders tell me he doesn't like the fact he had to say that either, and he just wants me safe. The final thought has me hesitantly nodding at him, and I step aside.

He walks in and studies the area.

"It's down the hall, second door on the left," I say, assuming he is looking for the bedroom. He turns toward me, thinned-lipped, and nods before stalking off to the room. He disappears, and then I drop myself onto the sofa which overlooks the sea. My eyes follow the movement of the waves, and I take calming breaths. I need to get out of here and away from him.

He thinks being here is so innocent, but it's not, just having him in there brings everything back. My guilt and confusion are the reasons I came here, and with him near, it's consuming me again.

I walk into my room and grab my towel, then head out of the double bifold doors. The warm air hits my face, and the smell of the salty water calms everything inside of me. There is no one in sight. I don't mind people, I am a people person and will talk to just about anybody, but I'm so happy no one is around. I can pretend Cash isn't only a few feet away and it's just me here.

I lay my towel out and then drop myself down. The white sand is silky against my palm as I run my fingers through it. It really is like being in paradise. The palm trees that overhang and provide bouts of shade throughout and the white sand that makes the blue in the sea stand out even more are a sight to behold. The gentle waves that ripple against each other and the glisten from the sun reflecting off the water that makes it appear like a sheet of crystal—it's stunning. I close my eyes, enjoying the whooshing of the waves and the squawking from the birds.

Jace's face pops into my head, but it doesn't make me sad, it makes me happy. I smile at the memory of us on the beach where he first told me he loved me.

*"You're so beautiful, you know that?" I drop my head, trying to hide the cheesy-as-hell smile forming on my face. I have only been with Jace for six months, and I swear the butterflies don't stop. Every glance, every touch makes me feel like I'm on top of the world. I haven't stopped smiling, and it all boils down to him.*

*"You did just tell me five minutes ago, but I'll happily hear you say it again." I side-eye him with a smirk, trying to hide how head over heels I am for him. He flashes me the sexy side grin that would have girls falling at his knees, and looks back out to sea.*

*I told Jace my love for the beach and how it helps me, so he brings us here a lot. He didn't see why at first, but since coming here, he understands now. He picks my hand up from the sand and laces his fingers between mine. We look down at our hands, and I grin at how perfect we fit together.*

*"You know . . ." I wait for him to continue. He looks back out to sea, with a small smile on his face. It's true what they say, the right person will come along when you least expect it. He glances over at me, holding eye contact.*

*"I never thought I would find someone as amazing as you, Rylee. I feel like you bulldozed into my life, knocking away every bit of bad in it." He smiles at me. His blue eyes sparkle like diamonds with the sea in the background. He has such a way with words, they send a shiver through me.*

*"What I'm trying to say is, I love you, Rylee Matthews." My eyes swim with unshed tears. A tear escapes and falls down my cheek, and he brushes it away. "Well, I didn't expect you to cry from telling you I love you." He smirks. Hearing those words brings more tears to my eyes.*

*"Ry?" His eyebrows draw together.*

*My smile breaks through the tears. "I-I love you too, Jace," I croak out.*

The crashing of the waves brings me back to the present. Wetness seeps into my cheeks as I let the silent tears fall. The waves lap at my feet; I didn't realize how close I was to the shoreline, but I welcome the shock from the temperature of the water. My fingers move of their own accord, and without even realizing, I wrote, *I miss you* into the sand.

# Chapter Twenty-One

# Cash

I walk into my room that will feel like a prison for the next week, then chuck my duffle bag on the bed and run my hands over my face. That was easier than I thought it would be. I expected her to put up more of a fight. Not that she would have won.

The room is pretty plain, nice though. Just white and blue—a typical beach house vibe. I stride over to the double doors that lead to the beach, and the white sand and sea are beautiful. Okay, if this is my prison for the next week, I won't complain. It beats the office. I go to turn around but something in my periphery catches my attention, and Rylee is sitting in the sand, running her hands through it, and staring out to sea. She looks so deep in thought like she isn't even here.

Rubbing my chest, my heart aches at her beauty, but also the guilt. Every time I think about her, or look at her, it floods my body. Giving into these feelings for her was one of the hardest things I've ever done. Now it's even harder because every time I look at her, I remember her sweet taste, her soft skin, and I shouldn't know what she tastes like or what it feels like to hold her. I know being here is bringing it all back for her too. The way she couldn't look me in the eye for longer than two seconds, and when I got near her, she would back away. I get it. Jace booked this place for them, and here I am. The ache intensifies the longer I stare at her, so I turn around and drop onto the bed.

Staring up at the bland ceiling, I grab my wallet, flip it open, and pull out what I look at every day. The big toothless grin stares back at me, the big blue eyes squinting from the large-as-life smile. A smile forms on my lips. How could it not, looking at this picture of Jace on his first birthday. He has icing from the cake smash in his hair and up his nose, but he was so happy. He just kept giggling, probably from the sugar rush. I run my finger over the picture; what I would give to see that smile again. The picture drags me back to the memory.

*"Oh, Cash, look how perfect my nephew is," Bridget says, grinning at Jace sitting on the floor the photographer placed him on to have his way with the cake. The round blue cake is smashed to pieces and everywhere.*

*"He loved it." I smile down at him bringing chunks of the icing stuck in his chubby hands to his open mouth. The dribble strings from his mouth to the cake, which makes me smile more. I bend down, and his big blue eyes find mine, then he lets out a loud squeal and flails his arms around, sending cake everywhere. The cake lands on my face and hair. Seeing him this happy swells my heart more than I could ever imagine. I run my hand down his face, and he stops moving and smiles up at me with his big toothless grin.*

*"Dada," he shouts.*

*A camera clicks as my vision blurs from tears. He just said Dada.*

*"Cash, Cash, did you hear him!" Bridget says next to me.*

*I look at her, the grin aching my cheeks from how big it is. "He just said Dada," I say in awe. Bridge smiles down at me as I glance around at the rest of the family. My mom and dad stand there mirroring my grin as Boh slaps an arm down on my shoulder.*

*"Dada, Dada," he says again, and everyone laughs because we know, no doubt, this is all we will hear now. I could hear this every second of everyday and never be bored of it. Bringing Jace up as a single dad has been a struggle, but my family makes it easier and his first word being Dada makes me surge with happiness. He opens his arms for me to pick him up. I lift him and give him a big kiss on his cheek.*

*"My boy," I whisper to him.*

My finger strokes over the picture again and again as I drag myself out of the memory. We were so happy in that moment. Tears roll down my face as I lie there with my eyes closed, imagining the word "Dada" that I would give my life to hear come out of his mouth again.

"What I would do to just see or hear you again, my boy," I whisper to the picture and place a kiss on it. Holding the picture to my chest, I let the silent sobs engulf me, and keep my eyes closed. The minute I open them, the guilt will eat me alive, and I can't cope with it right now. I block out the waves and the birds and turn over in the bed and keep the "Dada" floating around in my head until sleep takes me.

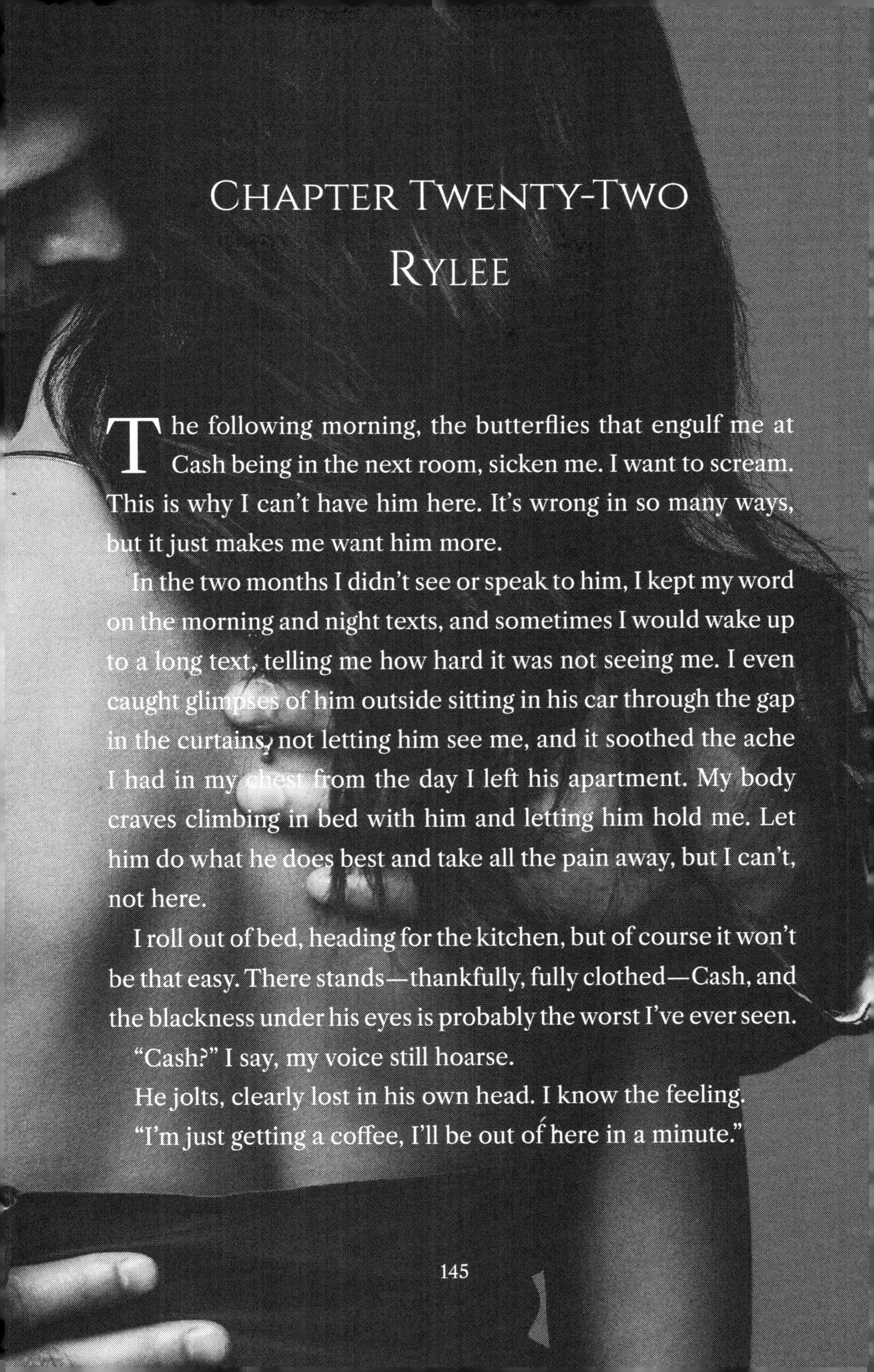

# Chapter Twenty-Two
## Rylee

The following morning, the butterflies that engulf me at Cash being in the next room, sicken me. I want to scream. This is why I can't have him here. It's wrong in so many ways, but it just makes me want him more.

In the two months I didn't see or speak to him, I kept my word on the morning and night texts, and sometimes I would wake up to a long text, telling me how hard it was not seeing me. I even caught glimpses of him outside sitting in his car through the gap in the curtains, not letting him see me, and it soothed the ache I had in my chest from the day I left his apartment. My body craves climbing in bed with him and letting him hold me. Let him do what he does best and take all the pain away, but I can't, not here.

I roll out of bed, heading for the kitchen, but of course it won't be that easy. There stands—thankfully, fully clothed—Cash, and the blackness under his eyes is probably the worst I've ever seen.

"Cash?" I say, my voice still hoarse.

He jolts, clearly lost in his own head. I know the feeling.

"I'm just getting a coffee, I'll be out of here in a minute."

I sigh. "Don't. I mean, you don't have to hide away in the room." I glance over his shoulder out to the beach. "It's too nice outside to hide away in there." I offer a soft smile.

Cash turns around, leaning against the doorway with the coffee in his hand, and stares out to the beach. "It really is stunning here."

I walk up and stand next to him, taking in the sound of waves. "He did good." I smile.

"Of course he did," Cash whispers. "He would have given you the world if he could."

I nod, knowing that's true, he would have done anything for me.

He jolts, then turns to me. "Oh, I almost forgot. Happy Birthday." He smiles. "Well, it's two days too late, but I went to your apartment to say it, then I realized you weren't there."

I glance at Cash, then back to the beach. "Thank you." Standing next to him has my stomach knotting. "I'm sorry I worried you." I text Toni last night, even though I know Cash would have text her, but hearing how worried she was, made me feel like a selfish bitch. She called me out, like I knew she would, and then told me to have my time but to meet up with her as soon as I got back. I knew before coming here what I needed to do, but Cash being here has messed everything up.

"It's okay. I was just really worried." He sighs, taking a sip of his coffee. "How long are you here for?"

"Not the full time. Jace booked it for two weeks. I told them I would only be here for five days." I wanted to keep the next thing to myself, but I need him to understand why I had to be here, why it was so important to get my time.

"I actually came here for a reason, Cash." I gaze over the waves.

"I have Jace with me." I feel Cash's stare on the side of my face, then I turn to him.

"I have some of his ashes that Bridge gave me a while back. I know you all have some, and of course I have my necklace"—I touch it around my neck—"but you know how much me and Jace loved the beach." I turn to look out to sea again. "I know nothing would make him happier if he was free here, Cash."

"You're going to scatter some of his ashes here?"

I nod. "Yes, I couldn't think of anywhere else more perfect. He booked this for us, so I want a part of him to always remain here." Cash clenches his jaw, and his eyes blink rapidly, swimming with unshed tears. I don't know how else to say this so I'm just going to say it.

"It also feels like a good way of me saying my goodbyes, Cash."

His brows furrow. "What do you mean, we said our goodbyes at his funeral." He just keeps staring straight ahead.

"I know that is what happens for most people, but I don't think I ever really said my goodbyes. This guilt—"

"It won't leave after saying your goodbyes, Ry." He stands over me, looking down and points to his chest. "It still stays there, eating away at you." His jaw clenches as he gulps. "I said my goodbyes, but I still feel riddled with guilt every single day," he mutters.

I nod again. "Except every single thought I have of you. Every single time I crave your touch or crave to hear your voice." Tears fill my eyes. "I feel like I'm cheating on him, I see his face, his disappointment, the sadness, the pain . . . It kills me." My voice breaks as the tears cascade down my face. His eyes roam over my face, like he wants to take the pain away, and one touch from him will, but the minute he steps away from me, it's back again. Then all I see and feel is Jace's pain.

I rest my hand over my heart. "He lives inside here, and it hurts," I whisper. Cash palms my face, and I let out a heavy sigh and lean into his touch. I close my eyes, and the pain slowly leaves my body. *No. No.*

"No." I step back so he can't touch me. "I need to do this on my own, please." His jaw clenches, his eyes go dark, and then he nods before walking past me and out of the kitchen. Leaving me to swim in the pain, and my heart breaks that much more because the one person who can stop it all, I can't have, not right now.

I haven't seen Cash since I went and laid on the beach, even though I glanced at the doors to his room a couple of times. They are open but no sign of him. A few people have been around the beach, and hearing their laughing and happiness has been nice. I stayed in my little bubble near the beach house.

I have had Jace's ashes next to me all day, waiting for the beach to clear so I can do this. Every time I look at the box, sadness engulfs me. I'll always have a part of him around my neck and deep in the depths of my heart, but doing this will be like setting him free. I have to. The crimson sun setting lights up the sky and creates a mirror on the water, the crystal-blue sea mixing in with the pink and orange. It's beautiful. I pull my phone out to take a picture of this moment, never wanting to forget it. A slight breeze cools my hot skin, and strands of my hair caress my face. I pull on my coverup, pick up the box, and walk toward the water's edge.

"This couldn't be anymore perfect, Jace." Jace loved a sunset, so I know this is the time. The cool water laps against my feet as I walk into it, my feet sinking into the sand. I stand knee deep in the sea and hug the box to my chest. Staring down at the fast current swirling around my legs, I know I need to let him go. I throw my head back as the tears fall. "Fuck," I cry out. My chest aches, my whole body aches. I try swallow the impending sob, but it doesn't stay down. Wailing, I let my tears mix with the sea.

"I can't do this," I cry. "I can't fucking do this," I scream out.

"Try for me, Ry, just try." Cash's voice eases the ache.

The tears continue to fall as I turn to the side, and he stands next to me.

"Cash, don't you see I'm trying? I'm trying everything I can to fight when all I feel like doing is flying," I cry out.

"Then fly, Rylee. I'll fight for the both of us." He pauses, his eyes flicking between mine. "But just remember, if you fall, I'll catch you. I always save you." Everything around me stops. My heart skips a beat, and my stomach does flips.

"Let me take the pain from you," he whispers. "You take mine, now let me take yours." My face scrunches as a sob leaves my mouth. He's right, he takes my pain away. Cash places a hand around me as I lean into him, letting him hold me, hold my pain.

"Let him swim free, Ry," he whispers into my hair. My shoulders shake as I weep into his chest. I lean away and open the box. Cash takes it out of my hand, and I take a deep breath.

"I'll go back inside if—"

"No." I swing my head to meet his gaze. "Don't leave me, please." He nods and places his hand on my shoulder.

I stretch my trembling hands out in front of me, staring at the sunset as it disappears into the water. I tilt the box and watch Jace fall into the sea, the gentle breeze scattering him across the water.

"Swim free, Jace," I cry as I empty the last of him into the water. Cash's hand slides down my opposite arm and squeezes tight.

"Swim free, my boy," he chokes out. I lay my head on Cash's shoulder, and his head leans on mine as we watch Jace dissipate.

"Thank you for being here, Cash."

"Thank you for allowing me, Rylee."

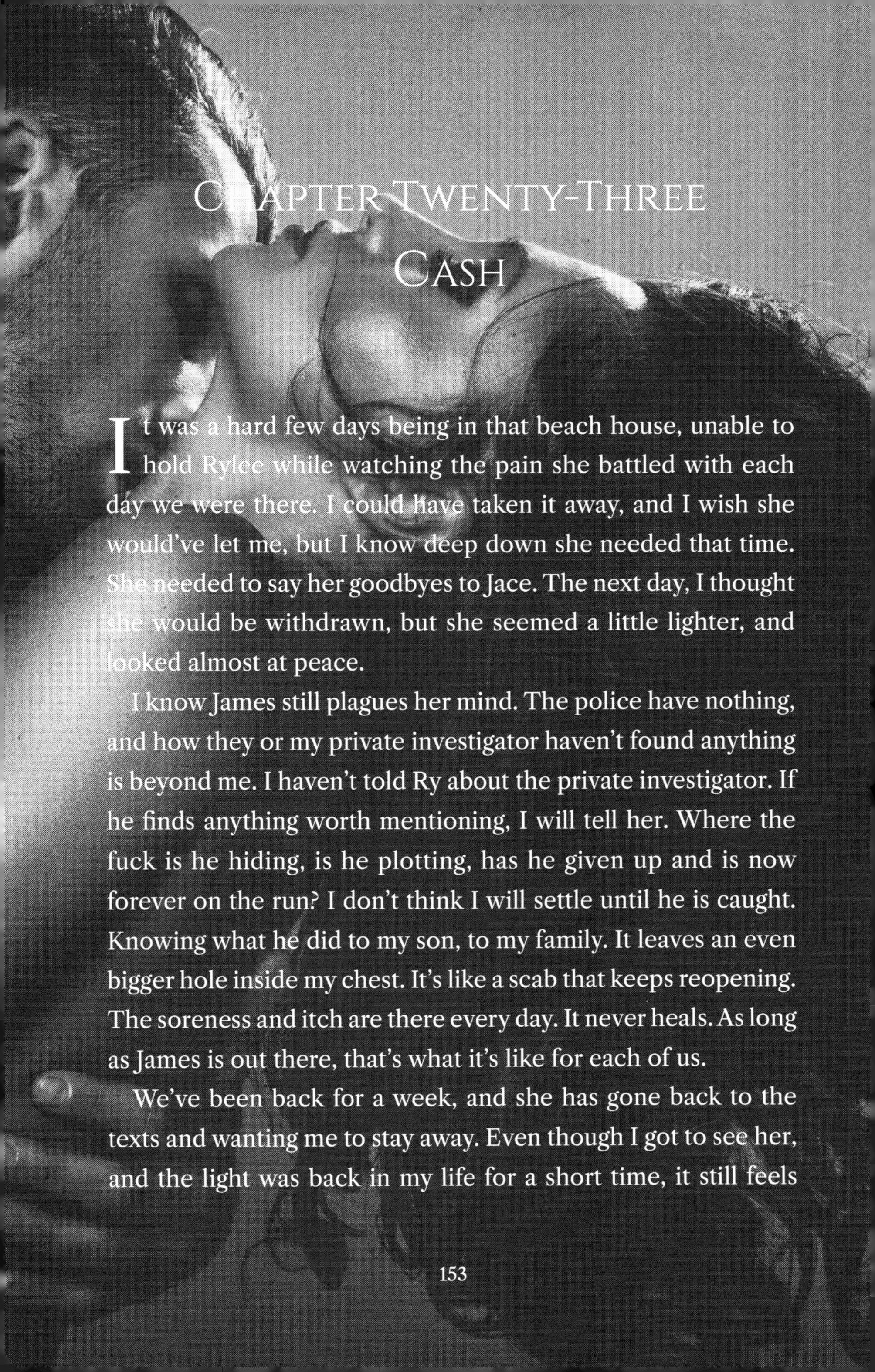

# Chapter Twenty-Three

## Cash

It was a hard few days being in that beach house, unable to hold Rylee while watching the pain she battled with each day we were there. I could have taken it away, and I wish she would've let me, but I know deep down she needed that time. She needed to say her goodbyes to Jace. The next day, I thought she would be withdrawn, but she seemed a little lighter, and looked almost at peace.

I know James still plagues her mind. The police have nothing, and how they or my private investigator haven't found anything is beyond me. I haven't told Ry about the private investigator. If he finds anything worth mentioning, I will tell her. Where the fuck is he hiding, is he plotting, has he given up and is now forever on the run? I don't think I will settle until he is caught. Knowing what he did to my son, to my family. It leaves an even bigger hole inside my chest. It's like a scab that keeps reopening. The soreness and itch are there every day. It never heals. As long as James is out there, that's what it's like for each of us.

We've been back for a week, and she has gone back to the texts and wanting me to stay away. Even though I got to see her, and the light was back in my life for a short time, it still feels like I've been without her for so long. It was so hard to not grab her at the beach house and demand she was mine. I've never had patience the way I do with Rylee, and it's killing me, and everyone around me. I'm constantly snapping at people; I lose my shit at least twice a day at work. I don't think people can stand to be around me. Well, good, I don't want any of them around me, only her.

I pour myself a second glass of whiskey. I didn't drink once in Mexico, but the minute I dropped her home and had to drive off and leave her, I walked into my house and poured myself a glass. I have continued pouring them since. My work is arranging the charity ball they do every year. We select a different charity every year, and the office does activities throughout the year to raise money for them. Jace was heavily involved with this and did all the arranging of everything. He dealt with the booking of the hall, the catering. I'm not good at things like that due to my lack of patience. Luckily, Boh wanted to take over for Jace, and I happily obliged. Bridge doesn't even work for the company, but she wanted to help. Arranging the auction is the only thing keeping me distracted.

People in the company and attending companies will donate holiday homes for a week, weekends away to luxury spas, and more. We've had great donations over the years and have raised hundreds of thousands. So far, we have twenty-eight donations, one being a week in a cabin in Whitefish in Montana, which is one of my most favorite places to go. I'm looking forward to the auction to see how much we will raise. Jace would be proud. It was one of his favorite times of the year. He always delivered the checks to the charity, and I know how happy it made him to see how excited they were. The auction is this Friday and I still have a lot to do, and I'm hoping it will take my mind off Rylee.

"Cash," Bridge shouts through the house. Does she not knock? I stay in the kitchen as her clicking heels gets closer.

"Oh, there you are." She beams at me and strides up to me to place a kiss on my forehead.

"Bridge," I greet her.

Her brows furrow. "You drinking again?" She glances at my glass.

"No, it's apple juice," I deadpan.

"Don't get sassy with me, Cash. I'm worried about you." Her voice softens. Bridget is a special woman, she worries about everyone and always puts other people's feelings before her own.

I sigh. "Bridge, I'm fine, it's just been a long week with the ball and stuff." I lie. It hasn't, it's been a long week because I haven't seen Rylee.

"I was just talking about the ball," she says, helping herself to a bottle of water out of the fridge.

"With Boh?" I take another sip of my drink.

"No, Rylee." That one name has me sitting up a little straighter, forgetting all about my drink. I try not to make it obvious how intrigued I am. Rylee used to come to the balls with Jace, but I assumed she wouldn't come this year.

"Oh, yeah. Is she coming?" I try ask uncaring, but my heart beats out of my chest waiting for the answer.

"Yes, of course she is. She always comes." She says like it was a silly question. The fact I will see Rylee in a few days eases the ache in my chest. It shouldn't be like this, it shouldn't feel like this, but it does, and there's nothing I can do about it. I was looking forward to the ball, but now I'm damn right ecstatic, just so I can see her face.

I nod. "That's good, I'm glad she is." I keep my voice neutral. Bridget's hand wraps around my forearm, and she gives me a gentle smile.

"You have been so good to her, Cash. You have helped more than I ever thought you could, and I can't thank you enough for that. She means so much to this family, and I don't ever want that to change."

I muster up a tight smile. I hate lying to Bridget. "It's what Jace would have wanted." I'm sick to my stomach even saying those words, but I can't tell her how I truly feel. I don't even know how she would react, but I can't see it being good. I can't see anyone taking the news well that I have feelings for Rylee.

"Did you come over for a reason or just to see me." I ask.

"I just wanted to come see how you were doing and, erm . . ." She sits down next to me. "See if you have heard anything from the police?" Her eyes meet mine, and her brows wrinkle.

I sigh, shaking my head. "Nothing." I take a sip of my whiskey. "They haven't had any leads, no one has seen him. He has a warrant out for his arrest, but that's it."

"I really worry, Cash," Bridge says, looking down at her drink. "I worry for Rylee and us as a family. I don't think it's settled in that Jace was . . ." She can't even say it.

I lean forward, grabbing her hands. "Hey." She has unshed tears in her eyes. "They will catch him, and he will get what's coming, Bridge. I won't stop until he does." She envelops me into a tight hug.

"I love you, Cash," she whispers.

"I love you too, Bridge." I hug her back, sinking into her smell that reminds me of home, or my mom. She always reminded me of Mom as she was growing up, but she has now turned into another version of her, and it makes me smile.

"So, how about you show me the donations. Boh mentioned they are good this year." She squeals.

"They are but hands off the cabin in Whitefish, that's mine." I wink at her.

"Ooo, so who will you be taking to the cabin, is it that nice girl from your birthday." She waves her hand around.

"Becky? No, no. I haven't spoken to her in a while."

"Well, you can't go to a cabin like that"—she points to the paper in front of her—"and not take a girl, Cash. There has to be someone?" Her eyes flick between mine. She has always had this way of being able to tell when I lie.

"There maybe someone, but it's early days yet." I lie, hoping it will dull her need to know who it is.

"Well bring her to the ball, I will scope her out and see if she is good enough for my older brother." She nudges me with a smile.

I glance at her. "Yeah, maybe," I whisper, then start going through the papers to show her the other donations to get her off the topic. Little does she know she already loves the girl like her own, she more than approves of Rylee, just not for me.

# Chapter Twenty-Four

## Cash

My eyes have been focused on the door for the last hour. She hasn't turned up yet, and I'm thinking she may not. I don't want to ask Bridget. A part of me wanted to text her back this morning when she texted me *morning*, but I was worried I might scare her off if I pressured. I'm trying to go at her pace even though it's killing me.

Everyone approaches me as if I'm a bomb about to explode. I'm the guy whose son was murdered only six months ago and his killer is on the loose. It's like people have forgotten how to have a conversation with me. A heavy thump lands on my back, and I glance over my shoulder to Bohdi. He nods.

"You good?" I take a sip of my drink, looking at him over the rim of my glass, something isn't right about him. Nothing is right with any of us, but Boh has always been good at keeping his head up and ours along with him. It's like the light has gone from his eyes completely. I nod, swallowing my drink.

"As good as can be, I guess, you good?" He nods, looking everywhere but me.

"Bohdi." His head snaps back to me.

"Yeah. All good." He rushes out.

"You and Bridge did amazing in here tonight." I glance around, taking in the hanging gold, silver, and blue decorations.

He nods, tight-lipped, and throws his thumb over his shoulder. "I'm just going to do the rounds. I'll see you in a bit." He slaps me on the shoulder before walking off. His head is no longer held high, his shoulders are downward. It's not the Boh we all know. Before I go after him to speak to him, Mike, one of my coworkers, stops me.

"Cash, my man. It's been a long time." I muster up as much of a smile as I can. The one good thing about Mike is he doesn't care about anyone else's life but his own, so you can guarantee he won't ask you how you're doing. He starts talking about his recent divorce and how he's getting himself back out there after being tied down for years, but his words fade when those doors open and I see her.

Rylee walks in the room, and every single bit of oxygen leaves my lungs. Her long brown hair that flows down to her waist in waves flips over her shoulder as she spins to say hello to someone. Her big green eyes shine and her smile lights up the room. The smile that erupts goose bumps over my whole body. I ogle her body, taking in the tight red ball gown she has on that accentuates every single sexy curve. When she turns back around, her slim silky leg is on display with the slit going up to her thigh. She's a fucking vision. I'm not the only person who notices; I clock at least five sets of eyes on her, women included. To top all this off, she doesn't realize how fucking stunning she is. She is oblivious. People approach her, introducing themselves, some are giving her condolences if her faltering smile and the deep breaths are anything to go by. I keep my gaze running up and down her legs, thinking of all the ways I want to sink my teeth in her thighs and the way my tongue would—

Who the fuck does this prick think he is? Matthew fucking Richardson. Of course it would be him. I down my drink, not taking my eyes off them. Rylee is laughing way more than she should; he's not that fucking funny. Come to think of it, he's not funny at all. He reaches up and touches her back. I see red, no one touches what's mine. No. One.

"Excuse me," I say to Mike as he goes on about God knows what.

I bypass Mike and walk straight toward Rylee. Mid-laugh, her eyes meet mine across the room, she stops laughing, and her eyes blow wide as she steps back from Matthew. *Too fucking late.*

As I approach, I don't take my eyes off her, and Matt shifts.

"Cash." His voice sounds hesitant, as if I caught him doing something wrong. In his head, he probably thinks this pissed-off look on my face is because he's talking to my dead son's girlfriend. If only everyone in this room knew how fucked up it really is.

"Matt," I say through gritted teeth. Still not taking my eyes off Rylee. "Excuse us." I take Rylee's arm and walk toward a set of closed doors at the back of the room.

"Er, Cash, what the fuck are you doing?" Rylee spits, trying to keep her voice down. I don't bother replying. She will find out soon enough. I don't slow my pace, so she's almost jogging as I pull her behind me. I have no doubt I'm not making this easy for her in her five-inch heels, but I don't care.

"Cash," Rylee spits, "you're making a scene." I know I am, and I know people will think this is weird, but I'm not thinking rationally. Seeing another man touching her and making her laugh has spurred something off inside me I can't control.

"You think it's okay for another man to flirt with you, Rylee?" I hiss, still not looking back at her, and push the doors open. My eyes scan the hallway, looking for a room. When I snag on a door, I storm toward it, praying no one is in there.

"Are you fucking kidding me right now," she screeches. "We were not flirting." Before she can spew any more bullshit, I open the door to the meeting room, thankful it's empty, drag her in behind me, and slam the door closed. I spin around and stare her down. She stares at me wide-eyed, as if I've just lost my fucking mind, and who knows, maybe I have. This is what she does to me. I take two strides toward her, and she pushes her shoulders back and raises her chin.

"Turn around and bend over the fuckin' table." I point to the long conference table behind her.

"Excuse me?" Her eyes bug out of her head more than I thought possible. The shock is evident on her face. "I don't know who—" I spin her around and push her head so she is bent over the table.

"I'm going to remind you who you belong to, Rylee," I hiss in her ear.

"Cash, what the fuck is wrong with you? This is not the way to go about this," she protests but doesn't move. I slip her dress up over her hips and bunch it up around her waist. My mouth waters at the sight in front of me, a thin G-string showcasing her peachy-as-fuck ass. I run my hands up and down her ass cheeks, spreading them and gripping them hard.

"Oww," she moans. "Ca-Cash what are you doing?"

"Tell me, you don't want this, Rylee. Tell me you want me to stop, and I will. I will walk out of the room and leave you alone." Like fuck will I. I let her think she has a say in this, but I know she wants me, I know she wants this. She doesn't have to say the words. No matter how angry she is with me, I know she will never say no. I slide my finger down the crack of her ass, and her fingers dig into the table. Then I hook my finger around the string and pull it back while running a finger through her pussy lips, starting at her clit, until I get to her hole.

"Everyone thinks you're so innocent, but you aren't, are you? If you were, your pussy wouldn't be dripping for me now, would it?" I push one finger into her soaking wet pussy. She rocks back onto my finger as I go to pull it out.

I bend over her, gathering her hair to lay over the opposite shoulder, and let my lips graze her ear. "Tell me how much you want it, Rylee." Her breaths stutter, and I smile. I have her exactly where I want her.

"I'm not fucking begging," she grits out through clenched teeth. I stand back up, taking my finger away.

"Cash," she moans. I glance down at her pussy lips glistening with her juices. There's no way I'm walking away from this, but I want her to beg for it. I want to know how much she wants me, even if I already know, I want to hear her say it.

I glide my finger up and down her slit, making sure I add more pressure to her clit as I rub over it. Quiet little moans come out of her every time my finger grazes her clit has me, and I grin.

"Tell me, Rylee." She moans, so I stop.

"Cash, fuck. I want you, goddamn it. I fucking want you, now. Please." I beam on the inside, hearing those words come from her mouth makes my dick twitch.

I unhook my belt and undo my pants. My dick is hard as a fucking rock. I jerk my dick a few times, reveling in the glisten of her pussy. I squeeze the head of my cock, already feeling the build up from just looking at her. There's no way I'm about to bust like a teenage fucking boy from looking at a pussy.

I rub my dick along her folds, gathering her juices. I knew she would be fucking perfect, but I didn't realize how perfect.

"Cash. Please tell me you have a condom," she pants, still squirming.

"No." I don't care about not having a condom. The first time I'm inside her, I want to feel everything.

"Cash. You can't without one, I'm not on anything." I don't know why, but those words rush through me with excitement, and eagerness? I have never thought of Rylee pregnant before, but the thought of filling her up and putting a baby inside her, has me thrusting into her in one swift motion.

"Cash," she screams. If there wasn't music and conversation in the ballroom, they would most definitely hear her, but I want them too I'm not thinking straight and wouldn't care if everyone knew it. Her pussy pulsating around my dick is like nothing I have ever felt before, like she was fucking made for me. I don't care how fucked up that sounds. I pull back slightly and slam back into her as I grip her hips and fuck her hard and fast. She moans and claws at the table, and her juices gather all over my dick. I want to capture this moment, I never want to forget it, it's fucking perfect. I let go of one of her hips and clutch her hair, pulling her hard so her back arches and her ass pushes into my pelvis even more, pushing me to the hilt, causing a gasp to leave her mouth.

"Oww, Cash." She moans.

"Does it hurt, Rylee?" I keep my grip on her hair and kiss down the side of her neck, keeping up with my punishing thrusts into her.

"Ye-yes," she moans out.

"Good. I want you to feel me for days. I want you to wake up and it hurt to walk. I want you to sit at your desk at work and feel the throb between your legs, remembering who was there." I bite her neck, bringing another gasp out of her. "Now, shut the fuck up and take this dick like the good girl I know you are." She moans loud as I increase my pace. A tingle starts in my spine, and I know I won't hold on much longer.

"Rub your clit, Rylee. I want you coming on my dick." She brings her hand under her dress and rubs at her clit.

Her moans get louder and louder, and her pussy clenches my dick. The sound of her wetness as I pull out and push back in, fills my ears. Her body trembles and her breath hitches. She's coming. Her body goes stiff and her pussy flutters. I bring my arm around her front, tilting her up, while keeping a grip on her hair as I spill my cum into her pussy, pushing myself in as deep as I can get it. I slowly pump in and out of her, allowing her pussy to milk every single drop.

Never has sex been like this. I have never come so hard in my life. Her weightless body hangs in my arm. I fall forward, pushing her front into the table and me on top of her. I lean on my arms, not wanting to crush her and we take deep breaths. My dick, tingles inside her, and I swear it's still fucking hard. I pull out slowly. I'll never get enough of her. My cum drips out of her pussy. I don't know what possesses me, but I rub my finger through her lips, gathering the juices and push them back inside her.

Her body jolts and a soft moan leaves her lips.

"I don't want you wasting a drop of my cum, Rylee." After pushing my cum back into her pussy, I put her G-string back into place and pull her dress back down. She gets up on wobbly legs as I put myself back together and fasten my belt.

A hiss leaves her lips. When she turns around, the sight of her sends my heart thumping in my chest. I did this to her, the redness on her cheeks gets redder as I take her in. Her mascara has smudged, and her hair sticks up and isn't silky soft like it was when she got here. I did that, and I have never been more proud. I lick my thumb and bring it to her face, wiping under one eye and then the other to get rid of the mascara. Her eyes follow my every move before snapping up and staying glued to mine.

I glance down at her mouth, realizing I haven't even tasted her today, so I dip my head and kiss her. It's not enough, though, so I run my tongue along her lips as they part on a gasp.

I lick my lips after, savoring the taste.

"I don't want you going to the restroom when you walk out of here." My gaze flits between her eyes. "I want you to go back into that ballroom with my cum in your pussy, so if Michael or whatever-his-fucking-name-is Richards tries flirting with you again, you won't have to think who owns you, you will fucking feel who owns you." I place a kiss on her lips again before smoothing down her hair.

"You're a fucking caveman, you know that." She seethes, more pissed off than she's ever been.

I smile at her, which only seems to piss her off more. She huffs before walking toward the door, and my face beams when she turns to me, an ice-cold glare penetrates me as her eyes narrow into slits and her lips thin.

"Have a good night, Rylee." She swings the door open, not saying a word before slamming it behind her.

I drop back in one of the chairs, run my hands through my hair, and laugh to myself. If I didn't know before, I have no doubt now: Rylee fucking Matthews is mine.

# Chapter Twenty-Five
# Rylee

I can't believe that just happened. With every step I take back to the ballroom, I wince. My legs are shaky, and my body feels like it's on fire and aches in every way. I can't believe how alive I feel.

Swinging the door open to the ballroom, noise floods out of it. Everyone having fun, drinking, and laughing. Paranoia sinks in thick and fast, who saw us walking out that door, who is watching me walk back through it. I scan the room, but everyone seems to be in their own worlds, oblivious to what just happened. I try and walk normally, but it's hard with how sore I am and Cash's cum running down my leg.

"There you are," Toni shouts. I jump out of my skin, my heart thumping out of my chest. "I have been looking everywhere for you." Her brows furrow. "Why are you so jumpy?" We came together but she went to the bar when we got here, then Cash dragged me out of the room.

"Girl, are you okay, you look flushed as fuck, do you feel ill?" Toni's hand rests on my head.

"Rylee, you're sweating and your mascara is smudged to fuck." She starts messing around with my face, rubbing under my eyes.

She pauses, her gaze darts over my face and then my hair, then she steps back, assessing me. I try and stand as still as I can. I move from one leg to the other, and the cum trickles farther down. Fuck, I need to get to a toilet. Toni's stare lands on my bare leg, and her eyes bug out.

"Rylee fucking Matthews." She gasps, her hand going to her mouth. I glance down and there on my thigh, clear-as-day, are fingerprints. I'm going to kill him. Toni grabs my hand and pulls us into an alcove hidden part of the room, then she glances around.

"Spill it now." My heart rate increases.

"I fucked Cash."

"Sorry, say that again." I go to say it again, but it truly settles in.

"Shit," I say, staring at Toni, my eyes bulging and my mouth opening and closing like a fish on dry land.

"Shit, Toni." I say dumbfounded.

"What? . . .What?" Her gaze sweeps me.

"I-I fucked Cash." My hand goes to my mouth. Toni smiles at me.

"It's about fucking time." She huffs. "But girl, could you have not waited until tonight?"

I rear my head back. "Hold on a minute, what do you mean about fucking time, you were the one that said I needed time."

"It's been nearly three months, Ry. You have been doing good lately, you are slowly getting back on track with your life and you have just left Cash waiting, and that man has literally done just that, he's waited for you. Fucking hell, he dropped everything and flew out to Mexico to make sure you were safe, and then you come home and tell him you need more time. You couldn't have expected him to wait around forever." She eyes me. Now making me feel like shit. She's right, I just left him there dangling, not giving him anything. I nod.

"You're right. Now I guess his reaction tonight is justified." I squint, thinking. "Weirdly enough."

"What actions?" Toni eyes me, eager as anything.

I let out a heavy sigh.

"Oh boy." She smiles.

"I can't tell you everything here." I glance around, paranoid I just admitted that out loud. "Maybe you could stay with me tonight?" I eye her. She gives me a tight-lipped smile, then drops her bottom lip.

"You know what, yes, I will. Hold please." She puts her finger up while digging out her phone.

"Hey." I snatch the phone out of her hand. "If you had plans, don't you dare cancel them." I scowl at her.

"It's only dick. You know you're more important than any dick to enter my life."

I shake my head. "No, you can come over tomorrow, and I'll cook us dinner," I say, holding her phone, waiting for her to agree with me.

"Okay, okay." She puts her hand out for her phone.

"So who is the guy, then?"

"Just some guy from work. No one special," she says, rolling her eyes. It never is with Toni. Whoever catches that girl's eye for longer than twenty-four hours will be very special.

"I need you to give me one thing, this cannot wait until tomorrow." She pauses, threading her arm through mine. "On a scale of one to ten, how Daddy was Cash." I shake my head, laughing. Only this girl could ask such a question. "I will leave you alone once you answer me. Just give me something, because I have this image of how he would be, I want to know if he lives up to what I think."

I laugh, only Toni could have an image of Cash having sex.

"Give me a number." She demands.

I stop laughing and look at her, raising my eyebrows. "Let's just say . . ." I stand closer to her and whisper, "I will think of him every time I sit down for the next week." A high-pitched squeal comes out of her mouth, drawing attention from a few people standing close to us.

"Shut your mouth, Toni." I keep glancing around, trying to smile it off like it's nothing.

"I knew it. Damn, I fucking knew it. I can't wait for the play-by-play." I laugh at her once again.

"Can I get everyone's attention please." Bridget's voice comes through the mic.

"C'mon," I say to Toni. We make our way back into the middle of the room, and Cash is nowhere to be seen. Bridge is standing on stage with Boh behind her, smiling, but it's not Boh's normal smile. I mean, no one in this family is the same, but it's only been the last couple of months that I've noticed Boh like this. His eyes scan the crowd, and when they land on someone, his jaw clenches and the small smile disappears. I lean up on my tiptoes to see who he is looking at—Cash. Maybe they had a falling out.

I've seen them have the odd tiff with each other, so maybe they disagreed on something. Cash's eyes squint, and then I glance back at Boh, who is back to smiling while looking at Bridget. I zoned out on what Bridge was saying.

"We have a total of thirty-four donations, and they are incredible, I can't thank you all enough. As you all know, the charity we are supporting this year is Shine Bright, a young children's cancer charity which provides clinical, financial, and emotional support for children and their families who are affected by cancer. This charity meant a lot to our Jace, so we wanted to do it again to honor him."

My heart aches at hearing his name, but then I smile because it's true; he loved this charity more than anything, and he would be beaming right now. Bridge finds me in the crowd, her eyes connecting with mine as I blow her a small kiss. She is an admirable woman, and I honestly don't know where I would be without her. "Now let's start the bidding." It's not something I've ever done because the men in this room are rich and the prices some of the gifts go for are insane, but I still like to see what's up for grabs and just dream it could be me going on the luxury holiday or whatever it is.

"First up, we have a stunning weekend away on this luxurious yacht donated by Benny O'Donovan." Everyone claps as a video on the projector plays, and to say that yacht is stunning is an understatement. It's something you would see in the movies. Toni stands on her tiptoes while using my shoulder to support her.

"What are you trying to look at?" I bunch my eyebrows together while following her eyeline.

"Can you see what that Benny O'Donovan looks like? Because that"—she points to the projector—"is a bit of me." I bring my hand to my mouth, trying to stifle the giggle that leaves me as I turn her body slightly and point at the old man whose gut hangs over his belt and is bald besides a few gray hairs left on his head.

"That's Benny, babes. I think you have a chance." I pause, eyeing her up and down and shrug. "Maybe." She punches my arm, letting out a huff.

"Where's all the young rich men at. It's the only reason I'm here tonight." I look at her wide-eyed. "And to support a great cause." She follows up quickly.

Bridge is up there for a while going through all the donations. Some take my and Toni's breaths away. Each person that donates, Toni scopes out, and I can see she already has her eyes set on one person. Boh even participated and won three nights on another yacht, smaller than the one Benny donated, but still stunning.

"Now this one is a favorite of mine. This has been donated by unknown." Bridge frowns. "We would all like to thank you but whoever you are, we appreciate this."

A stunning log cabin surrounded by mountains and trees lights up the screen. There are some pictures of it in daylight, and it's a complete dream, but when more pictures slide along to show it at night, it's breathtaking. Christmas lights surround the front as it sits in snow. It's like something out of a movie, like a fairytale cabin.

"This donation is extremely generous, it's for a week's stay in this gorgeous lodge. I think this causes for the bidding to start at 6000 dollars. Wow, what a dream that wou—"

"Six thousand." That gruff voice I know all too well, that was whispering the most sinful things in my ear not even an hour ago.

"Holy. Fucking. Shit," Toni whispers next to me. I glance at Cash looking up at the stage. Bridge stares at him wide-eyed with a huge smile on her face.

"My brother doesn't mess around." She jokes. "Will anyone beat that; can I get 7000 dollars?"

"Seven thousand," a quiet voice breaks through.

"Is he fucking kidding?" Toni laughs. I look up and it's Benny. "He would have a heart attack just walking up the stairs to the cabin.

"Toni," I hiss as a woman spins on her feet and scowls at Toni.

Toni shrugs. "What, it's true." She stares the woman in the face. The woman shakes her head and turns back around.

"Ten thousand," Cash's voice booms through.

"Well, well, wellllll . . . Daddy really wants you up in those mountains," Toni whispers.

"My brother clearly has good taste," Bridget says through the microphone.

"Benny, do we hear a 11,000?" Benny shakes his head.

"Going once, going twice. Well done, Cash," Bridget shouts while everyone claps. My gaze finds Cash. His stare heats up every inch of me and says a thousand words. I glance down.

"My nipples are actually erect from that stare. My god the sexual tension could slice through fucking stone," Toni whispers.

"Stop," I hiss. She chuckles next to me.

"Tonight has been entertaining, and it's about to get a whole lot more exciting for me." She raises her eyebrows with a smirk. I frown at Toni, what is she talking about.

"Now," Bridget says on the mic, giving everyone a devilish smirk. "We are changing things up this year. We are doing something a little different." *What is she up to?*

"Now this is what I've been waiting for." I swing my gaze to Toni, narrowing my eyes at her.

"What are you talking about?"

"Didn't Bridget ask—" She stops herself. "Of course, she wouldn't." She drops her head. "They are auctioning off people this year."

"They're what?" I say, shocked. They have never done this before.

"It's just a bit of fun, someone can bid to have a date with you, that's it. It's all for a good cause." Toni winks at me, then turns her gaze back to the stage with a big grin.

"I'm assuming you are a part of it." I raise one eyebrow at her.

"Do dogs bark?" she deadpans. "You know this is right up my alley. Hopefully a rich daddy whisks me away to Bali for the weekend." She elbows me in the side. "Keep those fingers crossed for me, my girl," she whispers. I laugh while turning back to the stage. She will need all the luck she can get because at least sixty percent of the men are over the age of sixty in this room, and not the hot kind either.

“Wait until you hear who we have up for bidding, guys,” Bridge says excitedly.

“Bohdi Stiles.” Women’s screams filter through the room, including mine. Bohdi takes a bow while laughing.

“Toni Delray.” I scream as Toni walks to the stage, purposely swinging her hips as she does a little spin and then blows a kiss to the crowd. Men whistle, and even some girls give her a cheer. A few other people are called up, and everyone cheers. Toni is lapping up the attention, and there is nothing more beautiful than seeing your best friend happy, and she’s glowing.

“We have one more person which I think is going to blow the roof off this place.” My interest is piqued. Who could that be? Everyone looks around.

“Cash Stiles.” As my stomach sinks to my feet, the smile falls off my face. Bridge was right about one thing. Every single person screams, and the roof almost blows off the building.

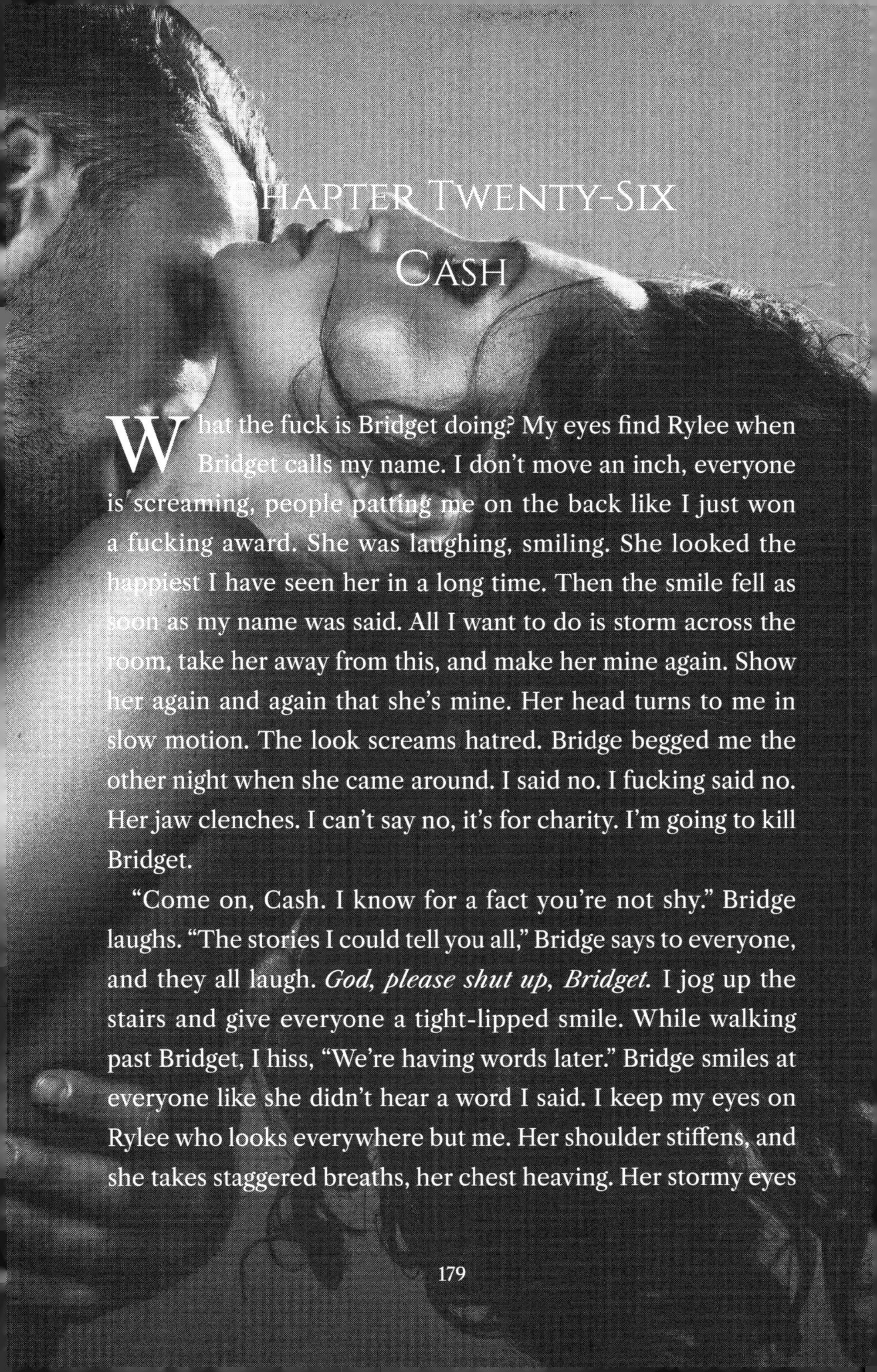

# Chapter Twenty-Six
## Cash

What the fuck is Bridget doing? My eyes find Rylee when Bridget calls my name. I don't move an inch, everyone is screaming, people patting me on the back like I just won a fucking award. She was laughing, smiling. She looked the happiest I have seen her in a long time. Then the smile fell as soon as my name was said. All I want to do is storm across the room, take her away from this, and make her mine again. Show her again and again that she's mine. Her head turns to me in slow motion. The look screams hatred. Bridge begged me the other night when she came around. I said no. I fucking said no. Her jaw clenches. I can't say no, it's for charity. I'm going to kill Bridget.

"Come on, Cash. I know for a fact you're not shy." Bridge laughs. "The stories I could tell you all," Bridge says to everyone, and they all laugh. *God, please shut up, Bridget.* I jog up the stairs and give everyone a tight-lipped smile. While walking past Bridget, I hiss, "We're having words later." Bridge smiles at everyone like she didn't hear a word I said. I keep my eyes on Rylee who looks everywhere but me. Her shoulder stiffens, and she takes staggered breaths, her chest heaving. Her stormy eyes take in everyone on the stage except me. I glance at Bridget but then catch Toni's face. If looks could kill, I would be twelve feet under, six feet from Toni and six feet from Rylee.

They start going through the bidding, and it's funny to watch how excited people get. Toni's up next, and she's bouncing on the spot. When Bridget was asking who I thought would like to take part, Toni was the first person who popped into my head. She's always up for a laugh and has to be one of the most confident women I know.

Bridget said that it might be nice for Rylee, but I shut that down straight away. If Bridge knew what was going on, she wouldn't be asking her, and if she knew the battle Rylee and I have been going through with each other, she would understand. I know it wouldn't be good for Rylee, seeing how much she has struggled lately, but I shut it down for my own selfish needs. Over my dead body will she ever go on a date with another man. Does witnessing the sheer anger that seeps from Rylee make me feel slightly good about myself? Yes, it does, I won't lie. Knowing it annoys her that I may be going out with another woman, makes me feel good about myself, but seeing her face drop and that beautiful smile disappear, isn't worth any of it. She still doesn't look at me as she jumps up and down while clapping. I zero myself back into the room.

"Congratulations to the lucky winner." She pauses, waiting for the guy to answer. I squint, trying to make out who it is, but I don't recognize him. He looks a bit young.

"Kaleb Hawks." His deep voice breaks through. I've never heard of him. Toni doesn't jump for joy, but her head tilts, sizing him up as if she's trying to work out if she's happy about him or not.

"Well, Kaleb, I can tell you that 15,000 dollars is worth every penny for the stunning Toni. You got a lot to live up to for the date. Have fun." Bridget laughs as Rylee's subtle laugh fills my ears, then my eyes find her beautiful wide smile and her eyes shining like diamonds. My eyes jump to Toni again, and this time, she is smirking at Kaleb, so I'm guessing she worked out she is happy. I kind of feel for the guy. Fifteen thousand dollars for a date, fucking hell. He has a lot to live up to.

"Now the one you have all been waiting for." Oh no, the one I've been dreading. Rylee's shoulders deflate. She drops her head to the floor like she can't stand to witness it.

"Who would like to take the grumpy, oh, I mean, beautiful Cash Stiles out." Everyone laughs because she couldn't be more right. "And, who knows, the lucky winner might be able to attend the cabin, because as far as I know, my brother is very much single." Fuck. I don't know what Bridge is playing at, I told her the other night there was someone. She asked me earlier if I brought anyone with me, and I said no. That doesn't mean I'm fucking single. I belong to one woman and that woman looks like she's about to tear every woman's head off in this room.

Toni raises a brow at me, offering me a sarcastic smile, shaking her head. She's not impressed. I can't blame her upset; I was inside Rylee an hour ago, claimed her as mine, and she's standing there with my cum running down her leg, and now I'm about to be bid on to go on a date with another woman and Bridge has announced that I'm very much single. She couldn't be more wrong. I'm confident but feel more awkward now because of Rylee. I stand there tight-lipped with my hands in my pocket, just wanting this to be over. I zone out as my eyes land on Rylee again. I try and tell her with my eyes that's it's only her. I know if she could, she would bid—if people wouldn't judge her, judge us. Hell, I would give her the money to win this date with me, but I know she can't.

"Eighteen thousand, wow, ladies. Wow," Bridge says in the mic. Can I get nineteen?"

"Twenty thousand dollars," a voice comes from the back of the room. Everyone turns around, and my eyes land on the woman—Miley Sweeney. Shit. Miley is one of the most successful women in Baltimore, but also my ex-girlfriend who I was with for two years, the last year being when Rylee and Jace got together. When Rylee spins to me, tears glisten her eyes, and my stomach sours at her sadness.

"Miley Sweeney," Bridget says through the mic. "This just got interesting." *Yeah, thanks a lot, Bridget.* "Come get your prize, Mills." Bridge giggles. Miley glides through the crowd in her short black dress, blonde hair flowing over her shoulders, and her mile-long legs that every man follows with their eyes as she walks past. She's stunning, there is no doubt about that, but she wants the family life. It's not something I wanted at the time or with her. There's only one girl I want that with. Miley walks up the stage, her eyes on me.

"Mills," I say as she approaches.

"Long time no see, handsome." You could hear a pin drop in this room, so I have no doubt Rylee heard that. Mills kisses me on the cheek as I kiss hers, my hand rests on her waist. I catch Rylee's eyes over Miley's shoulder, and she zeros in on my hand and then glares at me.

*You piece of shit*, she mouths before spinning on her heels and storming out of the room. She turns around to me one more time before exiting the door, and the fire in her eyes makes me sick to my stomach. There is no way I'm losing her now. I just got her.

"Excuse me, Miley, I need to go," I say as I walk off the stage, barging through everyone.

"Cash," Bridge shouts. *Not fucking now, Bridge.* I need to get my woman.

# Chapter Twenty-Seven
# James

My heart thumps as my eyes land on her. My chest heaves, watching her distressed state staring down at her phone. I clench my fists, thinking who the fuck did this to her. Why is she so distressed?

*You can make her smile again.*

I take one step and then another, ten more steps and I could touch her. I close my eyes, imagining my fingers trailing her soft skin. A shiver slivers up my back, as my body erupts into goosebumps when a breeze hits my face that smells like Rylee. She smells like a fresh summers day. My favorite. I need her, I need to feel her; I don't know how much longer I can go without Rylee in my life.

*She's yours. Go and make her happy.*

I allow myself to take her in again, my gaze tracks her body. How dare she leave the house looking like this; she is mine. I can only see this much skin. She should only dress like this for me. I close my eyes again and I grit my teeth as I take staggered breaths. Rylee has been testing me lately, I had eyes on her every single day, but one day poof! She was gone. Just like that and then days later she was back again. I found out a week later she had gone to that fucking holiday Jace was showing me the night he died. It made me sick to my stomach when I found out she had gone there. I found myself outside Casey's on one of the nights, I needed to calm myself and I knew she would help but after letting myself into her apartment, she wasn't there. It was a shame, she would have really helped. I don't think I can wait any longer.

*Calm down, you don't want to make her sad.*

My eyes flicker open, but she's gone. Where the fuck is she. My eyes frantically look around the front of the building, and then snag on her getting in a car. Fuck! I grab my car keys out of my pocket but as I go to take another step towards my car, I hear a bang and spin around, ducking behind a pillar.

Cash.

I watch him desperately looking around. This cunt isn't having her, I'm not having another Stiles man take what is mine. Soon enough, I will have her. Maybe not tonight, but soon.

# Chapter Twenty-Eight

## Cash

Walking out of the building, I look both ways but don't see her. Fuck, she can't have gone far. I jog down the stairs. It's taken a lot for Rylee to get her head around everything. She has a right to be pissed, but I just got her, and now she's slipping through my fingers again. I get my phone out of my pocket and dial her number. It rings twice before going to voicemail. "For fuck's sake." I sigh. I can only assume she is heading back to her apartment.

The streets are quiet, due to the time, but she promised if she ever traveled on her own it would be where there are people around. It's eerily quiet, and I don't like that she is by herself. I order an Uber, which is in front of me within two minutes. It's not far to Rylee's, but I just hope that is where she's gone, I can't imagine she'd go anywhere else. I don't have the key to her apartment on me, so what are the chances of her letting me up? Zero.

The Uber pulls up to Rylee's, and her lights being on relaxes me. My phone rings for the third time since being in the taxi. Bridget won't stop calling. The auction is the least of my worries.

I have one person on my mind, and I'm not settling until I have her in my arms.

I press her buzzer and wait. She doesn't pick up the intercom or let me in, but this is what I expected. My phone reads ten o'clock, it's a bit late, but I'm desperate, so I ring Miss Dainty. She is an older lady who Jace used to do odd jobs for, and when Jace died, I asked her to keep a special eye on Rylee for me, which she was more than happy to do. I press her buzzer, feeling shitty because of the time, but if I wait for someone to let me up, then I could be waiting all night.

"Hello." Her sweet voice comes through the intercom.

"Miss Dainty, it's Cash Stiles. I'm so sorry it's so late, ma'am, but would you mind letting me up, I'm a bit worried about Rylee."

"Of course, my dear, and don't be silly. I was just watching some good old TV while eating some biscuits." She cuts off the intercom and buzzes me in.

I take the stairs two at a time, until I'm outside Rylee's door, and raise my hand to knock but I freeze. I know her well enough to know she won't let me in. I glance over my shoulder as my eyes snag on Miss Dainty's door, knowing full well she has a key to the apartment. I try internally talking myself down from doing this, but I have no other choice. I walk over, giving the door a gentle knock. She answers the door, her hair in rollers, and she's wrapped up in a big fluffy dressing gown.

"Cash, my dear, are you okay?" Her brows furrow as she searches my face.

"I really am sorry to bother you again, Miss Dainty, but Rylee isn't answering her phone or the door, so I'm worried about her. Would you mind letting me borrow the key to let myself in." She walks away to grab the key. I know this is a shitty move, but I have no idea how else I will get into her apartment. Hopefully she doesn't have the deadlock on.

"Here you go," she says, grabbing my hand and placing the key in my palm.

I offer her an appreciative smile. "Thank you. I will drop the key back tomorrow so I won't bother you again tonight."

She waves her hand at me. "Don't worry about me, if anything is wrong, please let me know. I hope she's okay." Her face scrunches in worry.

"I'm sure she's fine, it's probably just me overthinking. Night, Miss Dainty, and thank you again." I wave to her as I walk toward Rylee's door and make sure she is out of sight and in her apartment before I let myself in. Who knows how Rylee will react to my entrance.

The last thing I want to do is scare her, so I shout her name when my foot crosses the threshold. She's stomping toward me, so I get myself in and close the apartment door.

"What the fuck? Do you just walk around with my key or something." Her big eyes roam my face, full of rage, but I can tell see she's been crying.

"Rylee, I—" She puts her hand up and closes her eyes while taking a deep breath.

"I don't want to hear your bullshit, Cash. Leave." She spins on her heels and strides away from me. I follow her into the kitchen.

"I said leave." She grits through her teeth.

"You should know me well enough to know that's not going to happen." I stay back, even if every fiber of my being wants to wrap her up and hold her.

"Why," she shouts as she spins to me. "Why the fuck did you do what you did tonight and then put yourself up to go on a date with another woman?"

"It was for charit—"

"Don't you fucking dare give me that 'it's for charity bullshit.'" She laughs. "Ahh, you really are a piece of shit."

"Rylee," I bellow. "Bridget asked me, I said no, but everyone thinks I'm single." Technically, I am, but I don't treat myself as if I'm single because there's only one woman for me.

"Well, you are. So, you can leave now."

"I think we know that's a lie." Her teary eyes find mine, softening.

"You are single. Go on your date, Cash, see if I care." Her voice breaks as she walks away from me, but I storm up to her, grab her arm, and spin her to me.

"Let go of me." She tries to yank her arm out of my hold, but I keep a tight grip.

"No. I will never let go of you." I bring my lips down to her ear. "You're mine, whether you have chosen to accept that or not. I have accepted it for the both of us, and that isn't changing. Not in this fucking lifetime." A sob leaves her lips.

"I had chosen to accept it. Tonight, I chose to, after what we did. I knew that was it, I was a goner for you." She pulls her arm out of my hold. "You know how much it took for me and yet you go and throw it down the drain by putting yourself forward to go on a date with your fucking ex."

"I did—"

"Cut the fucking excuses." She tries to sound angry, but her voice keeps breaking on sobs. I know tonight must have been hard for her, not just the auction but what we did in the conference room. I didn't want things to go down the way they did, but I was too far gone once I saw another man's hands on her. "Have fun in the cabin with Miley," she spits before stalking to her room.

I chuckle. Seeing Rylee jealous, I won't lie, makes me hard. Knowing this is riling her up because she thinks I'm going to that cabin with anyone other than her is fucking comical. I'll drag her there if I have to, but to clear it up, I will let her know exactly who I'm taking there. I stalk behind her.

"Go home, Cash. I need to have a shower and go to bed. I've had enough tonight."

I walk up behind her, wrapping my hand around her waist, and goose bumps rise on her arms. Her breath hitches as I bring my hand up her chest and grip her throat. She brings her hand to mine and tries prying my fingers away.

"Cash," she breathes out.

My lips skim her ear as I whisper, "Picture this . . ." I pause, running my other hand up and down her hip. "You arrive at the cabin. It's better than the pictures, it's stunning, huge. You look around and fall in love with it. You go out on the balcony, the crisp air touches your skin, causing you to shiver, you can smell the pine trees and hear the birds chirping. It tastes like freedom.

You glance down, and overlooking the stunning lake is a hot tub. It's bubbling, the steam warming your skin. The setting sun creates an orange tint on the world, it's almost perfect." I bring my hand around to the front of her dress, caressing her thigh.

"You strip down to nothing. No one is around, just us." I slink my hand beneath her dress, and her breath hitches as I get closer to the apex of her thigh.

"You place one leg into the hot, steaming water and all your troubles wash away. You stare out to the sunset, then a hand grasps your leg, and you're pushed forward to the edge of the hot tub. My hard dick glides between your ass cheeks." I grind her ass so she can feel how hard I am. "I tell you to watch the sunset and then slam my dick inside you. In and out." I collect my leftover cum from her entrance, rub over her folds, then push two fingers into her pussy. "You feel on top of the world," I say as she moans out, her head falling back as her mouth opens.

"I push my dick so far inside you, harder, faster. My fingers graze over your slit, causing a sensation to build in the pit of your stomach." Her moans get louder as my thumb rubs her clit. "Then I whisper I want you coming on my dick, and I want you to see stars. I graze your clit one more time as I pull your hair, and the scream causes the birds to fly from the trees. You open your eyes to the sky and all you see are stars."

Rylee moans, her pussy squeezing my fingers as she comes. "Fuck, Cash."

"Keep your fucking eyes closed. I want you to stay in that moment, looking up at the stars while you come down. I haven't finished with you yet, though; I drag you out of the hot tub and into the cabin." I lead her into her bathroom, unzipping her dress as we walk. When we stop in the bathroom, her dress drops to a pile at her feet. I unclasp her bra and slide her panties down. Her breaths come out in pants.

"Cash."

"I drag you to the bathroom. The stunning waterfall shower with black marble walls is in front of you. Candles surround the bathroom, it's like something off a film. I bring you to the middle of the shower." I lead her into the walk-in shower. "And I tell you to get on your knees." She drops to her knees in the shower, her eyes still closed. Her chest heaves, and her nipples are peaked. I strip out of my suit in record time and step in front of her. My dick as hard as rock. Her breath hitches when I shut the shower door, but she remains on her knees, her hands out in front of her resting on her legs. I touch her lips. She flinches but opens slightly, then I slide my fingers that were in her pussy into her mouth, pushing them to the back of her throat, and it contracts around my fingers as she gags. I pull them out and hold my dick in my hand, giving myself a few slow strokes.

"I tell you, you have never looked so beautiful on your knees before, lips red and plump, nipples begging to be pinched." My hand cups her tit, then I pinch her nipples, and she hisses. "I grab your hair from the back and pull your head back, and the water trickles down your body from the showerhead." I turn Rylee's shower on, and the water runs down her body, and she shudders.

"I then tell you to open up so I can push my hard dick into your mouth so you can finish me off." I wrench Rylee's head back by her hair, and the water hits her neck and flows down her tits. She opens her mouth as I smile. "Such a good girl you are for me, Ry." She keeps her mouth open, and a small moan comes from her throat. I slam my dick into her mouth, and it hits the back of her throat, and she gags before finding her rhythm. She bobs up and down as I watch in amazement; she's fucking perfect. I want to take a picture of this so I never forget it, even though I won't because I will make sure she's like this every week for the rest of our fucking lives.

"I want you to go faster, so I grab either side of your head, wrapping my hands in your hair as I fuck your face." I smile, Rylee knows what's coming next. I do exactly what I said and face-fuck her, and the water now hits her face. She chokes on my dick and the water, but I'm close, so I don't give a shit, she can take it. "I tell you how good you take my dick and I want you to swallow every drop of my cum when I come down your throat." I moan and pick up speed.

She pushes on my legs as the water flooding her face becomes too much, so I slide her back out of the water and continue to fuck her throat. "I'm close," I grit out. I pump two more times and then spill my seed into her mouth. I groan; her mouth is fucking perfect. I pump slowly, and her lips wrap around the head of my dick to suck me clean of any cum. I let go of her hair and bring my hands to her face.

"Open your eyes," I whisper. Her eyes flutter open as tears escape them. I was rough, but I don't care, I needed her to know how much it's her—only her. Her chest heaves as her swollen lips open slightly and she stares up at me.

I cup her cheeks.

"When I bid on that cabin, I pictured all of that, and I only pictured it with you."

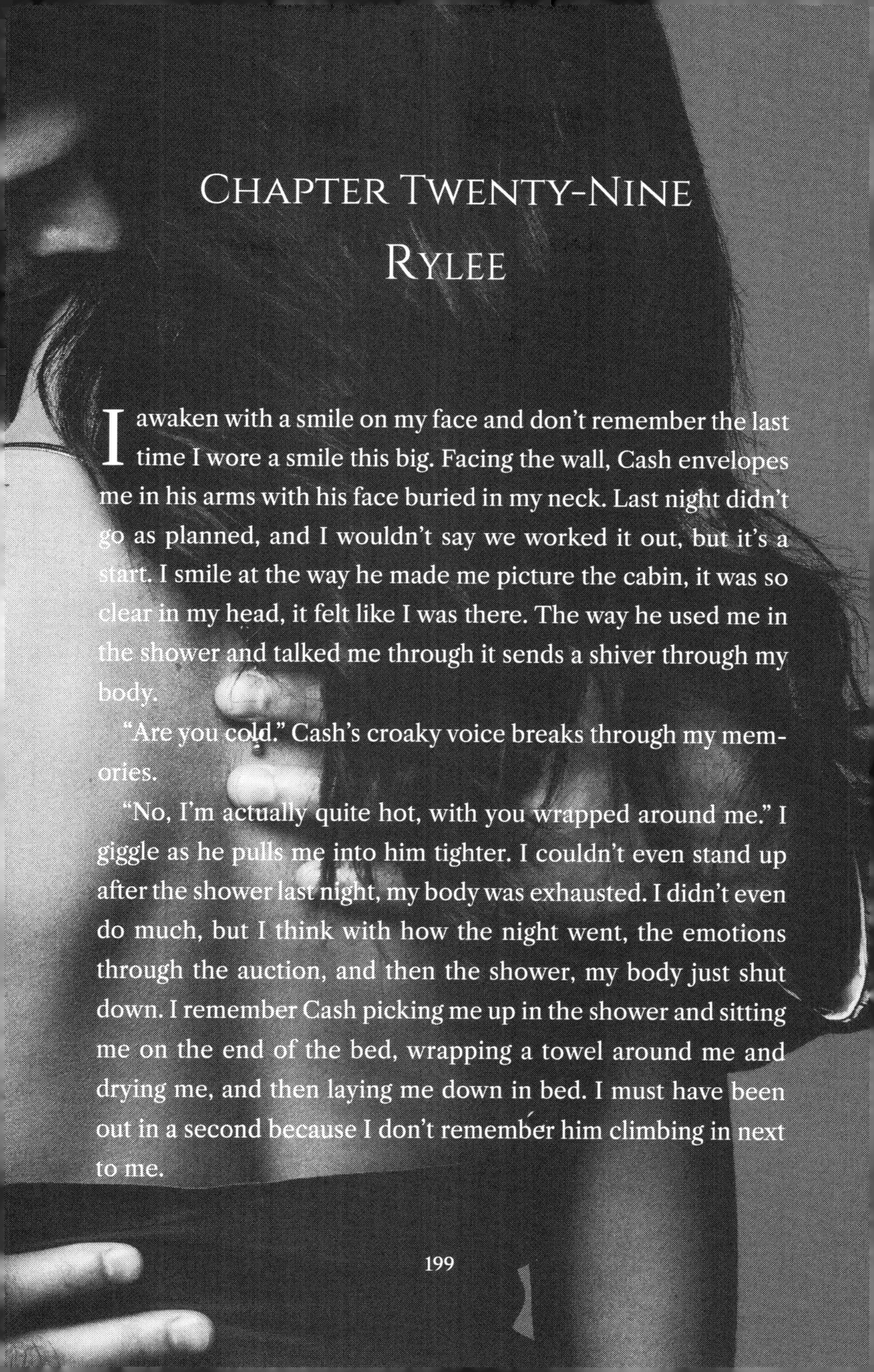

# Chapter Twenty-Nine
## Rylee

I awaken with a smile on my face and don't remember the last time I wore a smile this big. Facing the wall, Cash envelopes me in his arms with his face buried in my neck. Last night didn't go as planned, and I wouldn't say we worked it out, but it's a start. I smile at the way he made me picture the cabin, it was so clear in my head, it felt like I was there. The way he used me in the shower and talked me through it sends a shiver through my body.

"Are you cold." Cash's croaky voice breaks through my memories.

"No, I'm actually quite hot, with you wrapped around me." I giggle as he pulls me into him tighter. I couldn't even stand up after the shower last night, my body was exhausted. I didn't even do much, but I think with how the night went, the emotions through the auction, and then the shower, my body just shut down. I remember Cash picking me up in the shower and sitting me on the end of the bed, wrapping a towel around me and drying me, and then laying me down in bed. I must have been out in a second because I don't remember him climbing in next to me.

"Let me face you." I giggle out as he tickles my waist. He loosens me, and I turn to face him. His blue eyes are darker than usual. His hair is ruffled. I run my fingers through his stubble, and gaze at his face. We're naked, and I'm content being in his arms, happy. His eyes track mine, and we lie there in silence watching each other.

"I'm not waiting anymore, Ry." He keeps his gaze on me. "You're mine," he whispers. I smile. He's right. I'm his in every way, and I need to stop holding back.

"I'm yours, Cash." As I say the words, everything around me stops. His eyes flare open and the blue turns darker.

"Say it again," he says.

I smirk. "I'm yours," I whisper. I get lost in the blue depths. His stare burns into my soul, and I hate and love how my body reacts to him, like it calls to him and he can see and feel it. His gaze travels down to my lips and back up to my eyes again. My heart rate increases as he inches forward. His lips ghost over mine, as if he thinks I'll freak out at any minute. Not anymore. My whole body craves him, even my sick and twisted heart wants him. He pulls away slightly, and the heat swimming in his eyes mirrors mine. My body swarms in goose bumps as my breaths come out choppy.

Cash's lips descend on mine, his tongue aggressively probing my lips. I open my mouth, letting our tongues intertwine. The kiss turns frantic as he overpowers me, then he rises, leaning over me, taking my mouth like he owns it. He makes me feel alive, and every sweep of his tongue against mine makes the real world fade around us, the sound of the birds tweeting wanes. It's just us. Cash and me. I knew from the first moment we kissed it wouldn't be the last, my body craved him without me even realizing. Every time the pain comes back, he's there taking it away. The sudden realization has me halting my kiss. Cash stops and leans back. His expression sliding into a frown.

"You make it stop," I whisper into his lips.

"What stop?" His gaze holds mine, waiting for me to continue.

"The pain. You make it all go away." His next words make my heart soar because I know it's not just me.

"You make me feel alive, Rylee. I haven't felt this alive in a long time." His heavy breaths fan my lips. "My light," he whispers. His forehead rests on mine, and we stay like that for what feels like an eternity, with me feeling the most content and safe I have felt in a long time.

"You're not going on that date," I whisper into Cash's chest.

"I'll work something out."

I lean up on my elbows, frowning at him.

"That wasn't a 'No, I won't go on the date, Rylee.'"

He smirks at me. "Do you know how hot you are when you're jealous?" He smiles. I smack his chest. He laughs and pulls me in for a hug, and kisses my head.

"I promise you I won't go on that date."

"What will you do, she paid 20,000 dollars for you to go on that date. Fucking show-off," I mumble.

"Are you saying I'm not worth 20,000 dollars, Ry?" He pokes my waist.

"Hey, stop. I never said that." He pulls me in for a hug.

"Cash, have you thought what you might say to Bridget and Bohdi?"

He lets out a sigh. "I have thought about it once or twice. There's not really much they can say. They will just have to accept it. I know it's not what people will expect or approve of, but they will eventually, it just may take time."

I get that, but I don't think I'm ready to have everyone go against me just yet. "Can we wait a little while? I don't think I'm ready for everyone to hate me at the moment."

"Yeah, I think you're right." Cash sighs. "I want to spend time with you though. Just us. I don't want to have to sneak around each other's houses like we are eighteen."

"Neither do I, but what choice do we have."

"Can you see if you can get the second week of December off?"

Cash eyes me with a curious smirk. "Erm, yeah. I don't see why not. Why?"

His grin widens. "I want to take you to this cute little cabin in Whitefish." He leans in and kisses my neck. "Call it an early Christmas present."

The memories from last night, and knowing I'll get to experience them for real at the cabin, have me blushing. The reminders of yesterday have me flushing. Knowing that I will be experiencing all of that again, but I won't have to imagine it this time.

# Chapter Thirty
# Rylee

Toni grabs my face and gives me a huge kiss on the cheek.

"I have missed this smile," she says while wrapping me in a big hug. "I take it you and Cash worked it out?" She wiggles her eyebrows at me. I don't respond, and look down to the floor, trying to hide the schoolgirl smile that appears on my face.

She squeals. "I'm so ready for every bit of detail." We walk into the kitchen, and she pulls out a bottle of wine, and another, and ano—

"How many bottles do you think we are drinking tonight exactly?"

"Well, you have a lot to tell me, and boy, I have some to tell you too." She side-eyes me with a smirk. "You're not the only one who got dick last night." She grins.

"Shut the fuck up. Who?" I shout.

"No fucking way. You have basically been edging me for twenty-four hours. I want every single detail. Don't leave anything out. Including dick size." She pours us each a glance of wine. Once she is finished, we toast before taking a sip.

"Ahh, my faves." I smile after taking the first sip.

"Always, baby doll, you know I got you." We walk into the living room, place our glasses on the table, then flop down on the sofa. Toni crosses her legs and picks her glass up, then turns her body toward me.

"Go." She grins.

"Well, I think Cash got sick of waiting for me, and I don't think it helped that a colleague of his was chatting me up as soon as I got there. I didn't even see Cash, but I was there for all of about five minutes before he was in my face, raging." Toni smiles wide. I knew she would eat this up.

"It was embarrassing the way he more or less dragged me away like a rag doll to the conference room." Toni's eyes go wide.

"He fucked you in a conference room!?" Her jaw drops.

I laugh and nod. "Yep, over the table."

Toni closes her eyes and puts her hand on her heart. "This is going to be the hottest story. Oh my god." She opens her eyes, waiting for me to continue.

"It was animalistic, Toni, I swear to god. He pushed me over the table, and oh my god . . ." I shout.

"What!? What happened next." Her eyes are wide.

I place my hand over my mouth.

"What happened, why do you look so anxious?" She furrows her brows.

"Fuck! How could I forget? We need to get down to Walmart right now!" I jump up off the sofa and run toward my bedroom.

She gasps. "Rylee Matthews, did you not use a condom." Her voice gets louder as she walks toward my bedroom.

I pull my pants off to put jeans on. "No, and I fucking told him if he didn't have one, he couldn't because I'm not on anything."

Her mouth opens wide as she stares at me. "And he still fucked you?"

"Yep." I sigh.

"Oh my god, he has a breeding kink." She gasps, flapping her hands. "Fantastic," she says, rolling her eyes.

I screw my face up, wondering if I heard her correct. "What in the fucking fuck is a breeding kink?" Toni has many sayings and definitions for things I have never heard of before, so I dread to think what she comes up with for this.

"A breeding kink, have you not read any of those books I told you about?"

"No, reading hasn't been on my mind lately. Do they tell me what a breeding kink is?" I say, raising one eyebrow at her. "It sounds like something out of a zoo," I mumble, collecting my purse and slipping my shoes on.

"Wellllllll, men that have breeding kinks tend to act like an animal. What did he do when you told him you weren't on anything."

"Slammed inside me, and it fucking hurt, might I add." I think back to how much it hurt, for all of ten seconds.

"I can't tell you how fucking hot that is, my god. It's honestly something out of a book, Rylee. But Houston, we have a fucking problem here," she says while putting her shoes on. "Cash is such a dirty dog. I love it, but you cannot be getting pregnant. I don't know if I'm ready to be an auntie just yet, it's a big commitment." Her eyebrows draw down, as if alarm bells are going off in her head.

"Erm, yeah, and how big do you think the commitment is being a mom?" I roll my eyes. "Also, can we remember the whole situation I am in. A baby is not happening."

"Then you need to get on something because a man with a breeding kink is a savage."

I grab my keys and spin around. "Can you stop calling it a breeding kink. It sounds like you're referring to a caged animal."

She goes to speak. "Stop." I raise my hand. She sticks her bottom lip out.

"Okay, well, you need to get on something." She stops at my apartment door before closing it.

"Wait, I thought you were on the pill?"

"I was. I have been for the last six years, but I didn't think I would need to be on it and wanted a break, so I stopped."

Toni nods. "Yeah, I get that." She closes the door, and we walk toward the elevator.

"Rylee, my dear." I hear from behind me. I spin and there stands Miss Dainty.

"Hey, Miss Dainty," Toni says, taking her bags and helping her toward her front door.

"Hey, Miss Dainty," I say, following them. "How are you today?" Miss Dainty pats Toni's hand and gives her a kiss on the cheek when Toni takes the keys off her and opens the door and walks straight in, taking them into the kitchen. Miss Dainty has been here for years, way before Jace and me, and she is one of the nicest ladies I have ever come across. Toni loves her dearly and always wants to help her. I always tell her if she needs help with shopping, I will come with her, but she doesn't like to bug anyone.

I stand at Miss Dainty's door while Toni takes the shopping in. Miss Dainty stands next to the door opposite me.

"How are you feeling now, my dear. I was worried about you last night," she says, frowning.

"I'm fine, what makes you think I wasn't?" I question, offering her a smile.

"Cash stopped by here last night to get the spare key, and he looked worried out of his mind." Toni peeks around from behind Miss Dainty, her lips thinned, holding her laugh back.

"I was feeling a little unwell. Cash overreacted a little. I'm fine, Miss Dainty." I smile sweetly at her.

"He's a sweet man, that Cash. Making sure you're okay, it's lovely of him," she says with a big smile.

"Oh, Cash made sure Rylee was feeling perky as ever before he left, Miss Dainty." Toni walks out, shrugging while giving Miss Dainty a sweet smile.

"We need to be going now, Miss Dainty," I say grabbing Toni's arm. "If you need me to help with shopping, please do let me know in the future, I don't want you struggling." I place a kiss on her head.

"I know, dear, but I like to get some fresh air."

"Okay, well, so do I, so I will come with you next time." I offer her smile as I drag Toni toward the stairs, deciding I don't now want to wait for the elevator.

"Have a lovely day, ladies."

"You too, Miss Dainty," Toni and I say at the same time.

As we walk down the stairs, Miss Dainty shouts, "Oh, and Rylee, can you ask Cash to drop the key back when you see him."

"Of course, I will," I shout back. *The fucking dick.* Toni giggles as we jog down the stairs.

"Not a fucking word."

"I bet you feel right as rain now, don't you." She laughs.

"Of course, you couldn't just leave it, could you."

"Cash is smooth, I will give him that," Toni says as we exit the building.

"Don't think I haven't forgotten about you, missy. I want to know everything between you and—Oh, actually who is it? Do I know them?"

"Kaleb Hawks." She smirks as we get into her car. Why do I recognize the name?

"That name . . ." I squint. "Oh my God! That hottie from last night that won the auction." I stare at her wide-eyed.

"Yup." She smiles as she starts the car and heads to the store.

"So, was that your date, or . . .?"

"Do I look like a hoe?" Her eyes flit from me to the road.

I smirk at her. "Do I answer that, or . . .?"

"You bitch." She laughs. "No, it's not the date, just a tester, if you will," she says, waving her hand around like she always does. We burst out laughing.

"He did look a bit young from what I saw. How old is he?"

"Our age. Well, my age," she says.

"Thank you for correcting that."

"Bitch. You are only a couple of years younger; it will be your thirtieth before you know it."

"Eww, please don't." I snap.

I side-eye her. "Mmm, so he's twenty-nine?"

She nods. "Yep. How old did you think he was?" I think back to last night, but I didn't see him that well.

"I don't know, it was only a glimpse really, but like twenty?"

Toni lets out a loud laugh. "What twenty-year-old has 15,000 dollars to be spending on a date, Ry, come on."

I glare at her. "What twenty-nine-year-old has that, Ton."

She shrugs. "I don't know, but I will go on the date with him to find out." She wiggles her eyebrows at me. "He's not in town for long anyway, he's here on work."

"Well, didn't he tell you what he does?"

"Do you think I was worried about what he does for work when his tongue was working its magic like he was a professional porn star." She glances at me, one eyebrow raised.

"Exactly," she says when I don't answer her.

"So, when's the date?" I question, staring out the window, watching the world go by.

"I think he said he goes back home next Saturday, so I think we are going out on Friday."

"And where is his home?"

"Michigan."

"Interesting," I say.

"It is, first Michigan boy I've fucked, and I have to say, it was ten out of ten."

My eyes go wide. "You have never said a guy is a ten out of ten. What the fuck?"

"Honestly, I wouldn't be surprised if his full-time job is being a porn star. It was fucking amazing." Her eyes roll to the back of her head as the car swerves a bit.

"Okay, eyes on the road. You can have flashbacks later," I say, holding onto the dashboard.

"So do you think you may actually miss him . . . or his dick or whatever when he goes back to Michigan."

She bites her lip, thinking about it.

"Him, nah. His dick." She pauses and looks over at me. "I will weep into my pillow every night," she says straight-faced.

I burst out laughing. "Wow, that must have been some good dick."

She groans. "You have no idea."

"Let's not even talk about dicks anymore." The thought of going into a shop at my big old age of twenty-seven for Plan B makes me want to cry. "I want to get this over with." I sigh.

# Chapter Thirty-One
## Rylee

"I mean, if you tell me the rough size, I can go grab some for you while you get the pill," Toni says.

"I want to think you're just helping, but I know this is just to get out of me how big Cash's dick is."

She huffs and rolls her eyes. "You're such a spoilsport. I tell you the size of all dicks I encounter without you even having to ask."

I place my hand on my heart and gasp. "And I'm so lucky for that." I roll my eyes, then turn around to make sure there is no one I know nearby.

"Rylee, let me get this. You go browse, get those condoms you need." She offers me a small smile. She knows what I'm thinking without me even trying to give her any hints. Imagine what people would think if they saw me buying Plan B when I only lost Jace at the beginning of the year.

"Are you sure."

"Of course, my baby. I got you always, you know that." I walk away from Toni and browse the aisles. I get to the condom section, and there has to be at least twenty options. Do girls buy these; I've never done this before. What if Cash thinks I'm weird for buying them. What if Toni is right and he has this breeding thing. Oh God. I pick a pack up and examine the picture on the front, it has bumps on it. Why does it have bumps on it? "'For intense pleasure. You won't even know a condom is on.'"

"Rylee." My heart sinks. I stay looking down at the box, not wanting to turn around.

"Ry." I feel a tug on my arm as I turn around, and there stands Boh, staring at me, and then his eyes flick to the box of condoms in my hand. I feel my cheeks redden, and my heart thumps out of my chest. How do I explain this?

"It's not what it looks like, Boh," I blurt. But it is what it looks like, but I can't lose him. I can't have him thinking I'm a piece of shit, even if I am one in hiding. His eyes flick from me to the box again.

"I'm not judging. You're single now," he says without a smile. I stand there quiet, not knowing what to say.

"Who's the guy, then? He should be buying these, not you." He has a slight bite to his tone.

"I—Uh."

"There you are," Toni says from behind me. "Oh, hey, Boh," she says way too excited.

"You found them. Thank you, baby." She takes the box of condoms out of my hand. "Just doing the weekly shopping." She winks at Boh, waving around the Plan B in one hand and the condoms in the other. *The weekly shopping? Is she okay?*

"You ready." She eyes me, not looking the least bit embarrassed that she referred to Plan B and condoms as the weekly shopping. Boh's shoulders drop, and he smirks. They all know what Toni is like, so this all looks and sounds believable.

"Good night, Toni." Boh laughs.

"Always. Boh. Always," she says.

Boh nods, still laughing. "Well, I'll let you ladies get back to it." He starts to walk away. "Oh, Ry." I stop and turn slightly to face him. "You still coming to Cash's for Thanksgiving dinner?"

"Uh, yes, of course. Wouldn't miss it." I muster up a smile.

"See you then." Boh gives us a wave and walks away. My heart feels like it's about to thump up my throat and fly from my mouth. Even though Toni saved me, I still feel like every single lie was written all over my face in Sharpie. Toni links her arm through mine, pulling me along and dumping the condoms at the end of the aisle. I let her drag me out, still picturing Boh's face and how disappointed or annoyed he looked. I'm not sure, he's never given me that face before. My face must say it all.

"Don't you dare get inside that head," Toni says still dragging me through Walmart.

"Just get me out of here," I say, feeling like the weight of the world has placed itself firmly on my shoulders again.

"I really don't know if I can continue this with Cash." I may cry at any minute. My emotions are all over the place since seeing Boh. I can't stop thinking about his face, if he looks at me like that, imagine how others will look at me, or worse, say to my face.

"I told you in the car on the way home, Boh didn't suspect anything. He thought it was all me." Toni has a slight frown on her face.

"I know he did, but you didn't see his face when he thought they were mine." I pick at the nonexistent lint on my trousers. "He was so disappointed, and that's with him thinking it's a random guy, imagine if he found out it was his brother."

"Then that is a Bohdi problem, not a you problem," she states, eyes narrowed.

"What have I told you since we were young. Fuck what people think, Rylee. Fuck what Boh thinks, fuck what Bridget thinks, fuck what I think, fuck what Miss Dainty thinks, fuck what the dog next door thinks." I chuckle. "Your feelings are all that matters." She grabs my hand. "I get you don't want to hurt other people because that's the kind of person you are, but you have been and are still going through one of the hardest years of your life. Who are they to tell you not to be with someone who makes you smile again."

She grabs my cheeks, making me look her in the eye. "Because if anyone in this life deserves to smile again, it's you. It's too beautiful to hide away." I smile as tears well in my eyes. She wipes under my eyes, catching the stray tears before they fall. "It's time to put yourself first, Rylee," she says, smiling and bringing me in for a cuddle. "If anyone takes that smile away, I will kill them," she whispers into my ear, holding me tight. The joke is, I don't doubt that for a second.

# Chapter Thirty-Two
# Rylee

## Thanksgiving

"Rylee!" Bridget squeals as I walk into Cash's house. Bridge offered to pick me up, but I told her I was with Toni, so I would come by after, as I knew she was here helping Cash get the food set up.

"Hey, Bridge." It's Thanksgiving, and I knew Bridge wouldn't let me have it anywhere else but with her and the family. Toni said I could go to her mom's, but I wanted to be with the Stiles' family this year. It only felt right to spend the first one without Jace with them.

I give Bridge a tight squeeze before following her into the house. We're having it at Cash's, as he has the bigger place, so it made sense. This will be the first time I have been around Bridge and Boh since having sex with Cash, and I'm anxious. I feel like it's written all over my face. *"I fucked Cash, I'm a piece of shit."* I even practiced in the mirror to see what my face may look like seeing Bridge. It's made me crazy over the last few weeks. Cash laughed at me every time I would have a meltdown about it.

It's weird because we haven't spoken about what is going on between us. We haven't spoken about telling anyone. Not that I'm in a rush to, but the more time I spend with him, the more I fall for him and the deeper it gets. I have seen Cash every week since the night of the ball, and each time, we can't keep our hands off each other. I mostly come here, and I think he has fucked me over every surface in this house.

The minute I see him, my stomach somersaults. He has his back to me, fussing over some food in the kitchen. My heart races and my legs feel like jelly. I can't explain it, but whatever this high is, I never want to come down from it. It scares me because it's a high I want forever, and the thought of losing it is a sucker punch to the stomach.

There have been a few close calls with Bohdi. I spoke to Cash regarding him, but Cash has been avoiding him. Bridge had asked me over the phone why I left abruptly the night of the ball, so I said I felt sick and thought it was best to go home. I don't know what Cash said, but to be honest, the more I don't know, the better. I've never been able to lie.

"Hey, Bohdi," I say as I walk into the kitchen. Bridge walks over to the stove and fusses with some of the food.

"Ry. You okay?" He smiles, not his usual smile though. I wish I knew what was wrong with him. He used to text me, but I haven't spoken to him since the day after the ball when I bumped into him. I offer him a smile, trying to brush off the niggling feeling that something isn't right.

"Much better now I've seen you." I nudge his arm, trying to fall back into our fun banter, but he gives me a tight-lipped smile. He hugs me, but it resembles one of those hugs you give someone you just met. He goes to turn around, and I grab his arm.

"Boh, can I talk to you a minute." He squints at me and then nods before walking out of the kitchen. Cash is nowhere to be seen, which I'm glad for the moment, because I need no distractions before talking to Boh. As we turn the corner into the living room, I stop him.

"Hey, what's up?"

He examines my face before letting out a big sigh. "Nothing." He offers me a tight-lipped smile again.

"Boh, I know you. Something isn't right. Talk to me?" I plead with my eyes.

His eyes flick between mine. "You would always tell me the truth, wouldn't you?" His eyebrows draw downward. Why is he asking me this?

I nod and gulp, trying to plaster on a smile that says anything but the truth.

"Cash has been different . . . with you." *Shit. Fuck.*

"What do you mean." I frown, bringing my hands out in front of me and picking at the skin on my nail. Anything to ground this feeling right now.

"More protective, around you a lot. Since Jace, he's just been different, and it's a bit weird." He frowns toward the floor and places his hands in his pockets.

"I think it's just the James thing, with what James told me. He doesn't want James doing it again." I blabber, praying that Boh drops it. If he asks me to my face, I don't know if I can lie to him. My face will say it all. I'm already getting hot.

"Rylee."

I glance up and lock eyes with him. *Oh no.*

"Is anything going on—"

"Rylee, when did you get here?" Cash appears from behind Boh, walking over to me and giving me a kiss on my cheek.

My eyes flick from Cash to Boh. Boh's jaw tenses right before he nods a few times and walks back to the kitchen. He knows. He has to.

"Cash," I say, my eyes filling with tears.

"It's okay, he didn't ask. It's okay," Cash says, pushing my hair back from my face and cupping my cheeks.

I step back from him. "Don't." I put my hand out in front of me, glancing around, worried Boh or Bridge are watching.

"I stopped him from asking you. It's okay." He frowns.

"Were you listening?" I ask.

He nods. "I was worried he may ask. Every time your name is mentioned, he looks at me. He's barely talking to me at the moment," he mumbles, then takes a deep breath. "I think he knows."

"And now he hates me. He can barely even hug me anymore." My heart beats out of my chest, and I feel like a panic attack may set in any minute. My chest tightens.

"Calm down." Cash pulls my arm, and I yank it away. If he wasn't so fucking obvious, Boh might have never caught on.

"This is your fault," I grit out. "Don't talk or look at me for the rest of night. I mean it." I point at him. "I need to work out what to do about Boh. He means too much to me," I say as I go to walk past him. He grabs my bicep. I glance up at his face and relax at the way his eyebrows are drawn down. "What, and I don't?" he questions.

"Please just leave it for now." I walk away feeling like shit and the ache starts back up in my chest again.

"The food is great, Bridge," I say glancing sideways to her with a smile while cutting into my pork.

"Thank you, Ry," she says, bunching her shoulders up. The table is oddly silent, and I am doing all I can to avoid looking in Cash's direction. His stare is burning a hole into the side of my face. The only noise is the TV in the background. Bridge is squinting while looking between Boh and Cash. Boh is pushing around the food on his plate.

"Boh, Cash." Cash shifts in his seat. "Why are you both so silent?" she says.

"I'm fine, Bridge," Boh says, picking up his wine and taking a sip. He smiles at her like he normally does. Like the way he used to smile at me. I risk glancing at Cash, but he isn't staring at me. He's staring at the chair next to me. The one at the head of the table—where Jace always sat. His knife and fork still sit on the table as he swishes the whiskey in his glass. Staring at the spot. The empty chair represents the hole Jace left in all our lives.

"I miss him so much," Bridge says next to me, startling me. I glance at her and then at Boh. We all stare at the empty space, and that's what is wrong here. It's not because of Boh being in a mood, it's not because Cash is upset with me. It's because the life of this family, the heartbeat isn't here. His personality lit up a room. You couldn't help but be happy and smile around Jace. Now it's just empty.

"He wouldn't want this," I whisper.

Bridget takes my hand and squeezes. "You're right, Rylee. He wouldn't. So let's raise a glass to him and celebrate how he would want us to. Laughing, drinking, enjoying each other's company."

We raise our glasses. "To Jace," we all say before taking a sip of our drinks. Everyone seems lighter. Boh gives me his signature grin with a wink, Cash is smiling, and Bridge is telling us about one of her recent clients who asked her to design a sex room. We all laugh like we do every year, like Jace would want us to. We continue to talk about anything and everything, making each other laugh. It feels how Thanksgiving always does.

Something on the news catches my eye—Breaking News – Homicide. I stand up mid conversation with my glass of wine and walk toward the TV to turn it up. When I see the face that pops up, my body freezes and the glass slips out of my fingers, shattering at my feet, and the wine splashes my legs. None of that bothers me though because all I see is Casey's face plastered on the TV. Casey. Homicide.

Cash stands in front of me, his mouth moving, but I can't hear anything. My vision blurs with unshed tears as my gaze moves back to the TV.

"He-he's done it again." I choke up, staring at the TV, not blinking. I can't believe what I'm seeing. Hands grip my face as Cash stands in front of the TV.

"You're here. You're safe," he says. I nod as the tears fall, and Cash pulls me into his chest while I cry.

"He's done it again, and all she did was help us." This is all my fault, so I cry harder.

# Chapter Thirty-Three
## James

I sit in my car watching the local news on my phone. A small smile creeps up on my face when Casey's face appears on the screen.

"I hope you have seen this Rylee." It was bad enough that I didn't see Rylee for five whole days when she decided to go on that holiday, but to then learn that Cash was there with her for some of those days, sent anger through me like nothing before. I had a feeling something was going on with Rylee and Cash. I knew she had stayed with Cash for a few days, but that was after the cunt had found her with me, so I put it down to protection. After the ball, I followed Cash's Uber back to Rylee's and I watched Cash walk into her apartment that night and not leave until the following day. What sick cunt goes after his dead son's girlfriend? The more and more I thought about them, the more I couldn't handle it. I smashed up everything I own which caused me a small inconvenience. I thought of all the ways I could make Cash disappear. I could then make Rylee realize she is mine, but Cash made me take drastic actions before when he was around her too much and I wasn't thinking straight. I can't afford to mess this up again. I have been planning for months how I'm going to do this, and I just need a bit longer and then Rylee can finally see I am all she needs.

*She will realize how much you love her.*

I stopped drinking alcohol a while ago, it doesn't do me any good, but when I learnt that new bit of information, I lost it and once again I found myself outside Casey's. This time she was home. I let myself in and found her in the kitchen. I only asked her if we could talk, but she instantly began to wave a knife at me, screaming all sorts. She didn't make it easy for me. I look down at the bandage on my arm, the wound is still healing from where she tried to stab me. Sick bitch. I just wanted to talk, but by the sounds of her screaming and crying, she clearly wasn't in the talking mood. I tried to hold her down to calm her, but hearing her scream that Rylee will never be mine and that Cash will always protect her, didn't calm me at all. It made me worse. The images of feeling Casey's body convulse under me and watching the light die out in her eyes while my hands were wrapped around her throat did fill me with some sadness, her eyes were so similar to Rylee's. I quickly drove back to Rylee's house and anxiously waited to see her. When I did, I felt lighter again. She was alive and well and that's all that mattered.

I smile to myself as my eyes leave the screen, but the smile drops quickly as they land on Cash's house. Of course she is there, but this time next year, she will happily be with me.

# Chapter Thirty-Four

## Rylee

### December

"Have you ever been to Whitefish?" Cash asks as we take our seat on the plane.

I was confused when I realized he wasn't driving toward the city airport, and when I questioned him, he smirked and said wait and see. We arrived at a place I hadn't heard of before, but when I saw the air strip and realized it was a private airport, my jaw hit the floor. I can't imagine how much this must have cost, and I already know how much he paid for the cabin, but him shedding thousands on a plane ride made me kind of uncomfortable. I don't want Cash thinking he has to do things like this, I've never been a materialistic girl. He grabbed my hand and said, "Relax, I got a good deal from a client. It's their plane." That eased my anxiety some.

"I've heard it's stunning this time of year, though."

"Cold." He laughs. "Real fucking cold. Did you bring coats and sweaters."

"Of course. After you told me how cold it gets and after I went online and looked it up, I packed the thickest sweaters and coats I have. Hence the track pants." I glance down at my thick black pants. "Of course you would pick the coldest month to go." I roll my eyes with a smirk. I searched it, and it does look amazing in the winter. I prepared for snow, but we are only here for three days. Cash was given a week in the auction, but he had to split it, as he's busy at work. I told him we could just wait until he wasn't, but he wanted to come in December.

"You will see why tonight." He smirks before looking out the window. The stewardess comes out and tells us we are getting ready to take off, so we need to get our seat belts on. Cash and I smile and nod before clicking ourselves in.

I've never been on a private jet before, and honestly, I could get used to it. The seats are big and extra comfy with cup holders. There are two fridges stacked with drinks and food. I turn my head, glancing behind me, and there is a tiny sofa and two doors. I frown while turning back. Why are there two doors? Cash is staring at me like he knows what I'm about to ask.

"Two doors?" I question.

"Bedroom," he states, staring at me. His eyes say a thousand words. I don't know why I get so giddy around him, I'm a grown fucking woman, but in his presence, my stomach swarms with butterflies and a hot flush takes over my body.

"Oh, ye-yes of course. Makes sense, some people get tired on long flights." I nod while looking away.

"Real sleepy," Cash says in a sarcastic tone. I stay looking out the window. My cheeks feel like they're on fire. I can't keep going this red around him like I'm some inexperienced little girl.

"How long is the flight?" The plane moves down the runway.

"Around four hours, I think."

"Why, are you thinking of a nap?" Cash asks with a straight face.

"Uh, no. I'm okay?" He nods, like he doesn't know why I'm acting funny. I mean, why would he, he's a grown fucking man and I'm the one acting like a child. Cash leans forward, opening the fridge and pulling out a bottle of my favorite wine.

"You're really pulling out all the stops today." I smile at him.

He pours us both a glass of wine and passes one to me.

"Thank you for coming on this weekend away with me."

"Thank you for inviting me." I lean over and give him a kiss on the cheek.

We landed in Whitefish at a private landing strip, and to say it's cold is an understatement. The air bit my skin as soon as we stepped off the plane. Cash wrapped me up in his puffy jacket as we ran to the car waiting for us. Cash rushes ahead to open the car door. I slide in while Cash follows, then closes the door.

"Sir, ma'am," the driver says.

"Hey," I say, chattering as I blow into my hands. Cash nods while snaking his arm across the back of the seat. His fingers gently playing with the strands of my hair.

"Cold, isn't it," he says.

I bunch up my shoulders, shivering. "Freezing." Cash leans forward, turning the heat on, and I relax as my body flushes with heat.

"How far are we from the cabin?" I say, looking out at the snow-covered mountains that surround us.

"Only about fifteen minutes, I think."

The trees open up, and the white coated mountains blend in the background of the smattering trees that meet my gaze. The deep-green trees go on and on as the trail gets smaller. "It's beautiful," I whisper, mesmerized by the scenery.

"Beautiful doesn't even cover it." His breath against my neck sends a shiver through my body. I slowly turn to him, and his blue eyes trace my face. The heat in the car is suddenly too much. Cash smirks at me, as I sit next to him in a puddle of hormones and liquid lust.

Within no time, we are at the cabin, and I struggle to pick my jaw up off the floor. We're high up in the mountains, snow and emerald trees surround us, but it's the floor-to-ceiling windows at the front of the cabin which create this gorgeous modern look. You can tell the owner had work done on this to give it the modern touch. I didn't even realize Cash had gotten out of the car until he opened my car door. The pictures don't do it justice. Cash makes quick blowing noises.

"It's fucking freezing, let's get inside." He grabs my hand and drags me toward the door. When we enter, the vision takes my breath away. The wooden beams line the extra-high ceilings, and old brick work goes along one side of the walls. Huge ball lights hang from the ceiling. A large built-in fireplace runs along one wall, and an eight-foot Christmas tree decorated to perfection sits in one corner of the room near the floor-to-ceiling windows.

"Cash," I breathe out, not taking my eyes off everything in front of me. Cash takes everything in alongside me.

"It's beautiful," he whispers, sounding as much in awe as me. We slowly walk into the large open-plan living room, and I drop down on the sofa which faces the mountain edge overlooking the large expansion of the lake below.

This trip couldn't have come at a better time; it's been extremely hard since hearing about Casey's murder. We all know it was James, and the police know it too, even if there is no evidence. He is the main suspect, and they are on a wild goose chase trying to find him. It's like he has disappeared again. I felt like I was falling back into a hole when I saw Casey's face on the TV. Cash was the only person who could bring me back, and as always, he stopped the pain and helped me.

Cash presses a few buttons, and the fire in the wall blazes, creating an orange tint in the room.

"I think I could do with a shower, flying always makes me feel a bit icky." Cash nods and continues messing around with the buttons.

I head into the bathroom, and the pictures of the shower didn't do it justice. The stone wall and floor that makes up the huge walk-in shower is modern, but it still has the original wooden rustic beams, which gives it the old feel. I crave to be under that shower, so I make quick work of stripping. I turn the water on before stepping in, and the water heats up straight away. The steam swarms the bathroom instantly. A smile graces my lips as I step under the largest showerhead I've ever seen.

I stand there for a minute, head tilted back, letting the water run down my body. I let my head lull forward and my eyes open to Cash standing at the entrance to the shower. My mouth opens as his face appears through the steam, and my gaze runs over his very naked body. His dick bobs and smacks against my stomach as he walks toward me, coming chest to chest and pushing me back slightly so the water runs down his body. Cash is sexy every day of the week, but this man with water running down his body, it's a sight I never want to forget. The desire burns a hot spot in the pit of my belly, then his eyes open and his grin doubles the heat. He grabs my hand and brings it to his mouth, pressing a soft kiss to my knuckles. His lips feel like they burn my knuckles.

"Drop to your knees for me, angel." Every single hair on my body stands to attention, and every skin cell tingles. His gaze devours me as I melt to my knees, my gaze staying locked with his. He towers over me, devilishly smiling down at me. "I want to see those pretty lips wrapped around my dick, and your mouth full of me." The water hits his back, running down his body, and droplets drip from his hair onto his face. He palms his dick, moving his hand up and down. "Mouth open, princess."

My mouth drops open on his command, and he pushes his dick past my lips, the salty precum hits my tastebuds. He pushes in farther. "Can you take it all?" I push my head forward and take him to the back of my throat. "Fuckk," Cash groans. He threads his fingers through my hair, pumping his hips back and forth as feral moans leave his mouth. God, hearing him moan sends an ache to my core. I squirm on my knees, trying to rub the heel of my foot on my clit to get any bit of friction to ease the constant throb.

"How much do you want to touch yourself right now, Rylee?" Cash's gravelly voice flows through my body as he pumps in and out of my mouth. I nod, then he shifts, so the water mists my face.

"How about you come when I come down your throat." The devilish grin is back, and something glints in his hand. I continue to add suction while trying to catch on to what's in his hand.

"I brought you something." His voice has me moaning around his dick.

"Ahhh, fuck." He slams his dick in my mouth, making me gag, and holds my head in place with one hand. I breathe through my nose, but it's hard with the water when he holds his dick there.

Then he brings the chrome object in front of me. "Get yourself off, angel," he says through gritted teeth as I bring my hand up. He places the weighted pebble-shaped object in my hand and continues to fuck my mouth. "It's waterproof. Now use it."

I don't waste time, I turn it on, and bring it between my legs, and as soon as the vibration hits my clit, I rise up on my knees. Cash pushes on my head, so I'm in the splits on my knees. "Hold it there and don't move it." I moan around his dick and rock back and forth on the pebble. Cash grunts, using my mouth like his own fuck toy. He tilts my head back so the water is splashing in my face. "I want to see that pretty face when you come." He watches me as he punishingly fucks my mouth. The tension builds in my stomach, and I gasp around his dick. My eyes flutter closed as I feel myself peaking. "Eyes, Rylee," Cash growls.

I startle, opening my eyes.

"Good girl." Those two words have me falling over the edge. "Such a pretty girl," he whispers. The sensation pushes me into overdrive. I try to inhale sharply through my nose as Cash chokes me. I splutter, not being able to concentrate on my breathing as the orgasm flows through me.

"Fuckk, close your eyes, Rylee." I close my eyes, and he pulls himself from my mouth, and I hear a low, pleasant hum that warms my whole body, and then his cum lands on my face. "Fuck, Rylee," Cash pants, sounding like he just ran a marathon.

I flutter my eyes open, and Cash stares down at me in awe, his eyes sparkle as his gaze runs over my face. I continue to take deep, sharp breaths, trying to get my breathing under control. Cash's hand comes up to my face, and his thumb rubs into his cum before shoving it in my mouth. I suck, loving the taste of him.

"You're fucking perfect." He yanks his thumb from my mouth, and the next thing I know, he has pulled me up by my arms and his lips land on mine, tracing them with his tongue.

"I want you to taste like me forever," he says into my mouth.

# Chapter Thirty-Five
## Rylee

He washed me after the shower, and we curled up on the sofa with wine and watched the sun set from the living room. He fills me with contentment every time I'm with him. The images of the night of the ball have played in my mind whenever I'm alone in the shower or in bed. I touch myself, picturing it's him, but it never compares to the night he touched me. After that shower, I don't think those images will ever leave my mind.

I'm staring at myself in the mirror, and now regret everything. Why did I bring this barely there, strappy bikini? Does it make me look desperate? I mean, I guess I am for Cash. Cash is in the kitchen, so I tiptoe through. The fireplace heats the cabin to perfection, but the minute I open the doors, the air will feel like it's cutting me. I went out and turned on the hot tub ten minutes ago, which I know Cash saw, so I'm confused why he's messing about in the kitchen.

"Fuck." His gruff voice breaks through my thoughts, and I glance up at him. His jaw is clenched and the veins in his forearms bulge, with the sleeves of his sweater rolled.

His darkened gaze is like fire, tracking my body, and leaves a burning trail in its wake.

My heart rate increases, and I try to keep my breathing under control.

"I'm going to get in the hot tub," I say, turning around and walking toward the back door. As I slip sandals on by the door, he groans. The crisp air takes my breath away before I jump down the few stairs and run toward the hot tub. I take deep breaths, trying to calm my body from the shock, but the cold air filling my lungs doesn't help. As soon as I step in the steaming hot tub, my breathing calms and I let out a sigh. It's really fucking hot, but as I drop to my knees so my shoulders are covered, my whole body relaxes. I close my eyes, my head rolls back, and my whole body relaxes.

The images Cash painted come to the forefront of my mind as the bubbles caress my skin. I rub my hands up and down my stomach, wishing he was in here with me. My touch will never be enough. I huff and open my eyes, then yelp at Cash standing in a pair of swimming pants staring down at me.

"Is it nice?" My body erupts in goose bumps. He passes me a glass of champagne.

"It would be better if you were in here with me." I look up at him through my lashes. He gets in and sits down opposite me, arms stretched on either side of him on the edge of the tub, with one hand dangling a flute glass full of champagne. He ogles me like I'm his prey and is working out how to catch me. My breathing accelerates, so I take a gulp of the fizz, and revel in its taste before taking another gulp.

"The view really is stunning," I say, looking out at the lights from the town in the distance. It's a picture-perfect moment. I must remember to come out here and take some pictures tomorrow night.

"My view is better." Our gazes meet before his moves from my eyes to my lips down to my chest. My throat bobs as he brings the glass to his mouth, taking a small slow sip. I wish his lips were touching mine right now instead of the wineglass. His Adam's apple moves up and down as he swallows. I'm mesmerized by every little move he makes, and I can't pull my eyes away. My clit throbs, begging for him to touch me.

He places his arm on the side of the tub again.

"Is the temperature okay?"

"Ye-es." A smirk creeps on one side of his face.

"I want you to do something for me, Rylee." If he told me to bark, I'd do it. If it meant him touching me, I'd do just about anything right now.

I nod, not trusting myself to speak. If I do, I may just cry while begging him.

"I want you to touch yourself for me." My breathing hitches. Did I hear him right?

My eyes go wide. "You want me to?" I squeak out. Why can't he?

He nods. "Now."

I freeze, like I've forgotten what to even do with my hands.

"I want to see you touch yourself for me. Your eyes don't stray from mine."

I whimper. His words send a signal to my pussy. He smiles, and his gaze burns my skin.

I place the glass to the side of the hot tub and let one hand sink beneath the water. His eyes don't move from mine. My chest heaves, and my mouth goes dry. I run my fingers along the waistline of my bikini before dipping my hand beneath it. The water gliding against my clit creates a teasing sensation. As soon as my index finger touches my clit, my eyes close.

"Eyes. On. Me," Cash grits out.

My eyes fly open.

"Your eyes remain on me at all times." His voice has me rubbing at my clit with two fingers now.

"Keep your fingers on your clit, don't you dare fill that hole of yours, that hole is mine, only I do that." His authoritative tone has me whimpering as I rub my clit faster.

"Tell me how good it feels."

"Cash," I whimper. I don't want to rub my clit. I want him to.

"Tell me," he whispers before taking another sip of his fizz, his eyes not leaving mine once.

"It feels good, but I want it to be you." His jaw clenches. I moan at the tingle in my lower belly.

"Cash . . ." I let my head drop back and close my eyes.

"Eyes" is all Cash says, and my head snaps up, eyes wide. "If you close them again, I won't let you come."

I gasp. As if he could stop me.

He raises his eyebrow like he just read my thoughts. "If you want to come on my dick, then you best listen to me when I tell you to keep your eyes on me." I nod frantically.

"Tell me how much you want my dick, Rylee." I can't form any words because all I want to do is come, but I can't. I let out a frustrated moan.

"If you tell me, you can have it." My breathing increases and my fingers get faster at the thought of his dick filling me.

"I want it, Cash, I want you to fill me, and . . . " I stop myself for a minute but the way I'm feeling right now I want him to mark me as his in any way he needs too. "I want you to come in me." I'm on the pill now, and haven't mentioned it to him, it's not something I need to tell him, so having sex without a condom won't be the end of the world.

His jaw clenched as his eyes flare.

"Get over here now." I freeze to the spot.

"Don't make me ask you again." I shuffle on my knees to him, until his knees graze my hips.

"Come sit on me." I stand, then straddle him on the seat.

"Sit," he says. I drop onto him, and a moan escapes my throat as his erection presses into my center. His finger grazes my waist up to the side of my boob. My body shivers, then I grind on his dick. He chuckles and my eyes find his.

"So needy, Rylee."

I moan. "Please, Cash."

"Please what?" I don't know when he became patient, but I don't like it. I like when he overpowers me and fucks me senseless.

"Fuck me," I say through gritted teeth.

He tugs at the strings on my back, untying my top, then runs his finger up the length of my spine and undoes the strings at my neck. My breathing accelerates, and I continue gyrating on his dick as the top drops into the water and floats away.

My nipples stand at attention, and Cash devours them with his eyes. Water drips from each nipple as he comes closer, then his eyes flick up to mine and he blows on my nipple. His warm breath mixing with the cold air has me gripping his shoulders. He brings his lips over one nipple and sucks. A loud moan escapes me, then he sucks my nipple harder and his teeth graze it before he lets go with a pop.

He brings his hand up to the other nipple playing, pinching, squeezing. I move faster when the tingling sensation grows in my lower stomach. I allow my head to roll back, ready to come, but Cash grips my cheeks and yanks my head forward.

"I want you to watch me when you come." Those words send me over the edge, Cash's eyes track my face as he continues to play with my nipple. He pushes himself up so his dick rubs into me harder, prolonging the wave washing over me. I suck in a sharp breath.

"Fuck, Rylee. You're so fucking beautiful it hurts." He grips the back of my neck, pulling me to his mouth, devours my entire soul, and consumes me in every way. His finger traces my bikini line as he moves my panties to the side. His thumb grazes my clit, and I jolt, but his grip keeps me in his lap.

His lips leave mine as he says, "I'm nowhere near done with you. I'll never be done with you." In one swift movement, he fills me, and I gasp as my body molds to him.

"Fuck, your pussy is still fluttering."

"Breathe for me, angel."

I moan and move up and down, slowly adjusting to him. I crave every single inch of him. I wish we could stay like this forever. I look up at the stars that litter the clear night sky, Cash's grunts filter through as I bounce on his dick.

"I need every inch of you," he says before he picks me up while keeping me filled, and I yelp. The cold air hits my wet skin, but with Cash gripping my hips and his dick inside me, it doesn't feel as cold as before. He steps out of the hot tub and walks us back inside, closing the door behind him. I keep myself wrapped around him as he walks toward the living room. He kneels, then lays me on the rug in front of the fireplace. Cash pushes up, staring into my soul. The fire dances in his eyes, reminding me of the heat racking my body.

"I want to feast on every inch of you," he whispers before his lips attack mine.

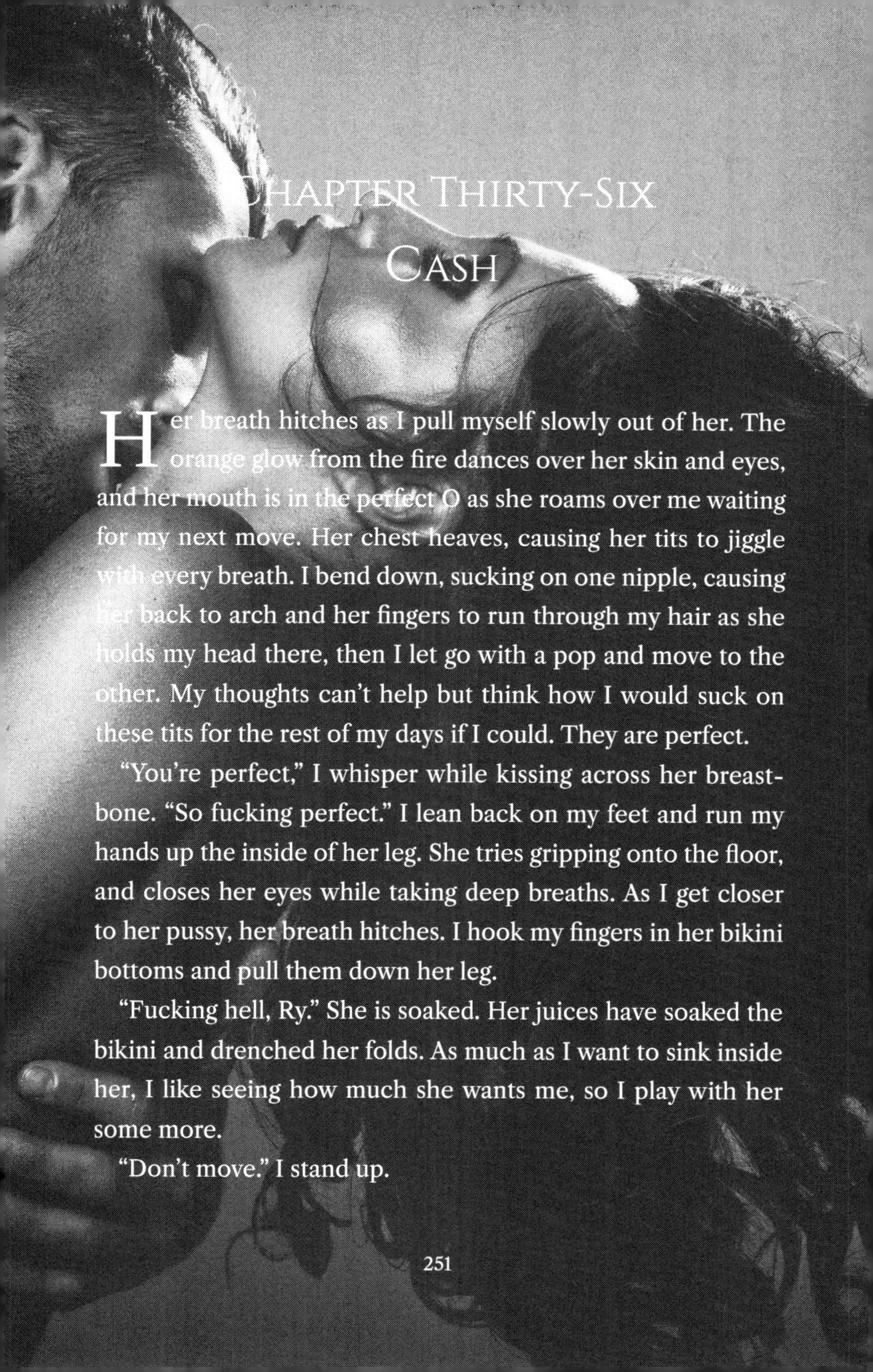

# Chapter Thirty-Six

## Cash

Her breath hitches as I pull myself slowly out of her. The orange glow from the fire dances over her skin and eyes, and her mouth is in the perfect O as she roams over me waiting for my next move. Her chest heaves, causing her tits to jiggle with every breath. I bend down, sucking on one nipple, causing her back to arch and her fingers to run through my hair as she holds my head there, then I let go with a pop and move to the other. My thoughts can't help but think how I would suck on these tits for the rest of my days if I could. They are perfect.

"You're perfect," I whisper while kissing across her breastbone. "So fucking perfect." I lean back on my feet and run my hands up the inside of her leg. She tries gripping onto the floor, and closes her eyes while taking deep breaths. As I get closer to her pussy, her breath hitches. I hook my fingers in her bikini bottoms and pull them down her leg.

"Fucking hell, Ry." She is soaked. Her juices have soaked the bikini and drenched her folds. As much as I want to sink inside her, I like seeing how much she wants me, so I play with her some more.

"Don't move." I stand up.

"Where are you going?" She leans up on her elbows.

"I said, don't move." I smirk at her as I walk toward the kitchen to grab a bottle of champagne out of the fridge and two glasses. When I get back, she lies there, staring into the fire. The flames flickering over her skin, lighting her up as she lies there in nothing has me wanting to drop to my knees and worship every single bit of her body. My chest aches, so I stalk over to her, and she licks her lip while gawking at my erection bobbing against my stomach. I swallow a groan. I'm surprised I don't walk around like this all day when she's around.

I untwist the cap and pop the bottle. While pouring the champagne, she watches me with wide eyes and her mouth slightly open. The unknown, the waiting, and being told what to do turns Rylee on, and I love it about her.

I take a sip, glaring at her over the rim of the glass. "Lay back," I say, bringing the glass down in front of me. She places hers on the floor and lies back, her chest heaving. I drop to my knees between her legs and bring my glass over her. Her eyes blow wide at me pouring the liquid over her stomach, and her breath hitches, causing it to spill down her hips but some collects in her bellybutton. Then I take the bottle and pour some over her tits, and revel in it spreading over her collarbone and down her neck. She lies still, not moving, letting me do what I want with her.

I take a gulp from the bottle, then bring the bottle to over her pussy and soak her wet folds with the champagne. My mouth waters, and I can't hold out anymore, so I discard the bottle and lean down. As soon as my lips touch her pussy, she moans, then I place my tongue in her hole, collecting all her juices and the champagne, and lick my way to her clit. She grips my hair, pulling at the scalp, and her back arches off the floor as she wraps me in her thighs, probably still feeling slightly sensitive from the hot tub. Her flavor is like nothing I've ever tasted before, and I want to taste her every fucking day. I want her to lie in wait, legs spread wide, waiting for me to get home from work every fucking day.

"The champagne tastes nice from the bottle, Rylee. However, from your pussy it is sensational." Her sweetness on my tongue, I glance up at her looking down at me, mouth open, chest heaving.

"Now, open up and let me eat what's mine," I say before I spread her legs wide and my mouth connects with her pussy once again, but this time, I feast on her like she's my last meal, like she's the sweetest meal I've ever had—and she is. Sucking on her clit, I revel in her moans, and she thrashes as I bite down on her inner thigh. I can't get enough of her. Within no time, she is screaming my name and ripping my hair from my scalp.

I don't want to stop, but my dick is pulsing with the need to be inside her, fill her with my cum, mark her as mine again. Sitting up, I grab the bottle beside me, taking a gulp and swallowing. Rylee looks at me through hooded eyes, taking deep breaths. Her juices coat my face, but I don't care, I want her scent all over me. I take another gulp, this time not swallowing. I lean over Rylee, coming face-to-face with her, and she gives me a lazy smile and opens her mouth, so I dribble it from my mouth into hers.

"Swallow," I say once I finish. She closes her mouth and swallows, then leans up to kiss me while wrapping one hand around my neck and pulling me down. I devour her mouth as she moans into mine.

"I need you." I position her between my legs while still kissing her and push myself inside her in one movement.

"Fuck," she screams. I want to fuck her frantically and claim her all over again, but I also want to savor every single moment I have with her. I don't want this to end. Pumping in and out of her slowly, her eyes lock with mine as I lean down on my elbows and lower my lips to hers. She moans through the kiss, our tongues tangling, and every swipe of her tongue, every moan that leaves her throat, makes my body ache for her all that more. I'm literally inside her and have her in my arms, but my body still aches—No, it's my chest that aches, my heart. I stop kissing her, and our eyes lock again. Why do I feel like this? I thrust into her, and her eyes close on a moan. My heart aches more. I've never felt anything like this before. Everything around us disappears, and it's just Rylee. She's all I see, she's all I've ever seen.

"Rylee," I whisper.

"Cash." She moans.

Her emerald-green eyes sparkle back at me.

"Cash, please don't stop."

"I'll never stop." I grunt. Not having the meaning she thinks. I fucking love Rylee Matthews, and I'll never stop.

My body erupts in goose bumps as she runs her fingers through my hair, tugging at the ends. Her breathing gets more erratic.

"Cash." Her pussy clenches around my dick, tipping me over the edge with no warning. I push myself as deep as I can into her, making sure I fill her. I want her in my life forever, I want her pregnant. I want this woman as my fucking wife one day, and I won't stop until it happens. No matter how fucked up that may be.

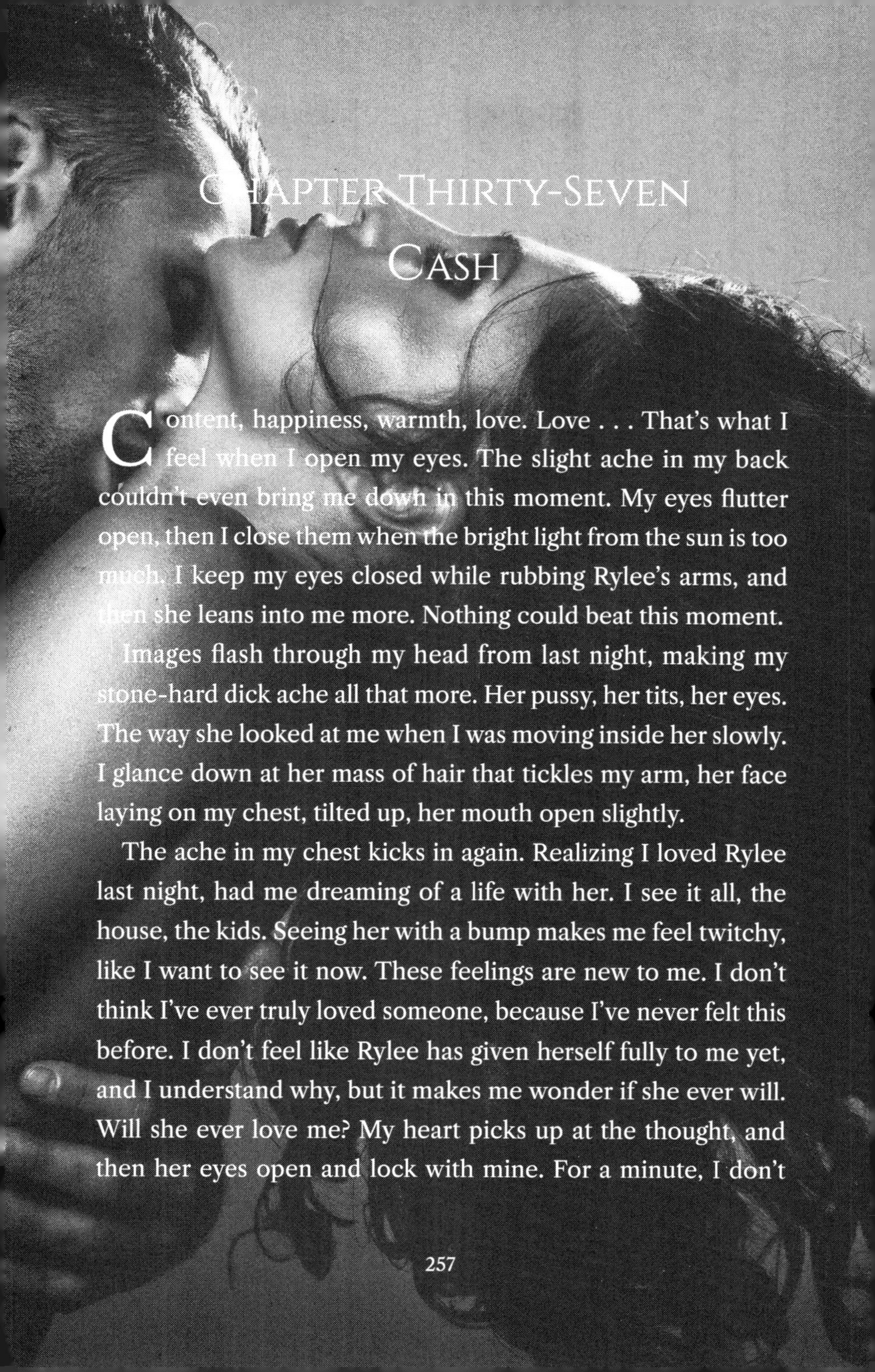

# Chapter Thirty-Seven

## Cash

Content, happiness, warmth, love. Love . . . That's what I feel when I open my eyes. The slight ache in my back couldn't even bring me down in this moment. My eyes flutter open, then I close them when the bright light from the sun is too much. I keep my eyes closed while rubbing Rylee's arms, and then she leans into me more. Nothing could beat this moment.

Images flash through my head from last night, making my stone-hard dick ache all that more. Her pussy, her tits, her eyes. The way she looked at me when I was moving inside her slowly. I glance down at her mass of hair that tickles my arm, her face laying on my chest, tilted up, her mouth open slightly.

The ache in my chest kicks in again. Realizing I loved Rylee last night, had me dreaming of a life with her. I see it all, the house, the kids. Seeing her with a bump makes me feel twitchy, like I want to see it now. These feelings are new to me. I don't think I've ever truly loved someone, because I've never felt this before. I don't feel like Rylee has given herself fully to me yet, and I understand why, but it makes me wonder if she ever will. Will she ever love me? My heart picks up at the thought, and then her eyes open and lock with mine. For a minute, I don't know why, but I panic that she may have regrets about last night until a small smile creeps up on her face.

"Morning, creep." She holds onto me tighter, closing her eyes again.

"I could stare at you every day while you sleep." My sleepy voice breaks through. I don't even think before saying that, but I don't regret it one bit. I would do anything to wake up in this position with her every day.

Her eyes open. The smile disappearing.

"Thank you, Cash."

"For what." I frown.

"Bringing me here, being here with me," she says before laying her head back on my chest. I don't say anymore because she doesn't need to thank me, but I squeeze her a little tighter. Then I remember I haven't given her, her late birthday present. I brought it the day I went over to her apartment, but with everything that happened, I didn't think it was the best idea to give it to her.

I lean up, causing Rylee to frown.

"Don't look at me like that." I laugh. "I'll be back in a minute, I just forgot something."

She narrows her eyes. "Mm-hmm. Well, hurry up," she says with a smirk.

I pace into the bedroom, feeling out of sorts without her in my arms. I'm so unbelievably fucked. I pick up the bag, juggling it from one hand to the other as I walk out to her on her back, with her phone in the air above her head. She glances sideways at me, frowning again.

"What's that?"

"For you." I push it out in front of me. She reaches up and takes it. Eyeing me.

"What for?" she asks, sitting up and crossing her legs, then placing her phone down beside her.

"It's a late birthday present," I mumble.

"This is enough." She waves around the room.

"This is your Christmas present." I frown down at her, knowing I already told her that. She raises her eyebrow at me again and digs into the bag. She pulls the box out and opens it. The soft smile she had on her lips disappears as tears glisten her eyes.

"Do you not like it?" I question. I had it made, not that I will tell her that, but I thought she would like it.

"Cash." Her voice breaks as she strokes it with her finger. "It's a wave bracelet."

I nod. "It's a type of wave bracelet, yes."

"I love it." She chokes. "I love it so much." She runs her finger along the wave and then spins the silver balls on either side. She squints as she brings it closer to her face.

"Are those—" Her eyes go wide. "Oh my God, is that sand?" Her face swings to me straight away and then back at the bracelet.

I nod. "Yes. It's from the beach in Baltimore and . . . the beach in Tulum. I know how much you love going to the beach, and I know Tulum meant a lot to you, so I thought you could have it with you at all times." I shift on my feet, worried she'll think I'm cheesy.

She turns it in her hand and then stops. "Happiness comes in waves," she says, and her eyes meet mine.

"It's perfect." She jumps up and into in my arms, wrapping her legs around me. "Thank you. Thank you. Thank you." She places kisses over my face.

I push the hair out of her face. "I need you to do me a favor, though."

"Anything."

"I need you to wear it and never take it off. Can you do that for me?" Her brows furrow, and then a smile creeps up on her face.

"That's not a favor, Cash. I was going to do that anyway," she whispers into my lips before her lips meet mine, then I carry her to the bedroom.

We haven't done much today. We fly back tomorrow. The fire has been going most of the day, and Rylee has been putting chick flick after chick flick on, and I have felt the most content I have in a long time. Now we sit outside with a hot chocolate she insisted on making, which I can't deny is one of the most amazing hot chocolates I've tasted. She said they had all the toppings, marshmallow, cream. So it seemed like a heart attack in a cup when she gave it to me, but she looked like a kid at Christmas, so there was no way I could turn it down, and I'm glad I didn't.

Rylee finished hers a while ago, and since it's cold, she curled up next to me on the long chair and wrapped herself around my waist. Her head lies on my chest while we stare out at the view. The water on the lake glistens from the sun, and you can see the reflection from the snowy mountains that surround us. It looks like something out of a film. I haven't stopped thinking about leaving this little bubble we are in, and what it's going to be like when we return home. I have to go back to seeing her when our schedules fit, and that kills me. How am I meant to let her go now. She shifts and her big green eyes burn into my face.

"You okay?"

She smiles and nods. Sitting up and rubbing her hands together. I grab them and rub them between mine to warm her up.

"Cash."

I raise an eyebrow at her to let her know she has my attention, and she refuses to make eye contact. Something about the way she says it and her refusal to meet my gaze is telling me she's a bit nervous.

"Go on." I urge her.

"Do you still think about him?" Her gentle voice breaks through the crisp air.

"Everyday," I whisper. She goes silent as we watch the sun disappear behind the mountains. A light breeze whips through the air, and Rylee's scent mixes in with it, creating this barrier around me, a content barrier. "I sometimes go to call him . . ." I think of the many times I tried to call him. "Then I remember, and fuck, it hurts, like physically hurts."

"Why does life have to be so complicated?" Rylee lets out a heavy sigh, and before I can even answer, she follows up with "Do you feel guilty?"

"About what?"

"Us?" she mumbles.

"Yes."

"It still eats away at me." She sniffles.

"Hey." I nudge her so she sits up. "Talk to me."

"Like you do me?" She injects. "I know it still eats away at you. You can't even look at a picture of Jace anymore." Her gaze drops down as tears track down her face.

"I don't want to be the reason you can't look at pictures of your own son anymore."

"Hey, look at me." I bring my finger underneath her chin, lifting her face. Her eyes look everywhere but me.

"Eyes, Rylee." Her watery gaze collides with mine. "I'm the reason I can't look at pictures of him. Not you, me." I cup her cheeks. "I want you to talk to me. Don't bottle it up around me. I want us to share our pain, together."

"I know, I just."

"Jace was the love of your life. You loved each other unconditionally. I know that. Don't ever think you can't talk about him with me. Tell me everything or nothing. It's up to you, but I know you will always love him, Rylee and I don't ever want that to change for you. You were perfect for my son, and I'm so thankful he got to share the last of his years with you. At least Jace was able to feel what true love was before he died. I had never seen him so happy as he was with you, so don't ever forget that." Tears continue to fall down her face as I brush my fingers against her cheek, trying to catch them.

"Do—" She gulps and drops her eyes to our hands linked together. "Do you think we should have waited." She glances over the lake. "Do you think this is the wrong time for us?"

"Do you?" An ache sets in my chest. I can't force her to stay with me, no matter how much I may want to, but I don't know if I could let her go now.

"I don't think there is ever a right or wrong time, whether it's two months or two years after, and I'm not dumb enough to not understand that a lot of people will see this as truly fucked up. Some won't understand, and the ones who don't, well, they can fuck themselves. Until they are in our shoes, they can't say shit. Their opinions are irrelevant to the feelings we have.

"I don't know what the future holds. I can't promise you there won't be days where I'll crash and burn, I can't promise you that a wave of grief won't come and take you under. I can't promise you that one day you won't look at me and break down with guilt. Those things hit us when we least expect it. But what I do know is, when you need me, I'll be there. When you think that wave will drown you, I'll pull you back to the shore. When you want to scream and cry, I'll be there to hear you scream and collect those tears. When life gets too heavy, I'll help you carry through it. And most of all—" I take a deep breath. I know this is the time, I need to tell her. "I want to be with you and . . ." I freeze. I've never been worried about what a woman may think or say, but I've never said these words to anyone, not in the way they mean anyway. I run my fingers through my hair.

"Cash . . ."

Her voice gives me all the strength I need. "Goddamn it, Rylee, I'm in fucking love with you." I exhale. "It's as simple and as complicated as that. I don't expect you to say it back, I don't expect you to say anything at all. I just needed to tell you. I fucking love you, Rylee Matthews, and that's never going to change."

She chokes on a sob before throwing herself at me and wrapping her arms around my neck, then pulls back, and her eyes dance between mine. "I don't know if I can say it yet, Cash, but just know, I'm not going anywhere." Then she wraps me in another hug.

"I don't think I could let you go even if you wanted to," I whisper, knowing in this moment, I'd burn this world down if she tried to leave me.

# Chapter Thirty-Eight
## Rylee

"Girllll . . ." Rachel drops down in the chair at our favorite restaurant. We have been saying for months we would go out for dinner, but our lives have been hectic, and she was in London for three weeks visiting family. I had let it slip about Cash and me. She was shocked to the core, and although I know Toni will always tell me the truth, a part of me wondered if Rachel would pretend it was okay and not speak her truth, but I was wrong. She said it was a lot to take in and I need to be prepared for what people will say.

"Catch me up on your life, how was the cabin." She smirks, and I can tell she wants every bit of detail. She's the calmer version of Toni, but those two together can be wild. "You have been beaming from ear to ear since being back, so I need to know what happened, and that little text telling me on your plane ride home you became a member of the Mile High Club, will not cut it, I need more." The waiter walks over at that point, so we order our drinks and food.

"Back to you." She points at me.

"He told me he loved me," I blurt. I got it off my chest to Toni, but it was over the phone. It wasn't as big of a relief as it is saying it to someone's face.

Rach stares at me, her mouth agape.

"Say something."

Her face breaks out into a huge smile.

"Broody Cash Stiles, who barely smiles, told Rylee fucking Matthews he loves her. Well, I'll be damned." She smacks the table. "And?" She stares wide-eyed at me.

"And I didn't say it back." I smack my hand over my mouth.

"You didn't say it back. Whaa-wha . . ." She flaps her hands around. "What am I missing?"

"Nothing, Rach. I don't know why, I just couldn't say it." I cringe.

"Well, do you love him?" Her eyes flick between mine. No one has asked me this yet, not even Toni. I can't believe how easy it is to answer.

"Yes." I smile. "Yes, I fucking love him."

Her smile meets her eyes. "You need to tell him. He needs to hear you say it."

I know he does. I just know once I say this, we will have to tell people, and I don't know if I can bear the hate from everyone, especially Bridget and Boh. Since the night I spoke to Boh, he hasn't said anything else about it, and if I tell Cash I love him, we will have to confirm his suspicions.

The waiter brings over our glasses of wine. "Can we add a bottle please? We're celebrating." Rach smiles up at the waiter. I laugh before taking a sip of my wine, eyeing her over the rim.

"You haven't said much about Harley." I raise an eyebrow. "Fucked him over any new desks recently?" I point at her. "I swear if you did it over mine, you're dead."

She smirks and winks.

"Oh my God, you didn't." I gasp. Her eyes crinkle as she howls while slapping her thigh.

"No, but seeing your face was worth that." She tops our glasses to the rim. She always says if you want a glass of wine, you want the full glass, not half.

"Harley is old news." She sighs.

I'm shocked by this, the last time we spoke about him, she seemed quite into him. "Oh." I don't know how to ask, so I just do. "His decision or yours?"

"Mine, he was great in bed, but that was it. If he ever decides to settle down, it will be years from now, and I'm not about to put my life on hold and wait for him."

I raise my hand in the air. "High-five, girl. I like it." We slap hands while giggling. We continue to chat about everything going on and I fill her in on my mile high experience which she eats up every word, especially when I tell her we barely made it to the bed. She tells me about a few dates she has been on from some dating apps. I told her she needs a night out with Toni. Toni always finds the men.

The waiter walks past. "Can we get the check, please?"

"Your table has already been paid, ma'am." I glance at Rachel, brows furrowed, and she looks as confused as me.

"I don't feel drunk enough to not have remembered to pay our check." Rachel laughs. The waiter chuckles.

"No, ma'am, a gentleman." He tilts his head towards the bar. "He's not there now. He said he knew you"—the waiter looks at me—"and wanted to pay." I frown at Rachel, but she just shrugs.

"Well, Happy Christmas." She giggles. I smile at the waiter, tell him, "Thank you," and then glance at Rachel.

"Don't you think that's a bit weird, if they knew me they would have come over and said something." She shrugs again.

"I wouldn't worry, Ry. Whoever it was, was just paying for our food and drinks." Her eyes flicker between mine. "Are you okay? You don't think it was James, do you?" She frowns, glancing over her shoulder and then around the restaurant. I scan over the guests.

"I don't think so, surely he wouldn't be so blatantly open, his face has been plastered all over the news as a person of interest in two homicides." An uneasy feeling washes over me, like I'm being watched. I scan the restaurant again.

"I best get back to the office, I have a lot to get done today." I want to get out of here as soon as possible. The walk back to the office, I can't stop looking over my shoulder, feeling tense. I send a quick text to Cash.

**Me:** By any chance, were you just at Gachos?

**Cash:** No, why?

**Me:** Someone paid for mine and Rachel's lunch and left before I could see who it was. They told the waiter they knew me. Maybe Boh?

My phone rings.

"Cash."

"Are you back at the office?"

"I'm just walking back now with Rachel," I say picking up my pace. I can tell by Cash's voice he isn't happy about this person paying for my food, and to be honest, neither am I.

"Can you work from my place for the rest of the day? I will come and get you from the office now."

"Cash, I can't just up and leave when something happens. I'll be fine in the office," I say, and Rachel stares ahead, smirking.

"Sorry, I worded it wrong before," he says. "You're coming here. I will come and get you now."

"Cash. No." I pull my phone away from my ear and look at the screen. *Ahh, he hung up.*

"Everything okay?"

I roll my eyes. "He wants me to work from his house this afternoon. He doesn't like what happened at the restaurant."

"I'm sure if you spoke to the police, they would have the CCTV looked at."

"Yes, that's a good idea."

# Chapter Thirty-Nine
# James

My hands tremble around the glass I hold while I sit at the bar. I can't believe she left me again. She went on another fucking holiday with Cash. I rub my forehead, taking controlled breaths. I needed to be near her, I feel like I'm losing her as the months go on, but our plans are not ready yet and I can't risk having her and then losing her again.

*Time is running out; you need to remind her who she belongs to.*

Her laugh filters through the air relaxing me as I slowly calm down. I glance carefully over my shoulder, I can only see the back of her, but it's enough. Soon enough I will be the reason she laughs like that; I will be the reason she is happy.

*Make her smile, buy her and her friend lunch.*

I smile. What a great idea. I finish my drink and stand up, but before walking towards the waiter, I feel the pull towards her so I give her one last glance. *Soon, Rylee.*

# Chapter Forty

# Rylee

## New Year's Eve

It's been three weeks since Cash and I got back from the cabin, and due to Cash's work, I have only seen him twice since Christmas Day at Bridget's, and then I stayed that night with him, then when he picked me up from the office the day I had lunch with Rachel.

The creeping around is getting harder, and the longer it goes on, the more of a cold shoulder Boh gives us. He gave his notice at work with Cash, telling him he needs a fresh start. Bridge said she would speak to him, but I haven't heard whether she has. I hate that Boh is being like this, as I've always had such a great relationship with him. He would always speak about stuff, but he hasn't texted me in two months. I'm convinced he knows, but Cash thinks it's something else. Bohdi won't talk to him unless it has to do with work.

I haven't stopped thinking about Cash and what he said. I'm finally going to tell him I love him tonight. I can't hold it in anymore, and I fall even harder for him every day, with the simple text messages he sends that brighten my day and the flowers just randomly showing up. He's already texted, telling me he's not drinking tonight, so he can "take me home," but that's the cover for me to stay with him.

Cash is having a New Year's party tonight. I'm not sure who all is going, but Toni will be here soon, as we're going together. Rachel has also been invited, but she is out with other people tonight.

Toni hasn't been herself lately. A part of me thinks it may have to do with Kaleb, but I've never known her to get like this over a boy. I keep trying to get it out of her, but she says it's just work. I'm hoping to get her drunk enough tonight to tell me what's wrong.

"Babycakesssss," Toni shouts through the apartment. I smile.

"In here."

"Wowza," she says from behind me. I spin around, doing a little twirl and moving from foot to foot, popping my hip, with my hand resting on it.

"You look hot as fuck. Mr. Breeder is going to want to fuck a thousand babies into you tonight."

I scrunch up my face. "Please don't ever call him Mr. Breeder again. Gross."

"Where did you get this dress, you look fire." Walking over to me running her hand up and down the backless dress. It's another red dress, but this time, it's short and tight. Cash said when we were at the cabin how much he loved me in red, so I wanted to wear red for him tonight.

"Silk." She hums.

"It's actually not new. I borrowed it from Rach." I turn around and start packing my clutch.

Toni's phone pings, she opens it, and a sad smile lands on her face. She isn't as chatty or as loud as she normally is.

"Ton," I whisper.

She looks up at me.

"Are you okay?"

"Of course, I'm always okay." She smiles but it's not her usual smile. I frown at her.

"Don't treat me as if I don't know you at all. What's going on?" Her eyes search mine, as if she's not sure what's wrong with her either. She frowns and huffs, and then her phones pings again.

"Uber is here." She jumps up, plastering on her signature smile, but I know.

"Toni," I say, frowning.

"Can we talk later? I want to have a good night." She frowns, staring into my eyes.

"Okay, but you promise you will talk to me later?"

"I promise." She kisses my head and walks toward my apartment door.

"Let's go get drunk, babyyy," Toni shouts while walking out of my apartment.

By the time we reach Cash's, the party is in full swing, there are people everywhere as we walk in, so Toni and I squeeze through. Some people from Cash's work stop me to say, "Hi." I search the room for Cash but don't see him.

"Rylee." Bridge comes out of nowhere, engulfing me in a tight hug. I squeeze her back.

"Hey, Bridge." Bridge sways slightly as I lean away from her.

"You on the heavy stuff already?" I smirk.

"Yeah, I was drinking while sorting the food. I hadn't realized how much I had actually drunk." She hiccups.

"Where are Bohdi and Cash," Toni injects, probably knowing I'm dying to see Cash. Bridge grabs Toni's and my hand and drags us toward the kitchen. People surround the island in the middle, chatting and doing shots.

"Cash, Boh," Bridge shouts, not directly at anyone. "Our girls are here." My eyes scan the large kitchen, and when they land on Cash, who's beer is midair until his eyes land on me. He slowly lowers his bottle, his eyes taking in my body from head to toe. He gulps.

"Cash." Bridge spots him as he breaks away from my stare and walks toward us. He leans in, giving Toni a kiss on the cheek and then turns to me. His eyes burn me from the inside out.

"Rylee." His gravelly voice sends my heart into overdrive as he leans in, but instead of kissing my cheek he says, "Meet me in my room in five minutes." I shake my head as subtly as I can. I'm not fucking him at this party with Bridge and Boh here. Bridge walks farther into the kitchen.

"What can I get you ladies," Bridge says.

"Wine please," we say at the same time.

"I'll go help, Bridge," Toni says, her eyes dancing between Cash and me.

"Did you shake your head at me, Rylee," Cash says while staring into the kitchen, taking a sip of his beer.

"I'm not . . ." I'm not even going to say it out loud, there's too many people around. "It's a packed party, have you lost your goddamn mind." I smile at a few people that walk by.

"I just want to talk." He walks in front of me. "You have two minutes," he whispers before stalking off. I stand there, staring at Toni talking and laughing with Bridget. I survey the room to see if anyone is watching me, which they are not. I glance back to Toni, and catch her eye. It's rare I actually have to ever say what I need her to do, and thank God, this time she knows. She gives me a wink before engaging in convo with Bridge again. I do another sweep before walking toward the stairs and then run up them, trying to hold onto the edges of my dress so it doesn't ride up. Once I get to the top of the stairs, I peak in the bathroom to make sure no one is in there, then tiptoe to Cash's bedroom.

Cash's bedroom door is shut, and I go to knock but then think twice and open the door. Cash stands by his window, staring out into the backyard where people drink and dance. The sound of laughing and music slices through the empty room. Cash turns on his heels, pinning me with a stare that says anything but talking.

"I missed you." He stalks toward me, wrapping his hand in my hair and pulling my mouth toward his. I have craved this, craved him all week. This is all I have thought about: his mouth on mine, his tongue sweeping against mine as he devours my mouth, bending my head to the side, so he can open my mouth wider. A moan escapes my throat before I can stop it. He pulls away, his eyes filled with liquid lust as they bore into mine.

"Are you trying to kill me in this dress? Did you do it on purpose, knowing it would torture me all night?" he whispers, trailing a finger up and down my bare leg. I smile and kiss on his neck, and he groans.

"Maybe." I lean back, smiling. "Why, is it working?"

He grins wide, clicking his tongue. "You will regret that later, when I have you laid across my lap while I tan your ass until you're dripping over this very carpet." The smile drops from my face. The thought has me clenching my thighs together.

Cash tilts his head to the side, his smile growing.

"I will be fucking you in this dress tonight, Rylee." He places an open-mouth kiss on my collarbone, which causes every butterfly in my stomach to flutter.

"I'll see you downstairs," he says before stalking off and leaving the room, not even glancing back at me. How he can say a few words and have me so uncomfortably wet and my legs feeling like they will give out at any minute, is beyond me. I wait five minutes before having a quick look to make sure the coast is clear. When I see it is, I leave Cash's room and walk down the stairs. As I get to the bottom, I do a glance around to find Toni, but I don't see her. She must still be in the kitchen. I head to the kitchen, but hearing Cash's name yelled has me halting. I know that voice. I turn on my heels, and a tiny woman throws herself into Cash arms, placing a kiss on his cheeks.

"Miley, you made it," Bridget squeals as she stalks past me, passing what must be my glass of wine to Miley. I grit my teeth as Miley hangs off Cash like he was fucking made for her. Why is he not stepping back from her? For fuck's sake, I swear to God if I find out Cash invited her.

"Cash you still owe me that date, remember." She winks. He laughs. *He fucking laughs.*

"Oh boy" comes from beside me. Toni stands there, taking in what just happened. She goes to take a sip of her wine, but I snatch it away and down the entirety of it. Not even wincing when it slides down my throat.

"Oh damn . . . Did you just down yours and mine?"

"No." I spin, glaring at Toni. "Bridge gave it to fucking *Miley*."

"I'm sure Cash wasn't even aware she was coming, Ry, calm down." She rubs my back.

"Fuck this, I'm going to get drunk." I spin around, and there stands Bohdi, staring down at me.

"Ahh . . . Boh. Hi." I smile, trying to douse the anger inside of me.

"Not a fan of Miley, I hear." He tilts his head toward Cash and Miley who are still in deep conversation, she keeps touching his arm, and I have never wanted to snap a wrist so bad in my life. But then I realize Boh must have heard our conversation, so I turn back.

"She's just one of those annoying girls, you know?" Toni waves her hand in the air, attempting to save the day like she always does.

"No, I don't," Boh deadpans, not taking his eyes off me. "From what I heard, it sounded like a lot of jealousy, Rylee. Why would you be jealous of Cash and Miley?" He squints, tilting his head to the side, assessing me. He knows. There is no doubt about it, but this is something Cash and I have to do together. I can't let this slip here, right in front of everyone.

"I just think Cash can do better, that's all."

"Who, like you?" he snaps.

Toni stands in front of Bohdi. "Whoa, whoa. I think you have had one too many of those." Toni taps Boh's beer. I don't tell Boh he's wrong, I just let my gaze flick between his, trying to tell him I'm sorry. He shakes his head, laughing to himself before stalking off. Toni turns around, eyes wide.

"That was close, but I think he definitely knows." Boh paces out to the backyard.

"Yeah, so do I." I breathe out.

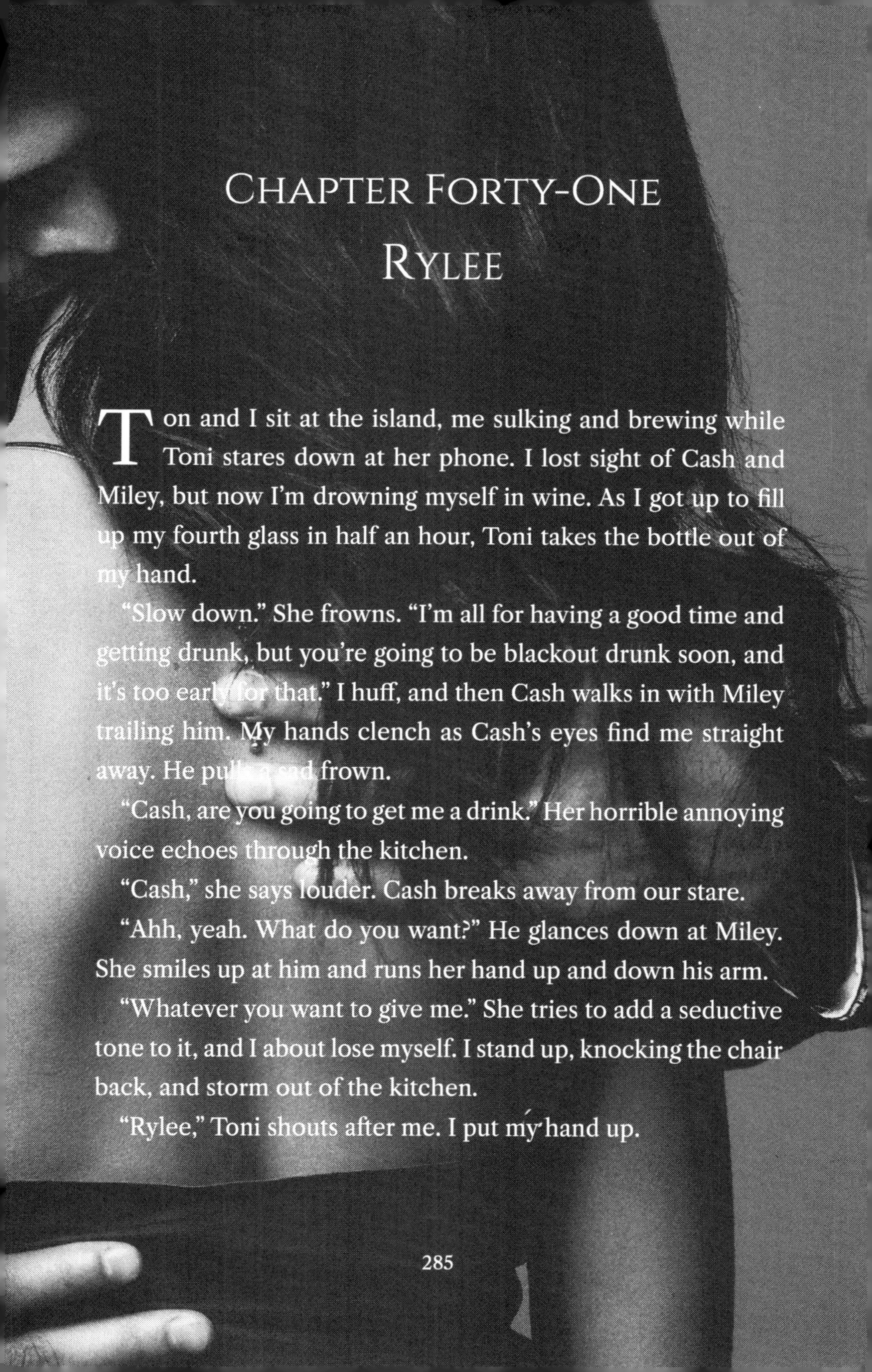

# Chapter Forty-One
# Rylee

Toni and I sit at the island, me sulking and brewing while Toni stares down at her phone. I lost sight of Cash and Miley, but now I'm drowning myself in wine. As I got up to fill up my fourth glass in half an hour, Toni takes the bottle out of my hand.

"Slow down." She frowns. "I'm all for having a good time and getting drunk, but you're going to be blackout drunk soon, and it's too early for that." I huff, and then Cash walks in with Miley trailing him. My hands clench as Cash's eyes find me straight away. He pulls a sad frown.

"Cash, are you going to get me a drink." Her horrible annoying voice echoes through the kitchen.

"Cash," she says louder. Cash breaks away from our stare.

"Ahh, yeah. What do you want?" He glances down at Miley. She smiles up at him and runs her hand up and down his arm.

"Whatever you want to give me." She tries to add a seductive tone to it, and I about lose myself. I stand up, knocking the chair back, and storm out of the kitchen.

"Rylee," Toni shouts after me. I put my hand up.

“I’m going to get some air.” I storm outside to the front yard and jump up on the front wall. The air whips against my face, and I’m hoping it simmers my anger. I know I wasn’t ready to tell everyone, but that doesn’t mean he can still flirt with other women right in front of my fucking face. What is that about?

“Fucking prick,” I mumble to myself, feeling a lot more drunk than I did before coming out here. I jump down, losing my balance as I giggle while trying to stand back up and pull my dress down.

“Ma’am.” I glance up in front of me but no one’s there. Am I hearing things? I turn around and no one is there.

“Ma’am.” I jump and spin around, and my whole world falls around me.

“Hi, Rylee.”

“No, no. Not again.” I go to scream but everything turns to darkness and then there’s pressure on my mouth. James has put something over my head and has his hand placed over my mouth over the bag.

“I will go into that house and kill every single person you love if you make a sound and don’t start walking.” I sob into his hand. He pushes me along, and within a few seconds, I’m being pushed forward and land on something soft.

“Lay there and shut the fuck up, Rylee.” I lie there sobbing as a door shuts, and then another one opens and shuts. I feel the rumble under me as the car starts, and then we’re moving. The alcohol is making me lightheaded and sick. With the way my heart is beating, I might pass out at any minute.

"Stop the crying, Rylee. You can remove the bag, just keep your head down." With shaky hands, I remove the bag. The only thing lighting up the car is the streetlights we whiz past every now and then. I can see James from the side, and at a quick glimpse you wouldn't even know it was him. He has buzzed his hair and dyed it white. It looks nothing like him, but I guess he had to do that to not bring attention to himself.

"James," I cry. I know it's pointless, but I still try. "Please just let me go, I won't say a word. Drop me off here, and I will go back and not say anything." A sob breaks out of me. I know he won't let me leave.

He laughs. "Oh, Rylee, Rylee, Rylee. You're mine and you will come to learn that. We are stopping off somewhere quickly, and then I have a private jet ready to fly us to our future." He grins. My brain tells me to fight, but my body has given up. I curl into a ball and sob silently. I feel the jolt of the car as we come to a stop, and then James is opening the door. I look up at James upside down.

"Don't even think about screaming," he whispers. He keeps glancing around; I sit up but he yanks me by the arm and drags me out of the car. He looks both ways again and pulls me into a tiny apartment. From the outside, you would think it was abandoned, but then we walk down a dark staircase and through another door, which I'm assuming is a basement. James drags me in.

"Sit there and don't move." He pushes me down on a chair as a small light turns on above my head. He scurries around the room, gathering up some bags.

He stops at his phone ringing, then pulls it out and yells at whoever is on the other end. "I paid you a lot of fucking money, make it happen," he snaps before putting the phone back in his pocket. I silently cry as my life crashes around me. Once we leave here, I know that's it, and as much as I know this is the end of my life, my body won't fight. I've lost everything.

"James." I sob. "Please."

"Rylee. Shut up," he bellows. "We don't have long, I need to get everything sorted. This would have been planned better if you hadn't of decided to fucking leave me again and take off on another fucking trip with Cash," He shouts and stops what he is doing, taking a few deep breaths. "Sit there and shut the fuck up," He says calmly. I choke out a sob and sit there, bringing my knees to my chest and crying. The thought of never seeing Cash again, seeing Toni, Bridge. Everything hurts as I breakdown while he just keeps rushing around me.

He moves over to a cupboard and pulls stuff out while looking at some other stuff, packing a large duffle bag. A noise comes from behind me, so I glance at James, but he doesn't hear it and keeps looking through the cupboard. I hear it again, then turn toward the door as it creeps open. My eyes go wide as Cash appears. He puts his finger up to his mouth. *He came for me.* I don't even question how. I turn and look at James, but he is still rooting through the cupboards. I turn back to Cash. He signals for me to come to him. I stand up as quietly as I can and take one step, but Cash's eyes go wide.

# Chapter Forty-Two
## Rylee

His voice brings the taste of bile to my mouth.

"Oh, Cash it's nice to see you again," James says from behind me, I turn and glance and see the gun in his hand. I close my eyes slowly. A tear escapes. I can't look at Cash. James walks up to stand beside me, bringing his hand up to my face, and I flinch.

"Don't cry, princess." My eyes flutter open, and Cash stands, jaw clenched. His fists opening and closing beside him.

"So what was it, Cash." James's venomous voice breaks through. "What was it like fucking your son's girlfriend." He snarls. "Oh, wait. Your dead son I should say." A sob escapes me as Cash lunges for him.

"You piece of shit," he shouts. James holds the gun up, pointing it at Cash.

"I would stay where the fuck you are if I was you," he spits. "Rylee. Did you always fuck Jace and picture his daddy?" I look past Cash at the wall behind him. My heart beats out of my chest, as the gun swings around every time he talks. How are we going to get out of here without him using it?

"Answer me, Rylee," James singsongs, the gun swinging my way. Cash flinches, which has my gaze colliding with his. I shake my head to not move.

"No." I grit through my teeth.

He tilts his head to the side. "Oh."

"So you're still in love with Jace, but his daddy is just the next best thing?" He looks up to the ceiling as if he is in deep thought while all I can do is helplessly stand here and not be able to do anything.

"No."

"Mmm. I think you are telling lies, Rylee. But we will park that for now."

"What the fuck do you want from her. She doesn't want you, so why go to all of this," Cash says. I try and get his attention, praying he will look at me. I don't want him to make James angry. We all know what he is capable of, and speaking to him like this will not help. But Cash doesn't look at me. He keeps his eyes on James and the gun.

"Because she was mine first." James's scream makes my body freeze. Tears stream down my face while I wish Cash would look at me, but he doesn't.

James points the gun at me, and Cash's hands go up.

"Bring it back to me, James. Point it at me. Not her," Cash says.

"No. No." I cry.

"She"—he thrusts the gun in my direction again, his eyes wide and frantic—"was mine first," he grits out.

"Jace always got it good. Always got the nicer girls. The better life. Everyone loved Jace." James laughs out. "I finally found someone I wanted, and who gets her? Saint fucking Jace." He rolls his eyes.

"Rylee," he shouts, causing me to jump. "Can you believe I even drugged your drink thinking I may be able to drag you away that night, but you still went home with Jace and woke up to him when you should have been waking up to me." He bangs his chest with the gun.

"You drugged me?" I now know why I was in such a state compared to the other girls. I had drunk the exact same as them, but everyone put it down to me being a lightweight. James fucking drugged me. Him being in the taxi. It all makes sense now.

"That's why you were in the taxi." He smiles, pushing his hands out to the side.

"I thought Jace might leave me to take you 'home.' But no. Of course Jace took you back to his place to make sure you were safe. I even offered to make sure you got home before we got in the taxi, but he was having none of it." The thought of that night, of meeting Jace and how my life changed for the better, but I basically signed Jace's death warrant.

"You see, I have grown up my whole life hearing how amazing Jace was, how I'll never be Jace." He bangs the gun against his head. "It's been ingrained in my fucking head and marked on my skin how amazing he was." I don't understand what he is saying. He's making no sense. My face must say it all because he laughs, but before he can speak, Cash interrupts.

"What do you mean all your life, you met Jace when he was in college."

"This is where it gets interesting." He winks at me, making me sick.

"Do you remember Roxanne, Cash?" James says.

By the look on Cash's face, he knows who she is. Who the hell is she? Cash's eyes bulge and shoot to James, and he doesn't answer right away. His mouth opens and shuts a few times before a frown mars his face.

"Yes," he states, his eyes narrowed.

He paces slowly in front of Cash, nodding to himself. James spins around to me. "Roxy was Jace's mom." He continues to look down at the floor, pacing. I glance over at Cash who eyes James with caution, his eyes darting with every movement James makes, but also, he keeps squinting, like he is trying to work out how James knows Roxanne. James turns his attention back to Cash with a sinister smile.

"You see, Roxy . . ." He pauses, spinning back to me again like this is some fun guessing game. "That's what the pimps used to call her," he says, laughing.

"She used to watch Jace from afar. He was always . . ." He uses the gun to point to his chin, as if he is trying to remember something. "'The son that got away,'" he says, waving the gun around in the air.

"What are you going on about, James? Where are you going with this?" James points the gun at Cash.

"No, please. No, James." I feel like my body is about to crumble. He then points the gun at me.

"Shut the fuck up, both of you. I'm getting to where this all fits," he spits, dropping the gun to his side as he paces some more.

James stares and squints at the floor, concentration marring his face as if he's going back to a time in his head that he doesn't want to. He freezes on the spot, his gaze darting to Cash.

"Roxy loved you, Cash," James states. "Yes, she loved the drugs, but she did really love you. Maybe if you would have stayed with her. She would have stopped the drugs and bettered her life. Did you ever think of that?"

"Of course I did," he grits out. "She was too far gone."

James nods, as if he's agreeing with him. "You're probably right." And puts his hands out either side of him. "And hey." He pauses with an evil smirk. "If you did, the world wouldn't have been graced with me." He stares Cash down, waiting for a reaction. Every emotion flickers across Cash's face: confusion, disbelief, disgust, hurt. Which has me confused, but I was too focused on Cash to take any of what James said in until now. This can't be true. He has to be lying.

"No." Cash sucks in a sharp breath, shaking his head. He eyes James, his gaze running all over his face, and then he rubs at his eyes with the base of his palms before eyeing James again. James smiles, letting Cash assess him.

"You see it now, don't you." James smirks. "You see Roxy," he states.

# Chapter Forty-Three

## Cash

I see it. Those soulless, sunken black eyes. That horrible big smile that once lit up my life. The smile that turned evil overnight. I see her.

"I feel you would have been a great stepdad, Cash." James nods, staring back at the floor, but then his eyes that now represent her glance up at me, creasing in the corners from that evil smile and then turn to Rylee. "Although, I would have had to keep him away from my girlfriends." He jokes, causing bile to rise to my mouth. I can't look at Rylee. I can't see the hurt on her face and the tears. It will gut me since I can't do anything right now.

"That would mean." Her jittery voice floats through the room as James turns back to her.

"Go on," James says.

"You-you're Jace's . . ."

All I want to do is hold her, tell her everything will be okay, but right now, I don't know if it will. I was meant to keep her safe, and now look at us. If he kills me, then who the fuck will save her. Who will keep her safe. Whoever it is, hopefully they do a better job than I have.

"Say. It," James spits.

"Brother," she sobs out.

"Finally. I feel a big weight lifted of my shoulder now it's out in the open." James bunches his shoulders up and down like it's a huge relief. How the fuck can he be my son's brother, and how could he kill his own brother?

"How?" I say. Even though I don't want to know the who or why's. In my eyes, he is nothing to with my son. Fuck what DNA says.

"Great question," James shouts.

"No one in this room knows what it's like to grow up with an addict that doesn't love you." He bangs the gun against his head. "It fucks with your head. Mentally and physically scars you," he says, pulling up his top. His whole body is covered in scars, some big, some small. Some circle shapes. He points the scars out.

"Cigarette burn." He points to the small circle.

"Pocketknife." He points to another one.

"Kitchen knife." He points to a larger one. "That one fucking hurt." He laughs. "What you are looking at is what it's like to live with an addict who will put drugs before their kids, even if it means men torturing their kids for fun." He pulls his top back down, and an ache starts in my chest. I can't even imagine what it must have been like for him growing up.

"You know, she had a picture of Jace." He stops. "A few, actually. I think she must have gotten them online. She had this specific one in a photo frame from when he was around sixteen in his football jersey." I've got loads of pictures of Jace in school in his football jerseys.

"She used to make me look at it and ask me why I couldn't be him. That I would never be him." His stare turns murderous. "She said if I hadn't come along, she might have been able to have another chance with you." He points to me with the gun.

"I ruined her life, apparently. Funny, because I didn't ask to be on this earth, and if I had the choice and it was with her, I would have much rather not. I didn't even know Jace, never spoke to him, never seen him, but I grew up in his fucking shadow. Constantly compared to him. How good-looking he was, how he was doing well for himself. 'You will never be like my boy, you worthless piece of shit.' That's what she would say every single day. I don't recall one day she didn't say that. I had to grow up staring at Jace's face every day while she would cry herself to sleep because all she wanted was him and you," he spits, eyeing me up and down.

"I would get weekly beatings from her and her pimps, or random men," he says.

I hate that some part of me deep down feels any sympathy for him, but how can I not? How can someone put their child through that?

"I was compared to him my whole life. He ruined my fucking life. If it wasn't for him, she may have loved me," he shouts. "Me." He points the gun to his chest. "Not fucking Jace, not you. Me!" Tears form in his eyes.

I choose then to look over at Rylee, and wish I hadn't. She is crouched down on the floor with her hand over her mouth, silently sobbing. I know Rylee. I know her heart, and I can guarantee she is breaking in half for not only Jace but James as well. I look back to James. Seeing her cry like that makes me sick to my stomach. The pain in my chest aches like you wouldn't believe, knowing there is nothing I can do about her pain.

"Then one day, it all stopped." His voice breaks me out of my internal thoughts. "I woke up one morning. Normally, I was woken by screaming or Roxy being beaten. Sometimes waking up to a man in my room. There was never a dull morning in that trailer, But that morning, it was silent. So silent. It made me feel weird and uneasy. I will never forget that feeling." He squints at the wall, as if he's taken himself back to the day. Rylee and I don't say a word, we just listen. Listening to how we got here, to what led us here, to why he took my son's life.

"I remember tiptoeing out into the hallway. I was starving, which wasn't anything new. I mostly ate scraps out of the bin or stole food from people at school." He shrugs like it's no big deal. "I didn't want to call out because if I spoke without being told I could speak, I would get beaten. So I kept my mouth shut and crept through that trailer.

"The living room was empty, the kitchen was empty, so I stood outside Roxy's door, shaking as I pulled that handle down. The sight changed everything for me. Her lifeless body lay on the bed. Her vacant eyes stared at the wall, the dribble of vomit that trickled out of her mouth. The needle that hung out of her arm. I will never forget that image. You know . . ." He pauses, breaking away from his daydream and staring at me. "I had no reaction, I just stared at her for what felt like hours until I heard a noise coming from the living room. I panicked and ran and hid in her closet. I heard some shuffling and some mumbles. I assume it was her pimps or whatever." He waves the gun in the air.

"They didn't find me. I waited until it was silent again, and then I crept out of that closet. Her lifeless body still lay there, not moving. You know what I did." A sad smile appears on his face. "I screamed at her, asked her why I wasn't enough, why she hurt me, why didn't she love me. Everything I had ever wanted to say to her, I screamed it until I barely had any voice left." The sad smile turns evil, and it's like seeing Roxy all over again, the day I found out who she really was, the smile she gave me is the exact smile I stare at now.

"But then, the anger settled in quickly. I was thirteen when she died, thirteen years she had put me through utter hell. I had no childhood memories." He pauses. "Well, that's a lie, I had plenty of being beaten and tortured, but no good ones. So, I went into the living room, picked up the bat that she used to use to defend herself if the men got aggressive toward her, then walked into that room and without a second thought, with every bit of strength I had in my weak body, I pounded it down on her head, and I didn't stop." He smiles. "Until I was covered in her blood."

He throws his head back as a roar of laughter leaves him. "Oh, that was a good day. I had never felt freer than I did in that moment. I had to obviously get myself cleaned up, which I did. I was able to have a shower which I had never been allowed one before. I was always made to wash in dirty cold water. Apparently, I wasn't worth the water charges." He shrugs again.

"Once I was cleaned up, I went in search of someone to help. I found someone and told them what had happened. Of course, leaving out what I had done. I wiped that bat and got rid of it in a river near where we lived. I knew the police wouldn't take it seriously because of what she was. She was always getting in trouble because of drugs or prostitution. I don't know what happened or if anyone got arrested. I don't even think there was a funeral. All I know is I was taken by the police and within a few days, I was in foster care with random people. I went through the foster care system, I was taken from home to home, never had a solid family. The last family couldn't wait to get rid of me. So when I was eighteen, I moved on with my life, and boy. I couldn't wait to start my revenge." The sinister smile is back on his face.

"My life changed from that moment. For the better?" He tilts his head. "Sure. But I always wondered what I did wrong. Why was I never good enough? I was the perfect kid. You never heard a peep out of me. So that brings us here," he says, bringing his arms out to the side and doing a little spin on the spot.

"How does that bring us here," I say. "None of that was Jace's fault. That was hers. That was your mother's." James storms toward me, and before I can even react, he smacks the gun over my head.

"Cash." Rylee screams. "James, please, please." She begs, not knowing what else to say. The shooting pain seers through my head, I put my hand out toward Rylee as she moves toward me. James must see it from the corner of his eye, as he points the gun behind him at Rylee.

“It was all his fault,” he shouts, spit flying everywhere. “If he wasn’t on this fucking earth, if he didn’t exist, I would have never been compared to him. I would have never gotten the beatings I did just for existing, for not being Jace. He made my life a living hell, so I planned to do the same to him. I stalked him for years. Worked out where he worked out, what school he went to, everything. Me enrolling in that college wasn’t a coincidence. I put myself there, to get close to Jace. Then I fucking started to see what people meant. He welcomed me more than anyone ever has. He helped me on days when I felt like shit and couldn’t get out of bed. He would be at my door, letting himself in, with a coffee and a bagel. I struggled to hate him. I struggled to want revenge, so I put it aside and became friends with him. I wanted to tell him so bad that we were brothers, but something told me not to, and I’m glad I didn’t because Jace showed his true colors the night we met you.” He spins around and looks at Rylee.

“I told Jace that night I wanted to get your number and he said, ‘Let the best man win.’ Once again, he stole what was mine, he put me back in the shadows that made me feel how I felt all those years ago when I was a young boy.” He stalks toward Rylee.

“You were talking to me,” I say as I walk toward James.

He spins on me, pointing the gun at me once again. “You stay the fuck there.” He turns on Rylee again.

“You were mine! I saw you first, before you even fucking bumped into each other, I saw you. You know Jace purposely put himself in your way so he could bump into you. Fucking prick.” He stands directly in front of Rylee. I can see the fear in her eyes as she looks up at him. They both stand sideways, and

James still has the gun pointed at me. He uses his other hand to stroke Rylee's cheek, causing her to wince and close her eyes. My whole body shakes with anger. I don't give a shit what he went through, all I can think about is putting a bullet through his head and killing him once and for all.

"Six years I waited for you. I was patient, don't you think." He narrows his eyes at a sobbing Rylee. "But then you had to fuck him, didn't you."

"I'm not fucking yours. I never have been," Rylee spits. James backhands her across the face.

"James!" I bellow. I run toward Rylee, but before I get to her, James hits me with the gun once again.

"Rylee." James pauses, staring down at her. "If I can't have you, then no one can. Starting with him."

# Chapter Forty-Four
## Rylee

James raises the gun at Cash. Everything happens in slow motion as Cash's blue eyes fall on me. He smiles at me. Fucking smiles at me.

"Cash." I weep, my whole body shaking.

"Say goodbye, Rylee," James deadpans. My world stands in front of me, the man who brought my life back, who made the pain go away, who made me feel again.

"I love you, Rylee. I will always fucking love you," Cash croaks out.

"I love you. I love you so fucking much, Cash," I cry out. Cash's eyes go wide at my words. Then bang. The gun goes off and I scream, my legs giving out as I collapse to the floor. Cash falls like a deadweight, hitting the floor, staring at me, eyes wide open. Blood pools around him as his eyes flutter close. I watch the biggest light in my world burn out. I watch the second love of my life leave this world, and this time, I don't think I will survive it. How can this be happening? I never got to show him how much I love him, how thankful I am to him for saving me. For making me feel like life is worth living again after losing Jace.

I've had someone else taken from me, and I don't want to be here without Cash.

"Kill me," I cry out. "Fucking kill me! Point that fucking gun at me and kill me." The anger invades me as I stand back up, wiping away my tears.

"I will never, ever be with you willingly. I will hate you for the rest of my life. I will do everything I can to make your life a living fucking hell. If you don't kill me now." His eye twitches, and then he's on me in a flash.

"You will fucking be with me. You ungrateful bitch. I have killed three people for you." He screams. I rear my head back and slam it forward, the pain searing when I make contact with James's head.

"You bitch," James says as he falls back slightly, and before he can gather his footing, I run to Cash's side. He lays there in a pool of blood.

"Cash. Cash. Please wake up. I love you. I love you. Please, I can't do this without you." I go to feel for a pulse, but then I'm being yanked up by my hair.

"Get up, you bitch," James spits. I glance at him and see the blood dropping from his nose. That little bit of blood sends satisfaction through me.

"I don't care what you thought, James. I will never be yours." I spit in his face, and again, he backhands me, but this time, it's with the gun. I drop to the floor, knowing he has split open my face. I hold my cheek as I cry again. My eyes land on Cash once more, and he still lays there, unresponsive, not moving. I've lost him, nothing will save us now. If James won't kill me, I'll find a way of doing it. I'm not living this life. He bends down and grabs my face.

"Look at him, Rylee. Fucking look at him." He pinches my cheeks as he turns my head toward Cash. "I didn't shoot his head for a reason," he spits. "I didn't want him to die straight away. I want you to watch him bleed out. I have waited years for you. Fucking years," he screams. "You can go through some of the torture I went through waiting for you." He shoves my face away.

"If I have to fucking force you, I will. I have waited over six fucking years for this moment. You are not taking it away from me." I'm confused what he means when I see him using one hand to unbuckle his belt.

"No. No." I shake my head. "Nooo," I scream as I crawl away, but James grabs me by my ankles, pulling me back. He drops to the floor, pushing all his weight on me. I freeze in fear, staring at Cash, the one thing good about his eyes being closed is that he doesn't have to see this. I don't bother fighting, I have no more strength in me. All I know is, once it's over, I will find any way and every way I can to end this all.

"Do you know how many nights I've pictured you. That night of the brunch when I picked Casey up from work, I pictured you. Every single time I was with Casey. You were all I saw." He kisses my ear as I stare blankly at Cash.

I let my mind take me to when Cash and I were at the cabin. When he would hold me when I was sad. I take myself back to when he bathed me and told me I was his light. My mind goes back to the good memories as James's hand slides up my leg and pulls up my dress. The tears start to fall as I close my eyes and try to picture myself in Cash's arms. James is saying something, but I have zoned him out. I imagine a made-up future with Cash, me in a wedding dress with him next to me. Tears continue to track down my face. *"I fucking love you, Rylee. It's as simple and as complicated as that."*

"I love you, Cash," I whisper as James hooks his fingers around my panties and pulls them down. Every tensed muscle in my body relaxes. I close my eyes once again and take myself away. I let myself be with Cash in every possible way I can. The mind is a scary place, but it can sometimes be a beautiful place to escape too.

"Mine," James whispers as he shuffles, and then all of a sudden, I'm being crushed with his weight. Why is he laying on me? What is happening? I wait for him to move but nothing happens, and then I start to hear again.

"Rylee. Rylee." I stare into Toni's big blue eyes.

"Am I dreaming?" I murmur, not moving as I feel my body get lighter, knowing the weight isn't on me anymore. Toni's eyes look frantic as she slowly pulls me to standing, but as soon as I'm up right, I drop back to the floor.

"Rylee. My babe, please look at me," Toni says, her eyes frantically flick all over my face. "You're safe. We got you." It's then I let my eyes gaze around the room, there are at least six police officers standing around, and then it feels like my heart stops.

"Cash!" I scream. I crawl toward people who surround him. "Get away from him. Get away." What are they doing to him?

"Rylee. They are helping him. Stop. The ambulance will be here soon. They are saving him." I scream and cry as Toni holds me in place on the floor.

"He's in good hands, Ry. I promise you." Toni holds me tight and doesn't let me move. I give in and sob into her chest, gripping on to her.

# Chapter Forty-Five
# Rylee

Beep . . . Beep . . . Beep.

I didn't think I would be hearing this noise so soon. I stare at Cash lying in that hospital bed. Eyes closed, tubes everywhere. How did this happen, how did we get here? I haven't left this chair for the last two days. I haven't washed. I haven't even brushed my teeth, but I don't care about anything other than Cash. I keep hoping and praying he will open his eyes, but with every given day, the panic sets back in. What if this happens again? I can't go through it again. Not with someone I love. The nurses keep telling me he will wake up and his body just needs to recover, but what if he doesn't? I can't help but think the worst.

The bullet punctured his lung and was still lodged inside him, so they had to operate to remove it. He also lost a substantial amount of blood, so he's had to have two blood transfusions. He has a breathing tube in due to his one lung being damaged and needing to heal, but seeing him like this, makes me think the worst.

Bohdi and Bridge have been here all day every day, but they go home at night. Neither of them have said anything about what happened the night I left Cash's or why I won't leave his side, why I cry holding his hand every day or why I tell him how much I love him and need him to wake up. Bohdi hasn't said one word to me. Bridge has, but she is distant. The thought of losing them crushed me before, but it's nothing like the pain I feel now. The fear of losing Cash. They could not speak to me for the rest of my life if it meant seeing Cash's eyes open, if it meant hearing his voice, hearing him tell me he loves me again.

"Ms. Matthews." I glance to the side, and two men in suits stand there, looking at me hesitantly. "I'm DC Lowen and this is my colleague DC Arman."

"Uh—hi," I say, trying to flatten my hair to make myself look partly put together. The night we came into the hospital, these two men were here, waiting for me outside my room after getting my butterfly stitches on my face, but all I could think about was Cash. I couldn't bear to think about talking to them or talking over what happened, but I know I can't keep putting them off. I know I need to speak to them.

"We would really appreciate it if you could come down to the station so we can get everything you know." I shake my head from side to side. "I'm not leaving this hospital. I will answer whatever you want to know, but it's done in this room or nowhere at all. I'm not leaving his side." I stand, pushing my shoulders back. DC Lowen glances sideways at his colleague and then at me and sharply nods.

"Okay. I will need you to start from the beginning. Please try and remember everything and don't leave anything out."

Three hours later, both detectives leave. I broke down a few times and had to stop when I had to recall everything that happened. Every interaction I could remember between James and me. They even questioned if I had ever given any false hope to him we could someday be something. I couldn't believe that was even coming out of their mouths. They reiterated that they didn't want to ask that, but they had to, and even if I had, none of this would have been my fault. I was crushed thinking back to all the times I had been nice to him, all the times I had even smiled at him. I had to explain what he told us about his mom. Everything that happened to him as a child. When they leave, Toni walks in, and at the moment, I'm crying so hard, I can barely breathe.

"Rylee." Toni rushes to my side. "Talk to me. What did those detectives say to you? Do I need to file a report?" I shake my head.

"They—" I sniffle, trying to gather myself. Toni pulls tissue out of her pocket, wiping at my face and nose like I'm a child.

"Take your time, babe," she says, her eyebrows drawn down.

"They wanted me to go over everything that happened," I say, turning my gaze to Cash. "With James, every single encounter I could remember."

She pulls me into her chest. "They spoke to me too." She sighs.

I sit up. "What, why?" Then I remember Toni slept with James that night I met Jace. "Oh my God, Toni, I'm sorry. I forgot." I watch her for any kind of reaction, but she is very tight on her emotions and doesn't always let them out.

"Are you okay?"

She looks at me, raising one eyebrow. "You are asking if I'm okay after everything you have been through?"

"Regardless of what I've been through, you still have every right to be feel sad and angry, and I'll always be here for you, no matter what is going on." It's me who pulls her in for a hug this time. She says nothing but lets me hold her.

"What's happening to him?"

"Well, he's been arrested. Was in hospital for a day. Apparently, some badass girl knocked him out, so he had to have stiches." She shakes with a laugh. "I wanted to do so much more, Ry. Believe me."

I sit up, realizing I hadn't even thought of this before. "Hold on. How did you find me? Actually, how did Cash find me?"

She glances at Cash and then back at me. She picks up my hand, playing with the bracelet Cash gave me for my birthday. "With this," she says, spinning it around on my wrist.

"What? What do you mean? It's a bracelet."

She nods. "It is, but it's also a tracker."

I gawk at her like she grew two heads. "Wh-what do you mean a tracker?"

"Cash told me about it before he had the bracelet made. He was worried about you. You were adamant that you go on with your life, and the only way Cash could rest even slightly was to know where you were when you weren't with him and not in the controlling way, in a way to know you're safe." She smiles.

"He really does love you, Rylee." Tears glisten her eyes as she pulls me back in for a hug. I nod, playing with the bracelet, thankful for how much he worried about me.

"I know, and I love him more than anything." I silently cry into her chest. We both put our feet up on the side of Cash's bed, lying there watching Cash's chest move up and down. I then remember something.

"Ton," I say, still with my head on her chest.

"Hmmm?" She brings her hand up to stroke my hair.

"Are you okay?" I lean away from her, bringing myself to sit up next to her and take her hand in mine. "Because I don't think you are." Her gaze connects with mine. She looks tired, fed up, sad, and her spark has gone.

"I'm not, but I will be." She smiles. "I don't want to talk about it at the moment, but I promise you when I'm ready, you will be the first person I come to." She squeezes my hand, and I have to accept her answer, even if I don't want to.

"I love you, Ton." I lean forward, placing a kiss on her cheek. "Have a kiss," I whisper.

"To make it all better," she whispers and smiles as I lean into her, and we hold each other.

# Chapter Forty-Six
## Rylee

I feel a pressure on my hand and squint my eyes open. The room is still dark, so I'm assuming it's early hours of the morning. I go to stand up, and then I feel it again.

"Wha—" Oh my God. He's squeezing my hand. I lean to the side and switch the bedside lamp on.

"Cash. Cash," I shriek. I squeeze his hand back which causes him to squeeze again—harder this time. I press the buzzer on the wall to call in a nurse. I stare at his eyes, waiting for him to open them, but he doesn't.

"Cash, c'mon. Come back to me. Please." My heart rate increases at the fact I may see his beautiful eyes staring back at me. The nurse walks in, glancing at me and then at Cash.

"He-he." I point to my hand, too excited and scared to say anything.

"My hand. He squeezed it. Three times." She nods, walking over and looking at the machine. She presses some buttons and leans over Cash to check his vitals.

She nods and smiles. "It's a great sign, Rylee. Give him time." She reiterates again.

"I have been giving him time." I throw my hands up. "Surely, if he's reacting, he should be awake." The nurse walks around and holds my hand in hers.

"I promise you, he is waking up. This is his body waking up, but slowly. His body has been through a lot of trauma. It just needs to go slow." She offers me a sympathetic smile. I nod.

"I know. I'm sorry. I don't mean to get frustrated. I just really want to see him smile again and hear his voice. I miss him and—" I sigh, feeling like I have the weight of the world on my shoulders. "I feel like something is going to go wrong and he won't wake up." I turn and look at him. "I'm scared he will leave me." A tear falls down my face as the nurse shuffles next to me. I turn to look at her as she pulls a tissue out of her pocket.

"His body is reacting extremely well to the treatment. He is fighting this like a pro. You have a strong man there, I don't doubt for a second he won't be back with you soon." She offers me another soft smile before looking at his records at the end of the bed. She writes something down and walks out. I turn back to Cash again and lean up. Placing a kiss to his head.

"Please come back to me soon, Cash." I sit back in my chair and rest my head on his hand, holding it tight, and let sleep take me back into a dream where Cash is awake and telling me he loves me.

"Rylee." Bridget's voice breaking causes me to jump up and look at Cash straight away, but he's still the same.

She touches my shoulder. "You need to keep that strength up." The bags under her eyes show she hasn't slept in the last two days either, but she always tries to keep a smile on her face no matter what.

"Thanks, Bridge." I take a sip of the coffee, feeling the effects as soon as I swallow. I put the bagel aside, knowing I need to eat it, but I can't bear it right now. Boh sits opposite me in a chair, staring at Cash. I grab Cash's hand and feel Boh's eyes fall on me. I'm done hiding it.

"I know this may be weird for you both," I say, keeping my eyes on Cash, holding his hand, knowing I will need his strength for this.

"When did it start," Boh says before I can even continue. There is a bite to his voice, so I glance his way, and he stares at me with his head hung low. Bridge glances at me and then Cash. She doesn't say anything, so she obviously wants to know now as well.

"I can't really pinpoint a date or time but—"

"When did you start to have feelings for my brother, Rylee?" Boh asks. My anger rises, and I push my shoulders back. If he wants an argument, I will give him one. I'm not ashamed anymore. I love this man, and no one will change that.

"Like I said, I don't know, Bohdi," I spit out. "It happened so quickly." My voice cracks as I squeeze Cash's hand.

"Wa—" Boh takes a deep breath. "Was it while you were w—"

"God. No." I rear my head back. "No. How—" The tears fall again. I can't be mad at them for thinking this, but it still kills me that this is the first thing people will think.

"I loved Jace, I loved him with all my heart, and I will always love him. That will never change, and Cash knows that." I sob. "I would never cheat on Jace. He was everything to me." I choke on a sob. "I miss him every day. Me and Cash talk about him a lot." Boh winces. "I know this is hard to accept, believe me, what you're feeling, I felt ten times worse. I still do, but . . ." I stare at Cash and reach my hand up, stroking down his stubble which has gotten longer since being here. "I love him so much. I honestly don't think I would have made it without him."

"I knew something was going on. I just kept praying it wasn't," Boh mumbles, eyeing Cash like he wants to rip his head off. He laughs, looking down at his hands which he has linked on his lap.

"The feelings may have not started for you when you were with Jace, but it makes sense why Cash was hostile with you for no reason." Boh glances at Bridge.

"Remember the odd times we pulled Cash aside for being snappy with Rylee. Now we know why, I guess." He glances back at me. "Because he couldn't have her." He chuckles to himself.

"Oh, this is truly fucked up." He sighs with a sarcastic smirk on his face. "My nephew hasn't even been gone for a year, and already you two are loved up."

"Bohdi, now is not the time for this," Bridge mutters.

"When will it be the right time, Bridge? Huh? It's a year next month, one fucking year, and he's already pounced on her."

"He didn't fucking pounce on me. Don't speak about him like he's some fucking animal. He saved me, Bohdi, what part of that don't you get. He made—" I cover my mouth trying to hold my sob in. "He made me feel what love was again," I croak out. "He took all my pain away. Without him, my chest aches. Physically aches. And as much as you don't want to hear this, and yes, it does pain me to say it, but it's not because I'm trying to fill the void of Jace. It's because I love him. I ache for Cash, When I'm not with him, he's all I think about. When I'm sad, one word from him makes me happy again. He brings the light back into my life. He makes life worth living. He makes me feel again."

"Fuck this," Bohdi says before standing and walking out of the room. I lean my head down and cry into Cash's hand. Normally, Bridge would comfort me, but she doesn't this time. I turn to Bridge, wiping at my tears.

"Bridge? Do you hate me?" Tears fall down her cheeks.

"Rylee, I could never hate you. You're one of the purest girls I have ever come across. You made my nephew the happiest person on this earth, and I'll always be thankful for that." She glances at Cash. "I should have known. He has been brighter lately. Happier. I knew losing Jace would kill him, but I knew something was keeping him going, and I couldn't figure out what." She looks back at me. "Now I know." She doesn't smile, but her eyes soften slightly as she looks back at Cash. "I think you saved him just as much as he saved you, Rylee." She stands up, walking around the other side of the bed and sits down where Bohdi was sitting and grabs Cash's other hand. She smiles while watching him.

"I couldn't have asked for a more perfect, big brother, Ry." She sighs and laughs as if she remembered something. "He was there to hold me when my heart got broken" she stops laughing again and to beat the shit out of the boy that broke it." This makes me laugh a little because that is Cash. He is one of the most protective people I know when it comes to the people he loves. "He was there to hold me up when our parents died. He was there on the days I couldn't get out of bed. He was always there on my worst days." She stops and looks at me. "But now, come to think of it, I don't ever remember anyone being there for him or holding him up. I don't ever remember anyone taking the pain from him. He just took everyone else's pain and put his aside because that's the type of selfless man he is." She silently cries, her gaze moving over his face.

"I know whatever he feels for you couldn't have been easy, and I bet he's beat himself up every day over it. I also know he would have never pursued his feelings with you if he truly didn't love you. He wouldn't want to hurt anyone. I'm glad he did." I'm taken back slightly with what she has just said.

"You're glad he's with me?" I stare at her with hesitation. She nods, smiling softly.

"He never put himself first, he always put others and their feelings before his own, and yes, if he did always have some kind of feelings for you while Jace was alive, then I'm glad he stepped away. But . . ." She pauses, sighing and looking down. "I'm glad that he finally got the chance to truly love, it wasn't in the best circumstances, but when is love ever easy. The side of Cash I have seen in the last few months has been different, for the first time in his life, he's looked lighter. He looked like he was carrying the weight of the world on his shoulders even before Jace passed away, and now he doesn't, and now I know what that look was." She looks up at me again. "It was love, Ry. He's finally fallen in love, and no one deserves that more than him. If my big brother was ever going to be in love with a woman, I could only wish it would be a woman like you."

"Bridge," I cry. She reaches over Cash and picks my hand up and places both of our hands over his chest.

"You feel that, Ry." I feel the soft beat of Cash's heart. I nod, offering her a small smile.

"That beats for you, and I know with every fiber of my being he's coming back to you."

# Chapter Forty-Seven
## Rylee

"Don't you think you should get home?" the nurse says after doing her checks on Cash. I offer her a small smile.

"I had a sink wash and brushed my teeth today in there." I nod over to the bathroom that adjoins Cash's room. "You will be pleased to know." She smiles and nods. "Did I smell?" I laugh. She chuckles while shaking her head from side to side.

"No, no. You just must be uncomfortable in that chair. It's been three days now." I shrug.

"I won't sleep at home knowing he is here." The nurse doesn't say any more and leaves the room. Bridge stayed in the chair opposite last night. We all know he will wake up and that his body is recovering well, but after what happened with Jace, I can't bring myself to go home. I keep thinking what if something goes wrong and I'm not here. Bohdi arrived half an hour ago. He text Bridget asking if we wanted coffee, but he hasn't arrived in the room yet. If this was a week ago, I would be beside myself, trying to get Bohdi to talk to me. Now it's like I don't care if he never talks to me again. As long as Cash opens those eyes, that's all I care about.

As if reading my thoughts, Bridget says, "Bohdi will come around. He loves his brother, and he loves you. It's a lot to accept."

I nod. "I know" is all I say. It is what it is. No one's words will change that. Bridge looks toward the door, frowning.

"I'm going to find Boh, he's been gone a while now." She stands. "Do you need anything else, a sandwich?"

I nod, smiling. "A sandwich would be great, thanks." As she walks out of the room, I turn my attention to Cash and lean up, placing a kiss on his lips like I do every morning. I didn't this morning because Bridge was here, and I wasn't sure how weird that would be for her this early on.

"Morning," I whisper into his lips.

"I miss you." I tell him this every morning. I rub my hand down his face, and then my breath hitches. He frowns ever so slightly. His eyebrows draw down and then rise back up.

"Cash," I whisper into his ear, "come back to me please." A tear escapes my eye as I stroke his face again, this time using two hands.

"Please, Cash." This time, nothing happens and that small bit of hope dies as my shoulders sag and I place a kiss on his head, holding my lips there but as I pull back, everything around me stops.

"Cash," I shriek. His eyes flutter. "Cash, come on. I'm here, please, please open those eyes." As soon as the words leave my mouth, his eyes open and then squint shut, but I see the blue.

"Cash." I slam the buzzer next to his bed, and within seconds, a nurse runs in.

"He's awake, he's awake," I cry. The nurse looks at Cash and sees him fluttering his eyes open again. She calls out behind her, and two other nurses come in. I get told to stand back, but I didn't realize I was holding his hand, and as I am letting go, he squeezes it, not wanting me to let him go. The relief leaves me in a wail of a cry. He's back here with me. I squeeze my hand out of his grip.

"I'm still here, Cash," I say through the tears.

"Mr. Stiles, can you hear me? I need you to open your eyes," the nurse says to him. Cash's eyes open, and this time, they open wider than before.

"That's it. Can you hear me? Nod if you can." Cash nods ever so gently, and in that moment, Bridge and Bohdi walk in and run to my side.

"Is he awake?" Bridge cries out, holding her hand to her mouth.

"He is Bridge. He's awake." I laugh and cry as Bridge pulls me in for a hug. We stand there holding each other as Bohdi stands next to Bridge, holding her shoulder and staring at Cash with hope in his eyes. It feels like the dark cloud that was over this room and over us is dissipating.

"Mr. Stiles, we are going to remove the tube from your mouth," the nurse says. His body convulsing makes me and Bridge squeeze each other. My heart aches at seeing his weak body in discomfort and reacting like that. I hold my hand to my mouth to try and silence the cries. The minute the tube is out, a nurse places something in his mouth. They speak quietly to him and ask him to follow their finger as they move it across his face.

We watch as they do checks and monitor the machines. After what feels like hours, which was probably only ten minutes, they all step away, and one glances at us. I don't even wait for what she is about to say, as soon as I see Cash's face, I jump forward.

"Cash," I cry. His head moves to the side, and his eyes fill with tears when he sees me.

"Rylee," he croaks out. I break down in tears next to him, pressing kisses to his cheek. His hands slide up my arms and move to my face. He stares at me, caressing my cheeks. Tears leak from both of our eyes. "You came back to me." I sob, overwhelmed he's awake. I cry and cry, as I'm leaned down with my head touching his.

"You need to be careful," the nurse says to me. "No sudden movements." I nod without looking at her. In this moment, I never want to let Cash out of my sight again. I want to be with him, every minute of every day. Cash doesn't say anything, just keeps staring at me.

"Cash," I say, a bit anxious since he isn't saying anything.

"I thought—" He swallows, and then a hand comes up and places an ice chip in his mouth. I glance up as Bridget and Boh are standing on the other side of the bed watching us, but I don't care. In this moment, I don't care about anyone but Cash.

"I lost you." He finishes, holding my face.

"You can't lose me. I'm here and I'm not going anywhere," I whisper as I let my lips meet his. The pressure from his lips has me crying against his. Having Cash here alive means everything in this moment.

"Cash," Bridge whispers. I know I need to let him go, but I don't want to. As I go to lean away, his hand reaches out and holds on to my arm.

"I'm staying right here, Cash." I sit down in the chair pulled up to his bed and hold onto his hand as Bridge fusses over him. For once, he's either in too much discomfort or he's too tired to tell her to stop because I never in my life thought I'd see the day he lets his baby sister fuss over him. I take in the tears and the smiles. Boh's face lights up as he speaks to his brother, as if he's forgotten everything. It's like an out-of-body experience. The family who has been broken more than anyone could imagine, is smiling, happy. I smile wide.

"Can we have a minute." Cash's voice is stronger now, but still croaky. Bridge nods and kisses Cash on his head. Boh nods and glances at me and then back at Cash again. His smile dropping from his face.

"Bohdi," Bridge says. He takes one stern look at me and Cash before stalking away. The room falls silent as my eyes find Cash's.

"Ry—"

"No. Please let me just say this." I stand up and sit on the side of bed. Cash follows my every move. Watching me in anticipation, waiting to see what I will say. "These last three days have been absolute hell. When I thought—" I gulp, taking a deep breath. Even the thought of saying the words makes me nauseous. Cash touches my hand and links his fingers through mine. I hold onto his hand tightly. Even his touch takes the pain away and gives me the strength to carry on.

"When I thought you died. I begged him to shoot me, I begged him to kill me." A stray tear streams down my face as I remember when Cash hit the floor. "It felt like my world had ended and I knew from that moment what you mean to me." His eyes move between mine, a small smile gracing his lips. "When you crash and burn, Cash. I want you to take me with you. When your world stops spinning, I want mine to stop with it. When you break, let me break with you and when it's time to build up those walls again, I want to be by your side building them up with you. I want to be with you at your lowest moments, not just your highest. When you hurt, I hurt. When you smile, I smile. We do this together. What I'm trying to say is—" I take a deep breath and smile. "I love you, Cash Stiles, and I'm so sorry it took me so long to say it. I fucking love you." I laugh and cry as every single light turns back on in my world. Cash's larger-than-life smile not only lights up this whole room but lights up my whole life.

"Come here." I get as close as I can get, but then he winces, and I jump up. "Don't you dare move away from me." He grunts as he grabs my arm, pulling me closer. I sit beside him and lean down.

"Kiss me." He smiles. I lean forward and kiss him, he opens his mouth for me as our tongues tangle, his soft lips brushing against mine. He breaks away.

"I love you, Rylee Matthews," he whispers, and then I feel like my life has come back.

# Chapter Forty-Eight
# Rylee

## One week later

Cash is home now, although he's meant to be on bed rest, I keep catching him walking around or trying to do things around his house. I've lost count of how many times I have had to walk him back to the bed. I can tell the way he keeps snapping that he hates me fussing over him. He had a serious operation and nearly fucking died, but he doesn't think about that, he thinks of everyone else.

We had a call yesterday from the cop station. They are charging James on one count of murder for Casey, one count of manslaughter for Jace, attempted murder for shooting Cash, two counts of false imprisonment and carrying a firearm with to intent to kill. James won't be seeing the light of day again and that makes us all breathe a little easier. A friend he had from high school was also charged with accessory to a murder, false imprisonment, and tampering with government data. He had James's history wiped from the database so no one could link him back to Roxy. James covered every step he could think of. The private jet he had hired was also through the friend and was booked in his name. We were going to Mexico of all places. He had hacked my work computer and laptop. We hadn't thought to send that in for checking as it didn't even cross my mind, but it makes sense. I put all my appointments in there, as it's linked with the calendar on my phone. James was always one step ahead because of it. It gives me the creeps knowing he was walking around in plain sight, watching me, waiting for a perfect moment. There will be trials in front of the judge for sentencing which won't be for a while yet, but James's bail got rejected, which we were thankful for.

Bohdi is coming over today to see Cash. Well, more watch him for me while I go back to my apartment and pack up the rest of my belongings with the moving van. Some people might say it's too soon, but as soon as Cash was home, I knew I didn't want to go bed or wake up again without seeing his face, and he didn't want me out of his sight, so it was agreed I would move in. Bridge has been over the moon for us, Bohdi still hasn't spoken to me all that much. He's there to help Cash but is a lot snappier and barely smiles. I wanted to grab him today before I left to have it out with him once and for all; I can't stand the silent treatment anymore.

I have been moving my clothes the last few days, Cash made some room in his closet for my clothes, but he asked Bridge to redesign his room to make it so we each have our own walk-in closet. He said we can knock one of the walls through to the next bedroom and use that for the space. Bridget has arranged for workers to come here next week to look at the walls and the frames to make sure it's doable.

"Come lay with me." I hear from behind me as I hang up the last top. I turn on my heels, smiling at Cash as I skip toward him, and lay next to him, running my fingers through his hair as he closes his eyes.

"How did I get so lucky to deserve you, Rylee."

"By being you. You're perfect in every way possible, well . . ." I stop, causing Cash to turn his head to me, raising one brow. "Minus the moods, even though I think I would miss them if you stopped." I laugh.

"I love you so much, Cash."

"I will never get bored of hearing that." He smiles.

"Good, because I won't stop saying it. Every single day until our last breath." I place a kiss on his lips, and it turns heated quickly, which happens nine out of ten times. I am craving him in every way possible, we haven't been able to have sex since the operation, and I know this is partially why he's moody. He said if I got in the shower with him, he could bend me over and fuck me from behind, but I wasn't risking his stiches opening up. I need him fit and healthy as soon as possible.

"Rylee, Cash." Bridge's voice echoes through the house. I stop kissing Cash and giggle into his lips.

"For fuck's sake," he hisses. "Don't let her come in here, I'm hard as steel right now."

I laugh, jumping up off the bed and glancing down at his obvious hard-on protruding through the tracksuit bottoms he wears.

"Sucks to be you." I tease as I walk backward out of the room.

"I'll remember you said that," he shouts as I disappear into the hallway, and I don't doubt for a second he will remember that, I hope he does.

"Hey, Bridge." I lean in to kiss her cheek.

"Is my brother still asleep?" As much as I would love to panic him by sending Bridget up there, I decide to not be such a meany.

"He is, I'm sure he will wake up soon. Can I get you a coffee before I leave?"

Bridge waves her hand around. "No, no, you get on, my dear. I can fix myself something." I nod, walking past her.

I stop and turn. "Where's Boh?"

She turns to me with a sad smile. "Just unloading the car."

I nod and tell her I will see her later.

I leave, and Boh is just closing the trunk with a load of bags surrounding him. They offered to do the grocery shopping for us, which was helpful.

"Boh." I approach him.

He nods. "Ry."

"Can I have a word?" His eyes meet mine, softening.

"Yeah, of course," he breathes out.

"I miss you," I say, trying to hold my tears at bay. I promised myself I would sort my emotions out and stop letting them get the better of me.

He nods, his jaw clenching as he looks down. "I miss you too, Ry."

"Then talk to me. I know this is all a lot and a shock, but you must see what me and Cash mean to each other." He winces as he looks around.

"I do. I really fucking do." He runs his hand through his hair. "I'm just struggling to come to terms with it all. To be honest."

He sighs. "I just need time. I know that's not want you want to hear. I don't know how to explain it. I just . . ." He pauses. "I need to get away, get a fresh start, I think, and clear my head."

I frown. "What do you mean get away? I thought you were starting back up your teaching job?"

He nods and a smile graces his lips. "I am." He stares at me. "In Michigan."

"Wh-what?" There's no way I can hold back the tears, but I try.

"You're leaving us?" I barely manage to say around the lump in my throat.

"I'm struggling, Ry. Jace was my nephew, but he was my best friend. It hit me out of the blue recently that I'll never see or speak to him again. I thought I could fill the hole he left behind, but I can't and I'm struggling because of it. Maybe if I go to a new city where there is no connection to Jace, it might help." He shrugs, pushing his hands into his pockets.

"When I was speaking with a friend who works there and I mentioned I was thinking of getting back into teaching, he said a vacancy had just opened up. It felt like fate, like it's what Jace wanted for me." My bottom lip trembles with the amount of strength I'm using to hold the tears at bay. "Everywhere reminds me of him, you, Cash, work. I need to get away from it all. I think I need time to grieve, on my own Ry." He walks closer.

"Come here." I fling myself into Boh's arms, knocking him back a few steps.

"I don't want you to leave me, Boh. Not when you're mad at me." I cry into him, soaking up his smell and holding him tight.

"I'm not mad. I love you and my brother. I always will. It's just hard seeing you together. I look at you and I see Jace by your side not Cash. It hurts, that's all. I'm sorry I have been a dick the last few weeks." I nod, crying silent tears. I understand it all.

"Can I still call you?" I mumble into his chest.

"Of course. I love you, Ry. Please don't ever doubt that. You're another younger sister to me. That will never change."

"When do you leave."

"My flight is booked for the day of Jace's anniversary. I will spend the morning here, and then I'm leaving."

"Thank you for staying for the anniversary. I will need you." I glance up at him. "You know you always have me, right? I'll always be here for you. I will only ever be a phone call away, no matter what the time is."

He nods down at me. "I know you are, just as I am you."

My Uber pulls up. I don't want to let go of Boh.

"Go on." He tilts his head to the side. "I'll wait for you to get back." He smiles. I sigh out in huge relief.

"I want a Bohdi and Rylee day before you leave." I stick my bottom lip out, and he flicks my bottom lip.

"I could never resist that bottom lip, could I." He rolls his eyes. "But yes, we will have a Bohdi and Rylee day." He places a kiss on my head and lets go.

"See you soon," I say getting in the Uber. Boh waves and stands there watching me pull away. How did I not see it? He's broke without Jace, and the difference between us is Cash and I had each other. Who does Boh have? He has Bridge, but he doesn't have someone to hold him at night, he doesn't have someone to take the pain away from him. He doesn't have someone to love. I just hope Bohdi can find himself again, and then hopefully, he may meet someone that takes it all away.

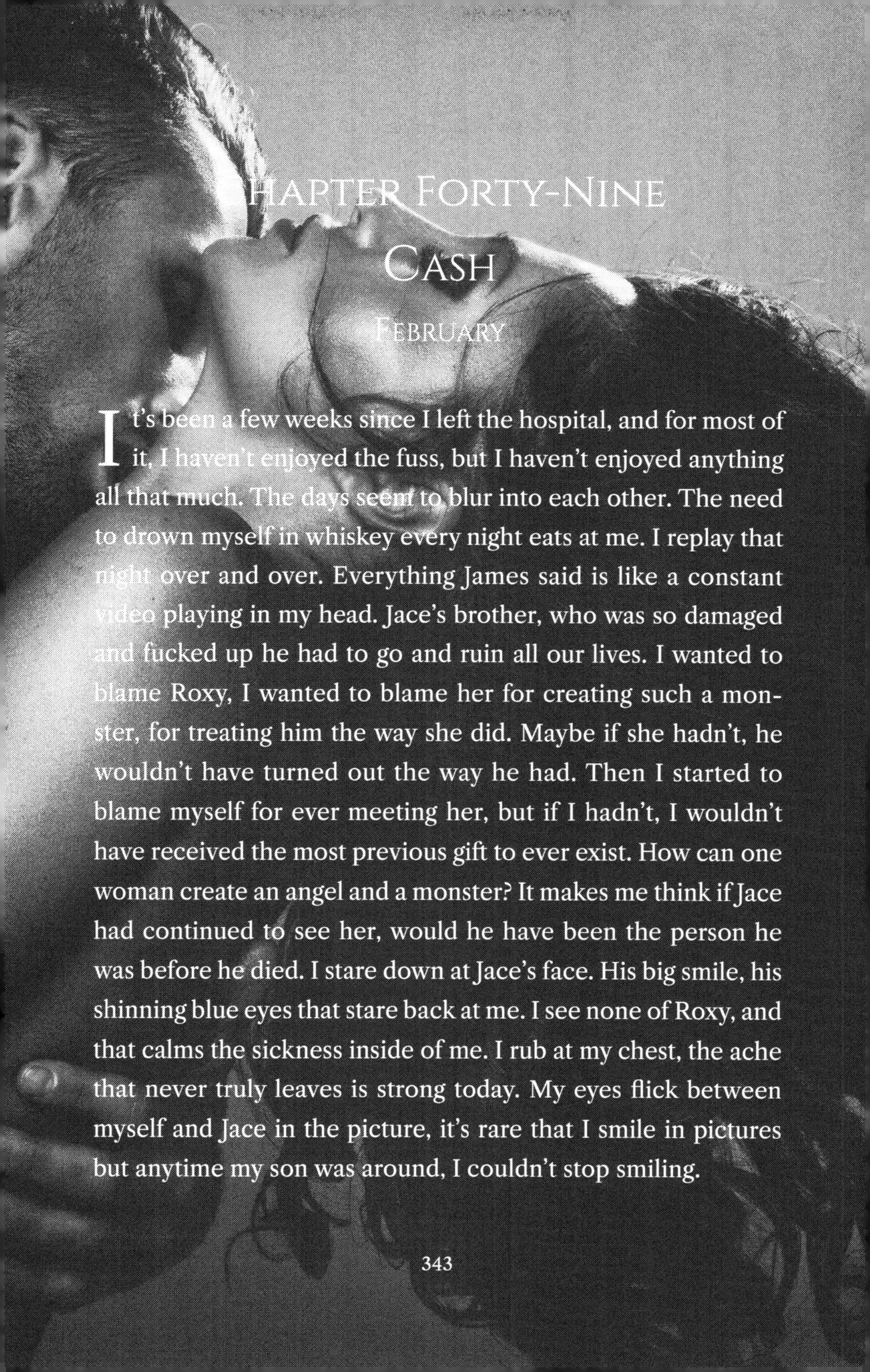

# Chapter Forty-Nine

## Cash

### February

It's been a few weeks since I left the hospital, and for most of it, I haven't enjoyed the fuss, but I haven't enjoyed anything all that much. The days seem to blur into each other. The need to drown myself in whiskey every night eats at me. I replay that night over and over. Everything James said is like a constant video playing in my head. Jace's brother, who was so damaged and fucked up he had to go and ruin all our lives. I wanted to blame Roxy, I wanted to blame her for creating such a monster, for treating him the way she did. Maybe if she hadn't, he wouldn't have turned out the way he had. Then I started to blame myself for ever meeting her, but if I hadn't, I wouldn't have received the most previous gift to ever exist. How can one woman create an angel and a monster? It makes me think if Jace had continued to see her, would he have been the person he was before he died. I stare down at Jace's face. His big smile, his shinning blue eyes that stare back at me. I see none of Roxy, and that calms the sickness inside of me. I rub at my chest, the ache that never truly leaves is strong today. My eyes flick between myself and Jace in the picture, it's rare that I smile in pictures but anytime my son was around, I couldn't stop smiling.

"One whole year without you, my boy." I rub my finger over Jace's face, wishing with everything he was standing in front of me now so I could hold him. Tell him how proud I am to be his dad; how proud I am of the man that he has become. My limbs feel heavier with every second I stare at him. This is the feeling I have felt every day since leaving that hospital. As soon as I arrived home, it was like losing Jace all over again, the pain, the emptiness, the darkness. The only time I ever see light is when Rylee is in my arms. Rylee. The girl who saved me, the girl who belonged to my son. The girl who now belongs to me and I love with every single inch of me. I roll my head back on the sofa, taking my eyes off Jace, and close my eyes.

*"Dad, I've met someone. I think she's the one," Jace breathes out, running his fingers through his hair. I frown and take a seat next to him at my island. "Why do you look so stressed about it?" I question. He peers up at me, and even though he looks stressed, his face lights up.*

*"Because I'm in deep way too quickly. She takes my breath away." He laughs. I grab him by the back of his neck, shaking him slightly. "Son, not many women come around and do that for you, you best hold on to that one."*

"Wasn't you right, son." I roll my head forward, and Jace's eyes shine back at me. The stab of guilt sears through me. "I'll look after our girl, son. I'll protect her with everything I have," I choke out as tears blur my vision. "I'll try love her the way you did. I'll love her the way she deserves. Just please don't hate me." The silent tears leave me as I close my eyes, Jace's life flashing before me, the day he was born, his first word, his first steps. His first day at school, his graduation, his first day working with me, our arguments in the office, our laughs at the bar after work. I lean forward and pick up the beer off the table, the tears falling faster.

"Cheers, son." I take a sip of the beer. "I'll carry you with me forever, Jace. Swim free, my boy," I whisper out, pressing a kiss to the picture.

"Cash." Bridge's voice breaks through her arm circling around my front. "Are you ready?" she whispers. I nod, taking once last look at Jace, and place the picture back on the table.

"I'm ready," I choke out.

# Chapter Fifty
# Rylee

"One whole year without you, Jace," I whisper into the cold breeze stinging my skin. The beach is deserted. It's the end of February, no one comes here this time of the year. The wind is icy and there are patches of snow on the sand, but how could I not come here today. It's Jace's day. The skies are gray, but in the distance, a bit of sun peeks out from behind the clouds. I smile, closing my eyes and raising my face to the sun.

"Hey, Jace," I whisper. "It's been one hell of a year." I open my eyes, squinting at the sun. "I keep questioning how the hell I ever got through it." I sigh, looking down at the sand, dragging my hands through the ice-cold grains.

"Things have happened, and I can't say you would be happy with them entirely. Maybe I have been telling myself if you could see us now, you would accept it. But who would accept their girlfriend moving on to their dad?" I laugh, trying not to cry. "I know it's not right, Jace. I know what some people say behind my back, and I have accepted it. People speak, lies are told. I know in time I will soon let it go over my head, but it still hurts hearing it."

I think back to the whispers in the coffee shop the other day when I was with Cash. I overheard a girl say I must have been sleeping with Cash for years behind Jace's back. Normally, I would confront anyone saying something behind my back, but I broke down. I ran out of the shop, collapsing to the ground, crying. Cash came out after me and held me until I stopped. He was furious when he heard what had been said, but that night, Bridge came over and explained that as horrible as it is, people who don't know us won't understand, and they don't see the love Cash and I have for each other and how much we have helped one another, and she's right. But it still hurts.

"I don't really know why I feel the need to say this, maybe so I'm saying this out loud? I don't know, Jace. All I know is I need you to know, nothing ever happened when we were together, and I never looked at your dad in any way at all." I keep my eyes on the sun, hoping it won't disappear. It doesn't, it stays shining down on me warming my face. "But you do have to know one thing. I love Cash. I have fallen hopelessly and utterly in love with him, and I can't picture my life without him." I close my eyes, picturing Cash lying in the hospital bed. "I honestly thought my life was over when I thought he was dead. There is no way I could go through losing someone I love again, and nearly losing Cash, made me feel realize that." I lay back on the sand, even if the coldness bites my skin.

"When I met you, it was like a fairytale, my very own story and every year of our life was a new chapter and I never imagined starting a new one without you. Now I'm starting a new chapter with someone new, but I can promise you, I will reread our chapters, Jace. My story began with you, and although you may have physically left me, you will always live on, your kindness, your love, the mark you left on each of us will never die. We will never stop speaking of you. We will never forget you. Your memory will live on through the rest of our chapters. I will always and forever love you in here." I raise my hand and rub over my heart.

I continue to lie on my side, watching the clouds move at a fast pace, my skin slowly going numb from the bitter cold. Then a dark shadow casts over me, but it doesn't make me cold. It makes me warm. Cash stares down at me.

"Cash." I smile. Bridge and Boh appear from behind him. I stand up quickly and am taken back. Toni appears, Rachel appears. Jace's friends and coworkers. Everyone that was at his funeral stands on the beach, all holding a tulip in their hand.

"We wanted to all be together today," Cash whispers, pulling me to his side. I haven't been affectionate with Cash all that much in front of people yet, but it doesn't bother me, and I know Cash doesn't care, if people love us, they will accept it.

"We do this together, Rylee." Cash places a soft kiss on my forehead, and I nod.

"Together." I smile up at him. He passes me a tulip, and I peep around his broad frame, everyone holding on to each other, standing on the shoreline, staring out to sea. Toni catches my eye.

She mouths, *I love you* before blowing me a kiss. I catch it and place it in my pocket as a single tear falls down her cheek.

Her hand disappears in her pocket, and then she pulls it out and places it against her cheek.

*I love you too.* My lips mime to her. We all huddle together and stare out to sea. Bridge has a few tulips in her hand, and I ask her for another one, and she smiles and passes me one. I walk toward the water and place one in the water.

"Rest in eternal peace, Casey." The tulip floats out, the waves taking it under as it slowly disappears. From the corner of my eye, I see everyone standing either side of me, and I peek up at Cash standing by my side, his hand sinks into mine.

"Together," we say as we bend down and place our tulips in the water, everyone follows, placing their own different colored tulips in the water. "Swim free, Jace." Me and Cash say together.

We all watch as they float in the waves, and then the sun shines brighter, causing me to laugh, but my heart beams when everyone at the same time says, "Hi Jace."

# Epilogue

## Rylee - Seven years later

"Thor, don't run too far," I shout as he plays on the beach. His little legs going too fast, and I see him going over before it even happens.

He lands flat on his face, and Cash next to me lets out a little chuckle. I swing my gaze so fast to him.

"Why are you laughing?" I screech, standing to get to Thor.

"Rylee. He's a boy. Let him be a boy."

I approach Thor and bend down, his face still flat in the sand.

"Baby, are you okay?" I turn him over, and his whole face, including his mile-long eyelashes I am constantly jealous of are covered in sand. I swipe off the sand, and his big blue eyes shine back at me before a smile appears on his face as he looks over my shoulder at Cash and laughs.

"Silly me," he says and pushes me off him. I stand up, and he takes off again. A warm hand slides around my waist as Cash places a kiss on my head.

"Why doesn't he need me anymore, Cash?" I say, frowning. "I don't want him to grow up." He's already too boyish, he won't need me at all soon. Cash chuckles and pulls me in for a hug, coming as close as he can, but my huge bump makes that slightly harder.

"I think in his own way, he's trying to be independent. He knows his little sister will be here soon, and he wants to be the best big brother to her and help you with her. Look how much he fusses over you when she is causing you discomfort." I smile, thinking back to last week when my ankles were swollen and I was struggling to stand on my feet for too long. My heart melted into mush on the floor when his little hand took mine in his and led me over to the sofa where he asked me to sit down and then picked up my legs one by one and placed them on the table with a cushion under them. He then told me, Daddy and he were cooking his little sister and me dinner that night. Which they did, and it was so special, even if it was nuggets and chips. Thor said it was his specialty.

Cash rubbing on my belly brings me out of my thoughts. "This little one is going to make me grayer than I already am." I smile up at him, running my fingers through his brown and slightly gray beard.

"I hope so," I whisper into his lips, a smirk forming on my face. Cash has aged like fine wine. He only gets hotter the older he gets. His wrinkles have become more defined around his eyes, and every time he smiles, my heart skips a beat. His hair is still brown but the gray specs shine through when the sun hits them and is a lot more prominent on his face. He still keeps up with the gym, so his body has never faulted. He still has the abs, but if I'm honest, I don't care. I'm so in love with him, my friends are still adamant it is sickening. I still gush about him seven years later, and even when he walks into a room, I get the same butterflies and still get nervous around him.

Cash looks down at me, raising one eyebrow. "You like me gray, Mrs. Stiles?" He smirks before following up with "I didn't know you had a daddy kink, interesting." I slap him on the arm, before pulling away and walking toward Thor, who is still barreling his way down the beach. I still get butterflies when he calls me Mrs. Stiles.

He took me back to the cabin in Whitefish for my birthday and proposed on the balcony. He had someone go out there and decorate it all in pretty fairy lights. It was perfect. A day I will never forget, because it was also the day I told him I was eight weeks pregnant. I had taken my pill religiously, but it felt like fate that it happened. He cried into my belly and kept kissing it all night. We then made love until the light was shining through. It was one of the best days of my life, and I'll never forget it. That and our perfect wedding, which Bridget and Ton organized to perfection.

Cash and I walk hand in hand, and Thor has stopped and is staring out to sea. I look out to see what he is looking at. The dark clouds that were there, are now disappearing as the sun breaks through. It's eight years ago today we lost one of the most amazing people in our lives. We still always talk about Jace, we want Thor to know about his big brother and how special he was. We have pictures of him around the house so he can know what he looked like. Cash always tells Thor stories about him when he was a kid, and the more I hear about Jace as a little boy, the more I see Thor in him. He always says how much Thor is like Jace in personality and looks. Thor and Cash have the most amazing father-son bond I have ever seen. I think Cash feels like this is his second chance at being a dad, not that he wasn't a great dad to Jace because he was, but he just always wants to be with Thor.

He stepped back from his position in the company, so he has more time with his family, which I love. Toni now runs things at Stiles Marketing. Cash needed someone with confidence and fire, and Toni was the first person who popped into his head, and I wasn't a least bit surprised. Toni had been wanting a career change and something to test her more, so when Cash gave her an offer she couldn't refuse, she took it. It took training and endless working hours on both parts to get her up to speed, but now she is loving life and has brought new opportunities to the company. He is over the moon with her, and they have such a great relationship. He does odd jobs throughout the company. Toni is in her element when she can boss him around, and I secretly love to see it. Cash has always been a man of control, so there were a few problems to start with, but when he realized what family life was like away from work, he was happy to do whatever he could to be at home more with us.

We come to stand next to Thor as I bend down and look at him. "What are you looking at, baby?" I run my hands through his mass of brown wild curls sitting on top of his head.

"The sun, Mommy," he whispers, looking deep in thought. "I know I'm meant to be the God of Thunder, Mommy, but I do really like the sun." I quickly glance up at Cash, and he doesn't look at me once. I told Thor we named him that because of his big brother. Cash then explained why Jace loved Thor, and then Thor wanted to watch the films. I told him he was too young, but he has been saying one or two things lately that is making me believe Cash has sat and watched the films with him. I will store that away for later.

"Look, Mommy, look," he shouts. I look out to sea and up in the sky, the sun shining bright and most of the clouds have nearly disappeared now.

A couple of nights ago, my emotions were all over the place knowing the anniversary of Jace's death was coming up. I still cry for him, I still miss him more than anything. Despite the fact I'm madly and deeply in love with Cash, I will always love Jace. That will never stop. I wouldn't change what I have for anyone, and I love my family more than life. I don't think I knew what deep love was until I held Thor in my arms and Cash cuddling us both in that hospital the day he was born, but I still cry for Jace. I still think about him all the time.

Mostly, I smile when I think about him but sometimes, I cry, and Thor walked into my bedroom when I was crying. His little face when he saw my tears made my heart break.

*"Mommy, Mommy, what's wrong." Thor rushes over to me, grabbing my hand. I hastily wipe away at my tears, not wanting him to see me cry.*

*"Nothing, baby, I think it's just Mommy's emotions playing me up again." I chuckle, putting on the biggest smile I can muster.*

*Thor jumps up onto my bed and brings his face to my belly.*

*"Storm, stop making Mommy cry," he whispers to her. I laugh and bring him in to cuddle me.*

*"It's not Storm, baby, I promise." Cash and I were struggling with a girl's name, but once again, it circled back to Jace. One of his other favorite films was* X-men *and Storm was another favorite character of his. Cash and I thought Storm and Thor worked together, so that's how we have ended up with Storm, but in all honestly, I love it. It's such a pretty and strong name for a girl.*

*"Then why are you crying, Mommy." His big blue eyes bore gently into mine, his eyebrows furrowed, not liking the tear that escapes my eyes.*

*"I was actually just thinking of your big brother, and it got me upset, baby, I miss him. That's all." He nods.*

*"It's okay, Mommy. Daddy gets upset sometimes too." He strokes the palm of my hand. "He looks at his pictures a lot and cries," he whispers. You don't realize how much kids really do see, as much as I don't want Thor to see me and Cash sad, I want him to know that it's okay to cry sometimes.*

*"You know." I cuddle into him more, holding him tight, breathing in his smell that grounds me and brings a smile on my face. "Your big brother has been the most amazing angel for me, that's why Mommy goes to the beach a lot, because when the sun comes out, that's your big bro coming out. He's the light in our lives, baby, and that's when I talk to him."*

*He leans away from me, looking up at me, his eyes wide and his brows drawn together. "He's your angel?"*

*I nod, smiling down at him. "He is, but now I want you to have him, baby." A big smile appears on his face.*

*"I can have my big bro as my angel." The excitement that shows makes my eyes sting with unshed tears. "But, Mommy." The smile disappears from his face. "What will you do with no angel, will you get another one?" He studies me, waiting for an answer.*

*"I don't need another one, I have you and Daddy. You are my angels, but that doesn't mean that sometimes I won't need to borrow yours now and again, is that okay?" I ask him in a serious tone.*

*He nods swiftly. "Yes, Mommy. That's okay." He cuddles into my side, drawing circles on my ever-growing bump. "I will share my angel with Storm, Mommy," he whispers as tears run down my cheeks at how perfect my little boy is.*

Something touching my face brings me back to the moment, and I realize it's Cash wiping a stray tear from my cheek. I hadn't realized I was crying but thinking back to that moment was so precious. I look over at Thor staring up to the all-blue sky with a big smile on his face. This moment right now, being here, couldn't be any more perfect.

On this day we come to the beach each year, the sun comes out. The sun makes me feel closer to Jace because it always reminds me of him, and now Thor associates the sun with Jace, and nothing makes me happier. I drop down on the sand next to Thor and stare up at the sky with him while Cash sits next to me and puts an arm around me, letting me lean on him. Thor comes between my legs and leans back on my bump staring up at the sky. Feeling each person I love most in this world around me in this moment makes me realize how perfect my life is, and when the next words leave Thor's mouth, my hearts soars.

"Hey, big bro." Cash squeezes me tight as tears fall down his face. His blue eyes fall on me as he smiles, pressing a kiss to my head and rubbing Thor's head.

"I love you, Mrs. Stiles."

"I love you more, Mr. Stiles."

I place my hands around Thor. "We love you, your little sister, and your big brother, Thor."

"Always, Mommy?"

"Forever baby."

## The End.

# Afterword

We made it!

I hope you don’t hate me now and you were happy with the end. My heart still hurts for Jace, and it always will, but I love Rylee and Cash. They healed each other without even realizing it and brought each other back into the light again.

The duet was challenging to write, but the outlet it gave me was amazing. Grief is a funny thing, and everyone deals with it so differently. Losing my Mum suddenly two years ago gutted me to the core. She was my best friend, and I never thought of life without her. I felt like, for a good year, I was dragging my way through life.

These characters healed a big part of me because it’s okay to be broken, but also, it's okay to move on and be happy again. You don’t always have to be sad or feel guilty for being happy.

The person you loved wouldn’t want you to be sad; they would want you to thrive in life and move on because life does go on. Being happy doesn’t mean you will forget or not care about them. A part of them will always live on with you. Never forget that.

Thank you so much for reading. I will never be able to tell or show you how thankful I am for taking the time to read this duet; I really hope you enjoyed it
. I love to hear from my amazing readers, so please feel free to reach out to me on Instagram, Facebook, or anywhere you can find me.
I will be putting some info out soon on Bohdi's book as that will be coming next, but also Toni's book will be coming after Bohdi's. I'm so excited for both!
I love you all!

# STALK ME

You can find me on the below platforms:
Instagram – @Authorps.black
Facebook – @PS.Black
TikTok – @PS. Black

Printed in Great Britain
by Amazon

31159623R00211